Rotherb[...] barely a foot away. "Would I offend you if I told you I returned to the Pump Room every afternoon for a full fortnight afterwards in hopes of seeing you again?"

Her heart took flight. "In what manner could that ever be offensive to me or to any lady?" she asked, meeting his gaze fully.

"Because I am not considered a proper sort of man. But that's right—you do not have a great deal of sensibility."

She merely smiled.

"Would you have permitted me to address you?"

"Yes, most certainly."

"My God," he murmured. "You knew then of my reputation, and you still would have come to me?"

"Of course."

"Where have you been all these years?" His voice was nearly a whisper.

"In Sussex."

"Are you telling me that all these years, had I been more nearly involved with my family, I might have had occasion to meet you again?"

"Undoubtedly," she breathed. "Indeed, I hoped for it season after season."

"Then I have wasted a great many years." He took a step closer and his hand touched the sleeve of her gown. "I would kiss you," he whispered. His right arm slipped about her waist and he caught her chin in his hand. "I have waited so many years to do so. Do I have your permission?"

"Yes," she whispered.

—from "THE ROGUE" by Valerie King

WONDERFUL AND WICKED

Carola Dunn
Valerie King
Isobel Linton

Zebra Books
Kensington Publishing Corp.
http://www.zebrabooks.com

ZEBRA BOOKS are published by

Kensington Publishing Corp.
850 Third Avenue
New York, NY 10022

First Printing: June, 2000
10 9 8 7 6 5 4 3 2 1

Printed in the United States of America

CONTENTS

THE PIRATE

by

Carola Dunn

One

London, 1814

"Very pretty-behaved girls," said Mrs. Drummond Burrell graciously. "I congratulate you, Lady Ransome." With a stately nod, the highest stickler of all the Almack's patronesses passed on, her train brushing the toes of Alicia Ransome's grey-satin slippers.

Alicia beamed after her. Of course she knew very well that her daughters were pretty behaved, but the encomium was not to be despised, coming from so influential a lady.

In front of her, the row of gentlemanly backs—blue, black, and Life-Guards red—shifted as another couple twirled down the centre of the set. Between two backs, she caught a glimpse of Emily and Frederica, their dark heads together as they chatted, awaiting their turns to dance. Though a trifle shortsighted, Alicia could tell from her seat among the chaperones that her girls were quite the prettiest within the sacred precincts of Almack's, besides having pretty manners.

The fashionable gentlemen of the metropolis had not been slow to discover the Ransome girls' charms—which included, admittedly, very handsome dowries. Since soon after the beginning of the Season, lovesick swains had swarmed about the Twin Goddesses.

Goddesses perhaps, thought their mother with fond amusement, remembering certain less than heavenly childhood mischief. Twins, no.

Though scarcely a year separated the two, Emily, the elder, was half a head shorter than her sister, with a slight figure and emerald eyes. Apart from the eyes, she much resembled Alicia in youth. Frederica was more like the late Viscount Ransome, tall for a woman and sturdily built, her shape, already at seventeen, distinctly curvaceous. A Pocket Venus and a Juno, the gentlemen agreed.

There went Emily now, in rose-petal pink with a crimson ribbon at the high waist. She skipped down the set on the arm of young Lord Ames, heir to an earldom, with a besotted look in his eyes. Alicia could not make out his expression just now, but it was plain enough when he was close. And Emma laughed up at him teasingly, but Alicia had seen the joy and tenderness in her face when Richard Ames requested the dance.

Frederica, in blue and silver, took her turn down the middle. Watching, Alicia's heart twisted in an involuntary pang.

Darling Freddie was already happily betrothed to Mr. Alwin Fairweather. Both Mr. Fairweather and Lord Ames were entirely unexceptionable gentlemen, well able to support her daughters and apparently deeply in love. Of course Alicia was delighted. But what would she do without her girls?

Up in the balcony, Neil Gow's band played a final chord. The dancers bowed and curtsied, and all over the room gentlemen delivered young ladies to their hopeful mamas. Before Emily and Frederica reached Alicia, she was surrounded by would-be partners for the pair.

Smiling, she shook her head. "I fear their cards are filled, Sir Adrian, Mr. Lambert."

"Dash it all, ma'am," sighed a third disappointed spark, "one must indeed arrive betimes to hope to dance with Miss Emily or Miss Frederica. The doors will not close for another ten minutes."

The girls came up and the beaux' attention turned to them. In the midst of the laughing, chattering group, Alicia was not precisely ignored, yet she felt herself apart. She was too young to be relegated to the ranks of the dowagers, she thought mutinously.

But she had forgotten how to rebel—since that last, fruitless rebellion which had ended in disaster.

Her daughters swooped down to drop a kiss on either cheek before going off with their new partners. "Pray do not look so sad, Mama," Emily whispered, "when Freddie and I are so very, very happy."

As the floor cleared to allow the dancers to take their places, Alicia noticed a stir on the far side of the room, near the entrance. At eleven o'clock, the patronesses closed the doors and admitted no one, once having turned away even so august a personage as the Duke of Wellington. A couple of gentlemen had arrived just in time. Alicia saw heads turn to stare at the newcomers, but at that distance she could not make out what made them particularly worthy of note.

The music started, and she gave herself up to the pleasure of the tune, hiding her tapping toe beneath the dove-grey sarsnet of her skirts. Emma was right; she must not succumb to melancholy when she had attained every mother's dream: to find excellent husbands for both daughters in their first Season.

Freddie was the first to return to her side. "Mama, who is that gentleman who cannot take his eyes off you?"

"Where? Do not point, Frederica! I am sure I have told you a hundred times."

"At least. Leaning against the pillar over there, beneath the musicians' balcony."

Alicia cast a quick glance in that direction, but all she could see was a figure in a dark-blue coat and the requisite black knee-breeches. "I cannot tell, not without staring rudely."

"Well, *he* is staring quite rudely, Mama. Why should not you, likewise? But there, how silly of me, I expect he is too far off for you to see clearly without your spectacles."

"Perhaps there is something amiss which only he has noticed?" Alicia patted her hair, still as dark as her daughters'. "My toque is not slipping sideways, darling?"

"Not at all. You are all perfection, Mama. Here comes Emily. Emma, do you see the gentleman propping up the pillar over there, who gazes so intently at Mama?"

"Yes," said Emily. "I am told he is but recently come to Town after many years abroad. I doubt he has not seen so charming a sight as Mama this age. It is not surprising that he should have no notion of manners, for he is a sea captain and only think, they call him Pirate Pendragon!"

The room swirled about Alicia's head.

"Mama, you have gone quite pale!" exclaimed Frederica. "It is only a nickname, you know. He is not a real pirate, I am sure, but even if he were the greatest rogue in Christendom, he could not make anyone walk the plank here, surrounded by the Beau Monde."

Emily, more perceptive, pressed Alicia's hand. "I believe Mama knows him, Freddie," she said softly, "or used to, rather. Dearest Mama, do you wish to go home? Frederica shall gather our wraps and I shall send for the carriage at once."

"No, no," Alicia said faintly, distractedly. "It would

look most particular. Your evening would be quite spoilt. I am perfectly all right. He can have nothing to say to me after so long. When we were children . . . Indeed, my darlings, go and dance. The music is starting and here are your partners patiently waiting."

The partners, seeing the ladies in earnest conversation, had held back. Now they came forward to offer their arms to Emily and Frederica. With many an anxious backward glance, the girls went off.

Alicia did her best not to look towards that slight, blue-coated figure, but despite her utmost efforts, her eyes turned that way.

The man known as Pirate Pendragon was talking to another, taller gentleman, who wore the scarlet coat of a guards officer. The girls were mistaken, then; he had not been staring at her after all. He could not possibly recognize her after so many years, and if somehow he had, she could not be more to him than an object of mild curiosity. His present interest had been momentary.

Or perhaps he had forgotten her altogether, she thought, not without a twinge of pique. But the moment of resentment quickly passed. He had shattered her world, left her desolate, and what she felt now was a deep sadness.

She had loved him. She had loved him for as long as she could recall.

Two

Cornwall—1781

It was the Honourable Miss Alicia Roscoe's fifth birthday. Mama and Papa were in London for the Season, but she already knew better than to expect any token from them. Her three elder brothers, who seldom agreed on anything, had clubbed together to give her the new cricket bat and ball they so desperately wanted. Rupert promptly borrowed them back, then grew impatient when she cried.

"Selfish little meanie!"

"It's not I don't want you to play with them," she sobbed, "but you never let me play, too."

"All right, if you stop blubbing, you can one day," promised James, "but not today because we're meeting the Pendragons for a game."

"But *today's* my birfday!"

"Now, now," said Nanny, tyrant of both nursery and schoolroom, dominating meek governesses and tutors alike, "you young gentlemen oughta be ashamed of yourselves. Miss Allie's old enough to go with you now. You just take her along of you this one day out of all the year." Nanny believed in fresh air and exercise for little girls as well as boys, which gave her time to nap.

So Alicia went along with the boys, and that was the first time she met Peter Pendragon.

He was the third of the Earl of Orford's four sons, just three years older than Alicia, the same age as her youngest brother, Edward. Orford's principal estate in Cornwall marched with Baron Roscoe's. Their lordships' sons played together whenever all were let loose at the same time. Seven boys aged from six to twelve—along with accompanying spaniels and pointers—were enough for all sorts of fun and gig, especially as a stream formed the boundary between the two estates.

That sunny day in May, their objective was not the stream but a newly mown meadow, perfect for cricket. When the Roscoe children arrived, little Alicia panting along behind in her wide, stiff skirts and petticoats, the Pendragons were already there, practising with their old bat and ball.

They gathered around to stroke the silky smoothness of the new white-willow bat, to admire the glossy red leather of the new ball.

"They're mine," Alicia announced loudly, hopping about on the outskirts of the group, trying to catch a glimpse of her proud possessions. "Bofe of them's mine. Rupert an' James an' Ned gived them to me for my birfday."

"Today's your birthday?" asked the smallish, green-eyed, gap-toothed Pendragon, turning to her. "Many happy returns! Are you going to lend them to us?"

"Ye-es," said Alicia doubtfully.

"That's Silly Allie," Rupert explained, "our sister. We had to bring her."

"An' you promised I can play," she reminded him.

"Oh, she can go out on the boundary, where she will not do any harm," said the biggest Pendragon carelessly.

"Let us choose teams. Not Roscoes against Pendragons. We shall split up the families."

Alicia never did discover which team she was on. Whoever was batting, it was never her turn, and the ball never came her way, though she had listened carefully when told she had to catch it and throw it back. She made a daisy chain long enough to go right over her head and round her neck and still she had touched neither bat nor ball. In fact, the dogs saw more of the ball than she did.

When Edward went in to bat for the third time, she lost her patience and marched up to the wicket.

"I want to hit."

"You are too little."

"Silly Allie, you're only a girl."

"The ball might hit you, and then we'd be in the suds."

"I would not cry," Alicia said bravely.

"You will spoil the scoring."

"Come along, Allie," said Peter Pendragon, catching her hand and pulling her away, "I'll bowl a ball for you to hit. We shall use the old ones, over there. They are just as good for learning."

Carefully coached, Alicia learnt the joy of hitting a ball into the thrower's hands. Her eight-year-old mentor was too kind to tell her that meant she was out. By the time she stumped homeward, weary but happy, in the wake of her brothers, she was already planning to marry him, in a year or two, when she was quite grown up.

Alicia had not made such a nuisance of herself on her birthday that her brothers were prepared to waste their effort arguing with Nanny next time they were told to take their sister along.

They had arranged to meet the Pendragons at the stream. It descended from the moors in a series of still, brown pools and white, rocky flurries, through a steep-sided, wooded valley. The widest pool was a foot or so deep and full of minnows. There, Sir Francis Drake (young Lord Pendragon, commonly known as Pen) once again led his fleet against the Spanish Armada, led by the Duke of Medina Sidonia (Rupert).

With a difference.

Peter Pendragon had recently been given a picture book about pirates. "You can all be admirals and things," he said as they took off their jackets, shoes, and stockings. "I'm going to be a pirate. I shall sink any ship I catch, English or Spanish, even Drake's, and steal all the treasure."

Sitting on a flat rock beside the pool, Alicia observed the battle. As each boy was a ship, its crew, and its guns, as well as its captain, there was a great deal of noise and splashing, with the dogs joyfully joining in. Alicia watched the pirate anxiously.

At first he did quite well. The battling fleets were too busy attacking each other to take much notice of the renegade. Peter managed to sink three dogs, Edward twice, and his own younger brother three times.

Then the Spaniards were forced to haul down their colours. As paroled prisoners, they joined forces with the English to suppress piracy on the high seas. Peter was very thoroughly ducked.

Alarmed, Alicia jumped to her feet and clasped her hands. "Are you awright?" she cried as he came up spluttering.

He squirted water through the gap in his front teeth, grinned at her, and said grandly, "Us pirates do not care if we get a wetting."

Pen promptly shoved him back down. While Drake was thus distracted, the Spaniards surreptitiously reneged on their parole. Led by Rupert, they scrambled over the rocks and surrounded Alicia.

"We've taken Queen Elizabeth captive!"

General battle once more ensued. Queen Elizabeth got her skirts splashed but suffered no other harm and was soon forgotten by most of the participants.

However, the pirate crept around the pool and sat down beside her, grasping her wrist.

"You are my prisoner now, Allie. I would make you walk the plank if I had one."

"What's that?"

"I shall show you the picture in my book one day. It has simply splendid pictures. Do you not mind getting your gown wet?"

"Not much. Not if it dries 'fore Nanny sees."

"Good for you. My sisters kick up a dreadful dust if they get anything on their clothes. I have three, and they have to be proper young ladies all the time. It is a dreadful bore. Maybe you don't have to be so prim and proper 'cause your father is only a baron. Mine is an earl."

"Maybe," said Alicia uncertainly.

"You are quite sensible for a girl. I shan't make you walk the plank if you don't want to."

"You haven't got one," she reminded him, and he laughed. Her brothers laughed at her all the time, but his laugh was different.

That summer, Alicia grew quite accustomed to being a captive of one sort or another. Lord and Lady Roscoe went straight on from the London Season to a series of country house parties, so the baroness did not see her daughter's face turning as brown as a berry, like any ragamuffin's.

Whether Alicia was a prisoner of the English, Spanish,

French, Indians (Red or otherwise), Saracens, Vikings, or Jacobites, Peter Pendragon usually managed to insinuate a pirate into the game.

It was James Roscoe who first christened him Pirate. The nickname stuck. Soon it was used so generally amongst the children that Alicia almost forgot his real name.

Now and then the older boys ordained a day of fishing. It was always Pirate who baited Alicia's bent pin for her. He would sit beside her on the bank and tell her marvelous stories from the Greek and Latin books he was beginning to study, and from the Arabian Nights, and of course from his pirate book. She didn't mind never catching any fish.

The magic summer drew to a close. That autumn Lord Pendragon went away to Eton, and the others were kept busy at their lessons. Alicia started to learn her pothooks and hangers, practising diligently on a squeaky slate, while her first sampler garnered its share of bloodstains from pricked fingers.

Three times a week, she went to the stables to learn to ride on the moorland pony Edward had outgrown. She loved Whitefoot almost as much as she loved Pirate.

Oh, the triumph of the day when she was allowed to ride out with the boys! For Roscoes, Pendragons, and dogs still met on Sundays and holidays, avoiding the dank woods and chilly stream in favour of fields and moors. The stable boy sent to keep an eye on Miss Allie was the only fly in her ointment.

"You can go home now," she told him when the Pendragons came in sight. "Pirate Pendragon will look after me."

"I've got me orders, missy," he said indulgently, but he fell back so that she rode to meet them alongside her brothers, as straight and tall in her sidesaddle as she could manage.

"Oh, you've got Ned's Whitefoot!" said Pirate, blotting his copybook.

Alicia gave him a hurt look. "He is mine now. He's a good pony, game as a pebble."

"So are you, and your seat looks good," he redeemed himself— almost, "for a girl."

"I hope you can keep up, Silly Allie," said William, the eldest Pendragon now that his brother was at Eton. "If you cannot, your groom will just have to take you home."

Grimly determined, Alicia kept up, following in the rear of the single file up the narrow, stony path between banks of golden bracken.

The others were all riding ponies not much bigger than Whitefoot, but not only was she smaller and new to riding, she had the disadvantage of the sidesaddle. If their mounts stepped on a loose stone and jolted them, they could grip with their knees. Alicia found herself grabbing Whitefoot's shaggy mane more than once on the ascent. It was not fair. Why could she not have been born a boy?

Rupert, in the lead, stopped at the top of the slope while the rest caught up. As Alicia emerged from the shelter of the bracken, a blast of wind sent her hat flying. She hung on to Whitefoot's mane again, afraid for a moment that she was going to fly after the hat.

"All right, Allie-oh?" asked Pirate.

"Yes," Alicia told him breathlessly, pride making her let go of the mane and regain the upright posture which had earned his praise. "Oh, what's that blue over there?"

It was a sparkling December day, the air as clear as glass. To the north, the brown heights of Bodmin Moor stood out against a pale blue sky. In the far west and south, a darker blue lined the horizon.

"That is the sea," Pirate told her. "Have you never seen it? That is where I am going to sail away to be a pirate when I grow up."

Alicia was dismayed. She did not see why he had to go away to be a pirate, when there was a perfectly good stream down in the valley. If he sailed off on the sea, how was she going to marry him?

"Do you *got* to go away?"

"You cannot be a pirate on land, Silly Allie."

He had never used that horrid nickname before. She blinked hard, with trembling lips. "Don't call me that!"

"Sorry, Allie-oh. I shan't ever again. I did not know you minded."

"I don't much, not when it is just the others. Will you come back again after you sail away?"

"Sometimes. I'll tell you what, when I capture a Spanish galleon, I shall bring you back some treasure. Would you like an emerald necklace?"

"Ooh, really?"

"I have already promised Ned some pieces of eight, because he is my best friend." Pirate looked round. The others were trotting away up the wide track. "But now come along, hurry up, we are getting left behind. Can you canter?"

"Yes," said Allie firmly, though she had only just learnt to trot and did not much like it.

Cantering was another matter. Whitefoot knew how, so she just let him have his head to follow Pirate, and it turned out to be much easier than trotting. They all rode to a circle of rocks believed to be an ancient fort, where Alicia became an Ancient British princess captured by the Romans. She was getting good at being a captive.

The following autumn, Rupert Roscoe and William Pendragon went off to Harrow and Eton respectively. With numbers diminishing, Alicia was occasionally allowed to be a warrior of some inferior kind. She was practically an honorary boy by then. When spring arrived, she was expected to bear her weight in a game of cricket.

Nearly seven, she had put on a spurt of growth and was taller than Johnnie, the youngest Pendragon, much to his disgust. She was also better coordinated. Thanks to Pirate's coaching, she was a good, solid batsman and a fair fielder, though tight sleeves prevented overarm bowling and throwing.

That May she turned seven. The timid nursery governess was dismissed. Lady Roscoe sent a new governess, whose job was to begin Alicia's training as a young lady. Not only history, geography, and French were added to reading, writing, and the modicum of arithmetic hitherto taught her, but she must learn to sing and play the fortepiano, to paint in watercolours, to do delicate embroidery, to move with grace, and most of all, to behave in a ladylike manner.

No more hoydenish gallivanting with the boys, decreed Miss Porringe.

Alicia quite enjoyed history—she already knew a great deal about the wars of the English over the centuries, from a captive's point of view. In geography, she learnt about the places Pirate would go when he sailed away, so that was interesting if sad. French might be useful if he ever let her go on a voyage with him.

She did not mind learning to be a beautiful lady like her seldom-seen mama. She remembered what Pirate had told her about his sisters, and she wanted him to be proud of her when she married him.

But nothing could stop her gallivanting, if that long word meant roaming the woods and fields and moor with Pirate, not to mention her brothers and his.

"She will have to lock me up in a dungeon with chains and rats and bats and things," she said passionately to Pirate, the first time she slipped away.

Fortunately, Nanny still ruled the nurseries, and Nanny still liked her naps. Miss Porringe was only in charge during schoolroom hours. On holidays, half-holidays, and Sunday afternoons, she usually shut herself away in her room writing endless letters to far-off relatives, so Alicia did not find it difficult to escape.

Bread and water for supper was a small price to pay on the occasions when the governess caught her returning home tousled and grubby.

Alicia was ten when Pirate's turn came to go off to Eton. At thirteen, he was still quite small and slight, scarcely an inch taller than Alicia. As well as missing him quite dreadfully—much more than she did Edward, who went to Harrow at the same time—she worried about Pirate. The older boys told horrid tales of the treatment meted out to juniors who could not defend themselves.

At last the boys all came home for Christmas. The weather was foul, with great gales sweeping in from the Atlantic and rain falling in buckets. It was not until the third day that the Pendragons seized a lull and rode over to visit, with tales of flooded meadows and downed trees.

Pirate and Edward fell to boasting of the hardships and joys of life at their respective schools. The two were equally lively and opinionated, yet to Alicia's anxious eye, Pirate's heart was not in their tussle.

Edward was summoned by Rupert to support him in some contention, and Pirate came over to Alicia, where she sat in the schoolroom window seat, watching and listening.

"Did the big boys at school pick on you?" she asked fearfully as he dropped to the cushioned seat beside her.

"Lord no, not particularly. It helps to have two older brothers there. Pen is a prefect, you know, in his last year.

Besides, he had told everyone I was called Pirate, and they thought that was funny. They teased, but they did not torment me."

"Do they call you Pirate at school, too?"

"Oh, yes," he said with a fine assumption of carelessness. Then his face screwed up as if he were trying desperately not to cry. "Allie, I found out I cannot go to sea."

Alicia's heart leapt. Though she was very sorry for his disappointment, she could not help but be overjoyed that he was going to stay at home. Perhaps they would be married after all, though she was old enough now to suspect such things were not simple to arrange.

"Why not?" she asked, hoping he saw only her sympathy, not her relief.

"I'm too old. Boys who want to go into the Navy become midshipmen by the time they are twelve, at the latest."

"But you do not want to," she said, astonished. "You are going to be a pirate."

"Oh, that was just a childish game!" he said with a touch of impatience. "The Navy is the only way to go."

"You are not *much* too old."

"No, and I daresay Father could arrange it, but I wrote to him as soon as I found out, and he said the Navy is not a suitable profession for the son of an earl. When I am old enough, he will naturally make me an allowance sufficient to lead a life of leisure, or if I insist, I may go into the Guards or the Church. The Church!"

"I cannot imagine you as a vicar," Alicia agreed. "Only consider, a vicar called Pirate!"

Pirate managed a wobbly laugh. He patted her hand. "I shan't do that, and I don't like the Army much better. I suppose I shall just have to be a gentleman of leisure. But I will say this for Father, he says he will buy me a dinghy so that I can go sailing on the Fowey next summer. Do you want to come out with me?"

"Yes, *please*," said Alicia.

Three

Cornwall—1786

Pirate never again spoke to Alicia about his disappointment. She was sure he did not forget it, but he appeared resigned. The following summer his stoicism was rewarded. Lord Orford kept his promise and bought a sailing dinghy.

The estuary of the River Fowey was a long, broad inlet reaching several miles inland from the port of Fowey at its mouth. Sheltered by hills on both sides, it was a perfect place for learning to handle a boat. The shallow stream which had seen so many battles opened into a creek, flowing into the Fowey, where the dinghy could be moored.

The next three summers, Pirate spent more time on the water than off it. Alicia joined him when she could, but now she was older, it was more difficult to get away.

Nanny had retired at last. In the big, empty schoolroom, Miss Porringe held sway, and Miss Porringe was not the sort of governess to make friends with her pupil. Alicia was bitterly lonely. She lived for the school holidays, but her brothers and the Pendragon boys were older too, and less ready to make allowances for a girl tagging along behind.

Sometimes the Pendragon girls' governess brought the three of them to pay a morning call on Miss Roscoe. Miss Porringe and Alicia always returned the civility, but Alicia had little in common with them. As Pirate had told her years before, they were very proper young ladies.

One day, in a spirit of daring, Alicia proposed a game of cricket. How wide their eyes, how round their rosebud mouths, how they oohed and aahed! Cricket was for boys. As for fishing . . . .

Lady Cynthia fanned herself languidly and observed, "Good gracious, what a tease Miss Roscoe is!"

So Alicia went fishing with Pirate, reckless of punishment. When bread and water for supper did not work, Miss Porringe made her stand in a corner with a book on her head, for hours, thus improving her posture as well as—the governess hoped—her behaviour. Alicia stood patiently. And galloped off again on her little mare, Comet, as soon as Miss Porringe's surveillance wavered.

Fortunately, the governess's authority did not extend to the stables, and all the grooms were on Miss Allie's side.

More and more often, though, Alicia would arrive at the creek only to be told she could not go sailing today.

"I am sorry, Allie," Pirate told her, "but I'm going out past Fowey, and it would be the act of a dastard to take a female with me."

"If it is so dangerous, you should not go either."

"It is different. I am a man."

At fifteen, though he would have been at sea for three years now had he been allowed to become a midshipman, Pirate still appeared a boy. Small and slight, as yet hairless about the chin, he was just about Alicia's height, since in the way of girls she had put on a spurt. He was every inch a daredevil, though.

Failing a direct prohibition, which his father had not thought to give, he often sailed the *Jolly Roger* single-

handedly out of the mouth of the Fowey. From Gribbin
Head to Pencarrow Head, he knew every cove and bay,
rock and inlet. But three miles of coast did not long satisfy
him.

The summer after her thirteenth birthday, Alicia rode
down to the creek early one sunny morning. She had little
hope, for she knew the tide was on the turn, perfect for
bearing the dinghy out to sea, and a steady breeze blew
from the west.

"I'm going to tack around Gribbin Head today," Pirate
told her, "into St. Austell Bay."

"Let me go with you, pray! I can help you row if you
are becalmed."

"Rowing at sea is not like on the river. You get wet. All
those petticoats would get tangled around you, and anyway, you cannot pull hard enough with those silly sleeves.
Tell you what, we shall sail up the river to Lostwithiel
tomorrow, if you can get away. I have plenty of pocket
money. I'll treat you to a nuncheon at the inn."

Alicia accepted gratefully, but she went straight home
and tried to get into a pair of Edward's breeches. Occasionally in the happy old days, she had dressed as a boy
so as to ride astride.

Alas, her shape had changed, she realized sadly. Hips
and breeches simply refused to cooperate. Whether she
liked it or not—and she most emphatically did not—she
was turning into a young lady.

That evening, after dinner, Alicia was allowed to join
her brothers playing at battledore on the lawn in front of
the house. As long as she did not run, Miss Porringe considered the game permissible for a young lady still in the
schoolroom. Alicia had just made a flying leap and hit the
shuttlecock a good whack, to cheers from her partner and

rebukes from the governess, when one of Lord Orford's grooms came trotting up the avenue.

Seeing them, he dismounted. They gathered round.

"Master Peter 'a' n't come home yet," he told them. "Do anyone know where un went today?"

"He was going out in the *Jolly Roger*, I know," said Edward. After being horridly seasick one breezy day on the Fowey, he had stopped accompanying his friend on the water. "I don't know which direction."

Alicia was torn. She knew Pirate's voyages out to sea were surreptitious. If she told, he might be well and truly in the briars. On the other hand, suppose he had come to grief out there in the wind and waves, on the rocks and shoals that regularly claimed their victims?

Her nails bit into her palms at the thought. "He was heading down to the mouth of the Fowey," she compromised.

"Thank'ee, miss." The groom rode off, leaving Alicia to explain to her irate governess just how she knew of Pirate's plans.

After a sleepless night, Alicia rose at dawn and rode down to the creek. No sign of the *Jolly Roger*. Her heart jumped into her throat and stuck there, choking her. What if he died, all because she had not told where he was going?

She turned Comet's head towards Pendragon House.

The earl's stablehands were already busy mucking out the stalls. They knew Alicia, and the head groom came to meet her as she rode into the yard. Even before he spoke, his grin reassured her.

"Master Peter come home around midnight, Miss Alicia. Stranded he were, over t'other zide o' the river, down Polkerris way."

"Is he all right?"

"He weren't hurt as I could zee, only plumb wore out and pretty mucky."

"What happened? Where's the dinghy?"

"I dunno, miss. Wi' his lordship waiting, he didn't stop to chat."

Alicia thanked him and turned homeward. Her worst fears were allayed, but now she worried about Lord Orford's reaction. If he banned sailing, Pirate's heart would break.

She did not expect to see Pirate that day, but he turned up shortly before midday. Alicia's brothers had all scattered to their various pastimes. She was walking in the garden with Miss Porringe, an incredibly boring occupation as she was not allowed to run, far less to climb trees, when she saw Pirate drive up in a whiskey gig.

Forbidden or not, she ran. Miss Porringe's remonstrances pursued her, but soon faded behind since the governess followed her own dictum, that a lady never raised her voice.

"Quick, drive on!" Alicia cried, as she scrambled up beside Pirate.

Grinning, he whipped up the horse and they raced down the avenue.

"I promised you a nuncheon in Lostwithiel," he said, "but we'll have to drive, not sail."

"What happened?"

He grimaced. "I misjudged the tide, like a regular lubber, and the currents and the wind, and the *Jolly Roger* got stuck on Par Sands. I had to wade to the shore, walk right across the peninsula to Fowey, persuade the ferryman to trust me for his fare, then walk all the way home."

"That is miles and miles! But oh, Pirate, what about the *Jolly Roger*? And what did your papa say?"

"He was mad as fire at first, but he had to admit he had never told me not to leave the estuary."

"I wager he has now. But you cannot, anyway, without the dinghy."

"That is the best thing of all. Father is a regular Trojan. Just a minute while I turn into the lane." Pirate slowed their mad career the merest trifle and swung around the gatepost. "There, driven to an inch!"

"Well, a foot, anyway," said Alicia as they trotted up the narrow, twisting lane, overhung with briony and old man's beard. "Is Lord Orford going to buy you another boat?"

"Not exactly. He is having the *Jolly Roger* towed off the sands for me, but best of all, he says he's going to buy a yacht!"

"He's giving you a yacht? Good gracious!"

"No, not giving," Pirate elucidated regretfully. "It seems yachts are becoming all the go, and besides, our Cornish roads are so bad that it is quicker to sail to London, or even to Plymouth and drive from there. But Allie, he says the son of an earl may be an amateur seaman, although not a professional. I may spend as much time as I wish aboard her, in the holidays of course, and he will have the captain teach me seamanship!"

For a moment, all Alicia could think of was that she would see less of him than ever. However, if nothing else, her life had taught her to swallow disappointments. Hiding her chagrin, she congratulated Pirate and resolved to enjoy today without thought for tomorrow.

It was a day worthy of lingering in her memory. The sun shone, the hedgebanks were bursting with foxgloves and campion, pheasants dashed across the lanes practically under the gig's wheels, and gulls wheeled overhead. Pirate was more cheerful than he had been in an age. He made an exciting story of his grounding on Par Sands, and a funny one of the ferryman's refusal to believe the salt-stained, brown-faced tatterdemalion was a lord's son.

The inn in Lostwithiel provided a perfectly splendid nuncheon. Alicia almost ate herself sick with sweetmeats. Afterwards she and Pirate walked along the river, playing ducks and drakes with pebbles, watching ducks a-dabbling and swifts darting after flying insects. They even saw a kingfisher, a flash of blue that gleamed as bright as Lady Roscoe's favourite sapphires.

"As blue as your eyes, Allie-oh," Pirate commented carelessly.

Best of all, as the gig turned into the avenue, Pirate said, "Of course you will be invited to take a trip on the yacht. Father said we might go down to Falmouth, or around to Plymouth, and back. You and Ned, if he has the stomach for it, and James and Rupert if they like."

With that to look forward to, Alicia did not mind in the least when Miss Porringe sent her straight to bed with no supper and nothing to read but a book of sermons.

The summer was nearly over. Pirate took Alicia out twice more in the rescued dinghy before he went back to Eton. The yacht had not yet materialized when he left, but at Christmas he rode over with news that she was bought and being fitted out in Falmouth.

"I am going to ride over to see her," he told Alicia and Edward, "whatever the weather."

"I shall come with you," said Edward, "as long as you don't insist on my going aboard, even in harbour."

"What is her name?" Alicia asked.

"She has been christened the *Seagull,* of all the dull names. Father says I may rechristen her, but I am not allowed to call her the *Jolly Roger.* Any suggestions?"

"The *Buccaneer,*" Alicia said at once.

Edward proposed several other names, but Pirate chose

Alicia's, to her delight. Perhaps at least he would think of her when he spoke of the yacht.

After Christmas, he and Edward rode off together. They were gone for several days. When they returned, Edward was quite unable to describe the *Buccaneer,* except that she was painted white with a red stripe and had three comfortable sleeping cabins as well as a day cabin.

Pirate made up for it with a wealth of minute detail. Alicia was ready to listen endlessly to his rhapsodies about her rigging and what sail she could carry, as well as her size and shape and living arrangements.

The *Buccaneer* was brought round to Fowey at Easter. As Alicia had feared, she saw little of Pirate during those holidays, just enough to know that he had suddenly grown four inches and started to shave. She consoled herself with the prospect of a cruise with him when summer came.

But long before that longed-for day, even before her fourteenth birthday in May, a great change came to Alicia's life. The boys had scarcely returned to school when, right in the middle of the London Season, Lord and Lady Roscoe came home to stay.

Four

Cornwall—1790

No one told Alicia why her parents had suddenly abandoned Society in favour of their isolated Cornish estate. However, she soon gathered through servants' gossip that they had outrun the constable.

The phrase at first made her dread their imminent arrest. Further listening enlightened her. As a peer, her father was immune to debtors' prison—for debt it was had sent him home: too many years of high living on a moderate income until the baron and baroness dared not step outside their London door for fear of duns. The town house had been let for the Season, might even have to be sold.

Further retrenchments were necessary. Miss Porringe was given notice.

"A great girl like you has no need of a governess," said Lady Roscoe in her languid fashion. "Indeed, too much learning is altogether undesirable. How shocking it would be to have a bluestocking for a daughter. You are not bookish, I trust, Alicia?"

"Oh, no, Mama!" cried Alicia, eager to please the beautiful, fashionable mother she scarcely knew. "I like best to be outdoors."

"Indeed! That is quite as bad." Lady Roscoe inspected her daughter closely. "I perceive your face is already grown shockingly brown, although spring is scarcely come. A girl's complexion is one of her most precious assets, child, and must be carefully guarded." With a faint smile she tilted her head, turning away from the bright spring sunshine pouring through the window. "Mine is frequently much admired. Of course, I married very young."

"Yes, Mama," said Alicia, a trifle less eagerly. She did not like the way the conversation was tending.

"Is it possible that you go outside without a hat and a parasol?"

"Sometimes, Mama," she confessed.

"Disgraceful! I can see it is most fortunate that I am come home to take charge of your education. Who better than your mama to teach you how to go on in Society?"

The question was unanswerable, but Alicia had no interest in Society. She wanted to be out sailing with Pirate, or fishing, or riding on the moors, preferably with him, but without when he was unavailable.

"Yes, Mama," she said glumly.

"Well, I am sure I cannot spare you any of my Distilled Water of Green Pineapples, for there is no knowing when I shall be able to replace it. You will just have to stay indoors until the colour has faded."

"Yes, Mama."

Lady Roscoe shivered delicately. "Fetch me my shawl, child. This house is horridly draughty. I do not know how I shall bear to rusticate here."

The baroness's instructions were not to be disregarded, as Alicia had so often disregarded her governess's. For the next fortnight, she never set foot out of doors. She did not even go out to the stables to see Comet and the dogs, now banished from the house.

She spent her time with her mama, running for shawls,

which her ladyship tended to discard about the house; disentangling embroidery silks, which seemed to knot themselves, for her ladyship scarcely ever set a stitch though her hoop was always by her; writing letters from dictation, when her ladyship discovered her hand was clear and reasonably elegant, if still a trifle childish; reading aloud from the gossip columns of the papers, which arrived five days late, to her ladyship's displeasure; and performing a thousand other small tasks.

Alicia bore all patiently, living for the day when her complexion had improved to the point that she was allowed out again. She would even put up with hats, veils, and parasols, though how she was to manage a parasol on horseback, she had no notion. Above all, she missed Comet and she longed for a long gallop.

Every day she scrutinized her face in the glass. It seemed to her to pale excruciatingly slowly.

However, one day her mother received a note from friends who were passing through the area on their way from Plymouth to Truro.

"The Dendridges will call tomorrow morning," exclaimed Lady Roscoe in delight. "How pleasant it will be to see civilized faces for once. I shall not need you, Alicia. You may take yourself off."

Lady Roscoe was still abed when Alicia hurried out to the stables early next morning.

Her mare had been sold.

Lord Roscoe, alarmed to discover the extent of his debts, had every intention of retrenching. All unnecessary expenses must be cut. By his reckoning, comparatively small outlays, such as his daughter's governess and her mount, would add up to hundreds over the years.

Unfortunately, many much larger expenditures were irreducible.

As eldest son of the house, Rupert was entitled to an allowance to enable him to reside in London, if not in high style. James would finish at Eton in July and was bound for the army. His lieutenancy would cost a pretty penny, and no junior officer of noble birth could be expected to live on his pay. Edward, willy-nilly, was to enter the church. The local incumbent was an aged gentleman who was bound to pop off the hooks by the time Edward took orders. In the meantime, the living still had to be paid, as well as Edward's school fees and then his university expenses.

Nor did his lordship, though free of the burden of the London house, succeed in cutting his household expenses by much. One must have carriages, and therefore carriage horses and the grooms to care for them. The indoor staff which sufficed for the four children, with only occasional short visits by their parents, was obviously insufficient with the baron and baroness in residence. And the gardens could not be abandoned to go wild. More fruit and vegetables than ever were needed, and her ladyship liked to have flowers about the house.

Furthermore, if she were forced to rusticate, then at least she must invite friends to visit. One could not entirely cut oneself off from decent society!

From Alicia's point of view, the one blessing was that when Mama and Papa had guests, she was free, comparatively. Hatted and parasoled, she went for long, solitary rambles through the countryside.

One day early in August, she was returning home when she heard hoofbeats behind her, then a hail.

"Allie, is that you under all the paraphernalia?"

She would know that voice anywhere. "Pirate!" Joyfully, she turned as he swung down from his horse.

"Not riding?"

The whole story poured out as they walked on. Pirate was deeply sympathetic.

"Parents do seem to have a knack of making a mess of things," he sighed. "Not that I should complain, I suppose, since Father bought the *Buccaneer*. She is a splendid vessel, Allie! That is what I have come about, to settle a date for the cruise I promised you."

"Really and truly? I feared Lord Orford must have forgotten."

"Well, I have not. She will be at Fowey for the next fortnight at least, so any fine day will do."

"Any day will do for me," Alicia said passionately. "I do not care if it is stormy. But I suppose it will depend upon Mama and Papa."

"Is Ned at home?"

"No, he is staying with a school friend in Somerset, and James has gone into the army, and I do not know where Rupert is, but not here."

"Poor Allie-oh, all alone and 'cabin'd, cribb'd, confin'd.' That is *Macbeth*—I have learnt *something* at school. I'm going to be at home for a while. If you can sneak out, I shall take you out in the dinghy one day."

"Oh, yes! As well as the *Buccaneer?*"

"Of course."

"I pray Mama does not say I may not go with you on the *Buccaneer!*"

The invitation from the Earl of Orford was too flattering to be declined. A day was named, after the departure of the present set of guests, with an alternate in case of bad weather. Alicia was *aux anges*.

At the last minute, Lady Roscoe discovered that Lady Orford and her daughters would not be present. They travelled in the yacht for convenience, but a pleasure cruise was another matter. The baroness was in two minds whether to go.

"Obviously, the outing is intended for gentlemen," she lamented.

Seeing her treat about to vanish, Alicia was on the point of daring to declare that, on the contrary, it was intended for her, when her father intervened.

"My dear, the invitation was directed to both of us. A little excursion will do your spirits a world of good. You may take your maid and the child for company, you know."

"Oh, very well. Life is so tedious, I have near forgot how to enjoy myself, I vow."

Alicia breathed again. Now all she had to worry about was the ever changeable weather, and whether her mother would rise in the morning early enough for them to reach Fowey to catch the tide.

A glorious day and the prospect of a change of scene brought Lady Roscoe from her bed at what she described as dawn. The landau to Polruan and the ferry across the river to Fowey brought them to the harbour in good time. Pirate and Lord Orford welcomed them aboard.

The earl was as eager to display the luxurious comforts below deck as Pirate was to explain the yacht's workings above. Lady Roscoe, far more interested in the former, accepted Lord Orford's escort down the steep stairway. Her abigail clambered after them.

Lord Roscoe and Alicia stayed on deck. If Alicia rather lost track of the technical details, she was more than happy just to be near Pirate, to watch his enthusiastic face and wonder at his knowledge.

A sturdy, grizzled man came over to them. "Begging your pardon, m'lord, miss—Mr. Pendragon, it's about time we cast off. Take the wheel, if you please."

"May I?" Pirate's already bright face glowed. "Oh, sir, this is Captain Denby. Excuse me, pray!"

As he hurried to the wheel, Captain Denby said, "M'lord, I'll ask you and the young lady to step aside here, if you don't prefer to go below. My hands will be running about raising sail."

"Oh, Papa, pray let us stay here—let us stay on deck!" Alicia begged.

He smiled, and seemed about to concur, when Lord Orford came up from the cabins.

"Your mama wishes you to step below, missy," he said. "Come, take my hand. The ladder is steep."

One glance at her father assured Alicia that he would not go against her mother's wishes. Bitterly chagrined, she accepted the earl's assistance and entered the cabin.

"My dear child," Lady Roscoe greeted her, "nothing, absolutely nothing, can be more injurious to the complexion than sea air! And those rough men rushing about . . . We shall be excessively comfortable here. See how charming Lord Orford has made everything, and he has ordered tea to be brought from the galley, which is what a kitchen is called at sea, I collect. Why, one might almost suppose oneself in the most elegant of drawing rooms on land."

A drawing room! That was not what Alicia had been anticipating for months. But it was no use arguing with Mama. She just stopped listening.

And Pirate was steering the boat, so Alicia would not even have the pleasure of his company. Blinking back tears of disappointment, she sat down by a window, where she could at least watch the little grey and white town receding as the ebb tide swept the *Buccaneer* down to the sea.

Then they passed St. Catherine's Point and met the sea swells. Lady Roscoe gulped and turned green.

"I wouldn't *wish* Mama to be seasick," Alicia earnestly

assured Pirate, standing beside him at the wheel, "but you must admit it is most providential. She has retired to a sleeping cabin and does not care to have anyone but her maid with her. She is in no case to wonder where I am."

"Most providential," said Pirate, grinning.

The *Buccaneer* tacked down to Falmouth, where Lady Roscoe was carried ashore, moaning and vowing never again to set foot on a seagoing vessel.

"I fear I shall have to escort her home by road," sighed Lord Roscoe. "She will not travel in a hired carriage, so one must be sent for from home." He glanced at Alicia. "I cannot think what I am to do with the child in the meantime."

"Allie shall sail back with us," cried Pirate. "Father, pray, may not Miss Roscoe come with us? I shall take good care of her, sir."

The earl indulgently agreed. Lord Roscoe demurred, but briefly. With a hasty admonishment to be a good girl and not cause her kind host any trouble, he followed his wife ashore, leaving a blissful Alicia aboard.

It was a wonderful day, and another two followed, for not until the evening of the third did Lord and Lady Roscoe reach home. Alicia spent both days with Pirate, sailing in the dinghy on the Fowey.

All too soon, life resumed its tedious pattern.

For the next three years, Alicia's life continued on the same humdrum course. Her mother grew more and more plaintive, her father more and more worried.

She saw Pirate at intervals, but he left school and was become a grownup now, a gentleman who rarely visited Cornwall. When he did come, it was generally with a house party which had as little time for a schoolroom chit as did Lord and Lady Roscoe's friends.

As Alicia's seventeenth birthday approached, her mother cheered up.

"It is such a pity your birthday is in May," she told her daughter. "You are just too young to make your come-out this Season. But next year you will be the perfect age. How I long to see London again!"

Alicia's training in the arts and conduct expected of a young lady suddenly became of vital interest to Lady Roscoe, as her ticket to Town.

Whatever the reason, Alicia enjoyed being important for a change. As she strove to meet her mother's exacting standards, she found herself quite looking forward to making her bow to Society.

After all, Pirate was part of the Beau Monde. He spent most of his time in London, he had told her, when he was not on board the *Buccaneer*.

One autumn day, at the dinner table—Alicia was permitted to join her parents for dinner now, when there were no guests—Lady Roscoe said to her husband, "I believe Alicia will do us credit when we go to London, Roscoe. It is a great pity you chose to sell our house, without recalling that we should soon need it for her presentation. It is time to order your man of business to look about for a house to let, or all the best ones will be taken."

"London?" cried his lordship. "My dear ma'am, there is no question of London. Your daughter will have to find herself a husband in Cornwall, for a Season is so far beyond my purse that London might as well be the moon!"

Five

Twenty years later, as she watched her own girls enjoying the sparkling society at Almack's, Alicia recalled her mother's fury and sighed. At the time, she had been quite frightened by Lady Roscoe's rage, as well as disappointed that she was not to have her Season after all.

Resilient by necessity, she had soon discovered a silver lining to the clouds. Find a husband in Cornwall, Papa said, and Alicia had been perfectly prepared to do so. Pirate might not come home often those days, but he was bound to be there for Christmas. When he saw that she was now a young lady, with her hair put up and her skirts let down, he would offer for her hand, and they would live happily ever after.

Alicia sighed again, for the eternal optimism of youth.

She had done her best to give her daughters an easier childhood than she had experienced. They were cheerful, good-natured girls, whose sunny natures drew the gentlemen to their sides as much as did their pretty faces. They had plenty of choice. Thank heaven Alicia could afford to let them follow their hearts.

The figures of the dance brought Frederica within a few

yards. Waiting for her turn, she darted out of the set to speak to her mother.

"It seems Mr. Pendragon is not a pirate after all, Mama, but he has been a privateer, which is the next best thing!" Laughing, she swirled back into the dance.

Alicia was not perfectly certain what a privateer might be. Girls these days were expected to be much more educated than when she was young, and to give her husband his due, Lord Ransome had not begrudged the expense of the finest governesses and schools. If he had known . . .

Mrs. Drummond Burrell approached again, apparently patrolling the room to ensure against infractions of the strict etiquette enforced at Almack's. A few steps beyond Alicia, she met Lady Jersey, a fellow patroness. They exchanged a few words; then Sally Jersey came on to take a seat beside Alicia.

The fifth Countess of Jersey was known as "Silence," because she only ever stopped talking for long enough to learn the gossip she then relayed. A beauty several years younger than Alicia, she fanned herself with a roguish smile which set Alicia's mind at rest. Silence was just as capable of stern hauteur as Mrs. Drummond Burrell if the rules were infringed. Since she smiled, presumably Frederica and Emily had done nothing to set her back up.

"My dear Lady Ransome," she cooed, "a little bird has whispered to me that you were once well acquainted with our latest Lion."

Hoping she had misunderstood, Alicia forced herself to smile, willed her voice to remain steady and casual. "Lion?"

"Or should I say our latest Dragon?"

Betraying heat rose in Alicia's cheeks. She fanned her face, saying, "One might almost imagine everyone here to be a fire-breathing dragon, it is so hot this evening."

"Excessively warm for the time of year," Lady Jersey

agreed with a touch of malice. "I speak of the Honourable Peter Pendragon, of course. Pirate Pendragon is an old friend of yours, I collect?"

"Yes, indeed. Lord Orford's estate marches with my father's, in Cornwall. The Pendragons and we Roscoes more or less grew up in each other's pockets. As children, we never stood upon ceremony."

"Ah, no doubt that would explain my informant's mis-apprehension. She was quite convinced of a romantic attachment, but a lack of ceremony might lead to that impression, might it not?"

"I daresay," Alicia managed to utter, scarcely above a whisper.

"A childhood friendship," mused Lady Jersey. "I am much inclined to believe the parties know altogether too much about each other for illusions to survive. It is not at all likely to lead to a flight to the Border."

"Not at all likely," Alicia echoed more firmly. She had lived out of the world, but even she knew that not only had Silence eloped with her husband-to-be, but her husband's parents had also married at Gretna Green. The maxim about people who lived in glass houses floated through her head.

She had just decided that voicing it could only confirm Lady Jersey's suspicions, when Colonel Lord Arthur Spence came up to them.

A fine figure in his scarlet regimentals, Lord Arthur was a friend of Alicia's brother James. He bowed to the ladies, and said something to Lady Jersey which Alicia did not catch. She was too startled at the sight of the slight, brown-faced gentleman standing half a pace behind him.

She had quite convinced herself that he had forgotten, or did not care.

"Lady Ransome," said Lord Arthur, "I think I need not introduce Peter Pendragon?"

"Yes. No! I mean . . ."

"Lady Jersey," he continued smoothly, "may I escort you to take some refreshment?" Lord Arthur and Lady Jersey departed, scarcely noticed by Alicia.

"Ma'am." Pirate's dark head, as dark as her own, bowed over her hand.

Her throat hurt. She managed to force out, in scarcely more than a whisper, "M-Mr. Pendragon." Then she blinked. "Why, sir, have you really been absent from England so long that you are still wearing your hair in a queue, in the fashion of twenty years ago?"

He grinned at her, and his grin had not changed by an iota. "We sailors still wear our hair long. None of these newfangled crops for us. Some of us privateers even wear an earring." He turned his head to display the gold hoop in his ear. "Shall we dance, Allie-oh?"

"Oh, Pirate!"

Six

Cornwall—1793

"Allie-oh, shall we dance?"

"Oh, Pirate, yes, please, but it is the middle of a set, you know."

"Dash it, so it is. I did not notice. I am not much in the petticoat line, you see. Next dance, then?"

It was Christmas. The Pendragons had brought a large house party to Cornwall, and they invited their neighbours to a Christmas ball.

The great hall was decked with evergreens and holly, and a Yule log burned in the vast fireplace. Alicia had never seen so many people in one place, almost all of them strangers. Feeling intimidated in spite of her new gown, she hovered at her mother's elbow.

Lady Roscoe was in her element, laughing and chattering and avidly acquiring gossip about Society acquaintances. She had to catch up on the latest *on-dits,* for they were to go to London after all.

Three things had changed Lord Roscoe's mind:

The first was the latest fashions smuggled from France. France and England might be at war, but where ladies' dress was concerned Paris still led the way. In Paris, sport-

ing silks and satins could lead to the dreadful guillotine.
Simple muslins erased the visible difference between the
hated aristos and the hating populace. So in England, ladies
at the forefront of fashion were passing their silks, satins,
and velvets to their abigails and wearing simple muslins,
high-waisted and straight of skirt. The cost of outfitting a
wife and daughter for the Season plummeted.

The second factor influencing Lord Roscoe was an invitation to stay at his brother-in-law's town house, thus ob-
viating the expense of leasing a suitable residence.

The third was desperation. No matter how hard he
struggled, he was deeper in debt each year.

Alicia, while in her father's eyes she would never match
her mother's fair beauty, had turned into an unexpectedly
attractive young lady. In London, she might—she must!—
catch the eye of a gentleman wealthy enough to bail out
his bride's family.

So Alicia was at the Pendragons' Christmas ball, testing
the waters and feeling very much as if she had plunged
in over her head, until Pirate materialized at her side. At
twenty, he was still slight and not above middle height,
but for all that, a good-looking, well set up young gentleman.

"Here, Allie, let me put my name down on your pro-
gramme, so you don't forget."

"As though I could!" Alicia proffered her humiliatingly
bare card. The only names on it were those of her brothers,
all home for Christmas, and her mother had written in
those.

"Rupert don't want to take you in for supper," Pirate
declared. "I shall scratch him out and put him in here instead, and you will take supper with me." He scribbled for
a minute, then turned to her with a smile. "I'll be dam . . .
dashed if you have not turned out quite well, Allie-oh. Dev-
ilish pretty, in fact."

Blushing, Alicia said breathlessly, "Really? Do you really mean it, Pirate?"

"I don't deal in Spanish coin, even if Spain's our ally at present."

"Is it? Mama does not let me read the political news. It is not proper for a young lady to know much about politics. She says if I am interested and my husband approves, there is time enough for that after marriage."

"Marriage!" Pirate frowned. "But you are not getting married. You are much too young."

"I shall be eighteen next May. I am going to London in the spring to look for a husband."

Alicia did not exactly expect him to tell her on the spot that she need look no further, so she was not too downcast when he laughed.

"Off to the Marriage Mart, are you?" he said. "Bedamned if I don't put in an appearance at the odd ball or two, then. You must let me know which you mean to attend."

"Will you, Pirate? I shall not feel half so terrified if I know you will be there."

"Nothing to be terrified of, Allie-oh," he said indulgently. "I daresay you will take very well. Come along, and I'll introduce you to a couple of friends of mine. Between us, we shall see that you don't sit out too many dances."

Brought up with a swarm of boys, never having learnt to be bashful, coy, or flirtatious with the opposite sex, Alicia was a great success with Pirate's friends. Between them they nearly filled her dance card, and drawn by their example, three other young gentlemen soon took the rest. She danced until supper, ate ravenously—to Pirate's amusement—and then returned to the great hall to dance again. And each of her partners in turn manoeuvred her beneath the bunch of mistletoe dangling from the musicians' gallery.

They kissed her on the cheek, boldly, shyly, apprehensively, smirkingly. All except Pirate, who kissed her teasingly, on her lips.

"Privilege of an old friend," he claimed, laughing.

Her lips burned. They still tingled hours later, back at home, when she tumbled sleepily into her bed, to dream of Pirate. She had thought she loved him before. Now she knew what true love was.

London was bewildering at first. The noise was what most struck Alicia. The racket of roisterers seeking their beds merged with the early morning cries of street sellers, peddling everything from clean sand for scouring pots to milk fresh from the cow. The din of iron-clad hooves and wheels on cobbles never seemed to cease.

Soon Alicia grew as oblivious to these sounds as she was to the birds' dawn chorus or the wind in the elms at home. Almost as quickly, she grew accustomed to the life of a young lady making her come-out.

There were endless fittings for gowns, as "simple muslins" turned out to be not so simple after all. Moreover, the whites and pale colours now in favour dirtied so quickly, one had to change one's dress half a dozen times a day. And the presentation gown was another matter altogether—Queen Charlotte still required silks and velvets, hoops and feathers, of all those making their curtsy to her.

Then there were pelisses, shawls, gloves, stockings, boots and slippers, fans, and a hundred other oddments to be purchased. The choosing of a single hat or bonnet could take an entire morning.

Lady Roscoe was in heaven. Lord Roscoe looked blacker and blacker.

As soon as the ladies had a couple of new gowns apiece, the morning calls began. Lady Roscoe knew all the important hostesses. Alicia became accustomed to being introduced with a deprecating, "Of course, I married young, and the dear child is scarcely out of the schoolroom."

What did her mother say when accompanied by Rupert, now four and twenty? Alicia wondered, as she curtsied to yet another of the Society matrons upon whose approval all depended.

Having passed this initial scrutiny, she was made acquainted with their daughters, the dozens of young ladies in the same situation. Unused as she was to the company of girls her own age, she was shy. Though she was quickly accepted as an unexceptionable companion for a stroll in Hyde Park or a visit to Hookham's Circulating Library, she made no particular friends among them.

It was quite otherwise with the young gentlemen. True to his word, Pirate called, bringing a couple of friends, one of whom she had met in Cornwall. Another of her Christmas ball partners heard she was in Town and dropped by to pay his respects. With them she was at ease.

Word spread that she was a comfortable sort of girl, as well as pretty. Youthful sprigs of fashion begged their friends for introductions. Alicia had the inestimable felicity of going to her first London ball with every single dance spoken for beforehand.

Neither Lord nor Lady Roscoe appeared to be as pleased as might have been expected. Not until much later, looking back, did Alicia guess why.

Alicia's court rivalled her mother's, and the baroness looked upon the callow youths with a jealous eye. She soon realized with relief, however, that her daughter was ill at ease with her own cicisbeos, mature men of the world who reminded Alicia of her father. She had never in her life held a proper conversation with her father.

On the other hand, the baron's disappointment rose from the youthfulness of Alicia's beaux. Most were of modest means, but even the two or three wealthy enough for his needs were young enough to be still under the influence of older relatives. They would not be permitted to marry a penniless bride and dissipate their fortunes in rescuing her family.

Scarcely aware of her parents' concerns, Alicia drove in the park with a different gentleman each day of the week, and danced each night away in the splendid ballrooms of Mayfair and St. James's. She was thoroughly enjoying herself.

If she occasionally felt guilty at the pleasure she found in frivolity, it was because of the news from France. Even the most sheltered young ladies knew that in the autumn Queen Marie Antoinette had followed King Louis to the guillotine. As the Terror's grip tightened on France, some fashionable ladies in England took to wearing red ribbons around their necks in sympathy with the victims.

However, for the most part gentlemen saved their talk of the Terror and the war against its perpetrators for occasions when ladies were not present. The only visible effect in England was the flood of emigrés fleeing across the Channel.

Alicia was less sheltered than most young ladies. Her beaux liked her because she was not missish. She did not expect a stream of extravagant compliments, or bridle at the odd oath inadvertently dropped into a conversation. They could talk to her without minding their tongues, and inevitably they talked of war.

Some spoke of joining the army. Two of them were actually subaltern officers in the Guards, and a third a lieutenant in the Royal Navy, waiting ashore while his sloop was refitted at Deptford.

Pirate bitterly envied the latter.

"If Father had let me go into the Navy when I was young enough," he said one breezy afternoon when he was driving Alicia in the park, "I should be with Admiral Hood now, fighting England's enemies."

Since Alicia was glad he was here with her instead of risking his life in storms and battles, she said consolingly, "At least you have the *Buccaneer.*"

"Yes, and I am to carry some of the fellows down the Thames from London Bridge to Greenwich on Monday, taking a look at Jerry's sloop on the way. You know most of them—would you like to come?"

"I wish I could, Pirate, but Mama would never permit me to go with you," Alicia said with a mournful sigh.

"I suppose not. Dash it, I keep forgetting you ain't a schoolroom chit any longer. It is a great bore, that young ladies have to be chaperoned."

"And I cannot imagine Mama ever again setting foot on the *Buccaneer*, even on the river."

Pirate laughed heartily. "Not a chance! Wait a bit, there is Freddie Datchett and his mother and sister. Don't despair yet, Allie-oh—I have a famous notion."

Mr. Datchett was one of the young sparks Pirate had invited aboard the *Buccaneer*, and also one of Alicia's admirers. She was also well acquainted with Lady Datchett and Miss Sophie Datchett. As Pirate drew up his gig beside their landau, she greeted them and then turned to speak to Mr. Datchett, who was on horseback and rode around to her side.

She heard Pirate say, "Just the ladies I hoped to meet. I daresay Freddie has mentioned, ma'am, that I am making up a party for a day's cruise to Greenwich in my father's yacht. May I hope you and Miss Datchett will join us?"

Mr. Datchett shot his friend a look of outraged betrayal which made Alicia giggle. The trip must have been proposed as a gentlemen-only chance for a frolic.

In answer to a query from Lady Datchett, Pirate started to expatiate upon the *Buccaneer*'s luxurious appointments.

"Shall you go, Miss Roscoe?" Mr. Datchett asked in a low voice.

"If your mama does." Alicia's mother would not care where she went as long as she was respectably chaperoned.

"Ah," he said with an air of enlightenment. "Well, I daresay it will not be so very bad, then. Sophie!" He raised his voice to address his sister. "You have not been at Greenwich, have you? It is a charming place. You are certain to enjoy it no end, I vow."

"We shall dine alfresco in the park," promised Pirate with reckless abandon.

"Mama, do let us go!" cried Sophie. "I adore eating out of doors, and I have never been on a sailing ship. I should like it of all things."

Pirate succeeded in answering Lady Datchett's further concerns, and the invitation was accepted.

"*Thank* you, Pirate," said Alicia a trifle tremulously, as he drove on.

He smiled down at her. "I like giving you a bit of fun, Allie-oh. You have always been a taking little thing."

Misty-eyed, she beamed back at him.

He groaned. "Dammit, did I say we shall dine out of doors? I have not the least notion how to go about providing a suitable dinner."

"I should consult your mama's housekeeper and cook," Alicia advised. "They will know what to do, but they will want to know how many you wish to feed."

"I had best invite Chaz's aunt and two cousins. He will not be pleased, but doubtless Lady Datchett will expect other female company. Besides, she might fall into a megrim or Miss Sophie throw out spots or something, and ruin everything. The excursion cannot very well be postponed, not for less than a month. One cannot count on the wind, but the tide will be just right on Monday."

Lady Roscoe considered an outing to Greenwich under the aegis of Lady Datchett unexceptionable for her daughter. (Alicia "forgot" to mention Pirate and the Buccaneering aspect.)

No one threw out spots. No one fell into a megrim.

The tide was just right, with a breeze to help the yacht downriver on the ebb, a breeze which kindly dropped when they went ashore at Greenwich. The sun shone. Lord Orford's household provided a magnificent repast and two footmen to serve it. The party rambled about the park and the splendid buildings of the hospital; then the breeze rose again in time to waft them homeward on the flood tide.

To Alicia, it seemed that the whole world had conspired to give her a perfect day.

Pirate drove her home from London Bridge. At her uncle's door, she jumped down from the gig and turned to thank him one more time.

He held up his hand, laughing. "Not another word, Allie. We all had a jolly time. Do you go to the Devonshires' ball tomorrow?"

"Yes. Mama says it is always the most splendid of the Season. She would not miss it for the world."

"I shall see you there, then."

He saluted with his whip and drove off, leaving Alicia to take herself inside. In spite of dancing with her at dozens of balls, he still had not quite grasped that she was a young lady now, not the child he had known forever.

Not that Alicia minded. Other escorts might hand her carefully down from their carriages, accompany her to the front door, knock for her, and see her safely bestowed

within before leaving. Pirate was in another class altogether.

A footman admitted her; then her uncle's butler came
into the entrance hall to inform her that her father wished
to speak to her. "His lordship is in the drawing room, miss."

Drawing off her gloves as she made her way upstairs,
Alicia wondered if Papa had somehow discovered her
omission as to the nature of today's outing. But she did
not think that would vex him much, though Mama might
scold. After all, her father had enjoyed the voyage to Falmouth.

Still, she could not recall when last he had sent for her.
A trifle apprehensive, she entered the drawing room.

"Papa, you wished to see me?"

"Alicia, my dear!" He strode to her with arms outspread
and embraced her jubilantly. "You have contrived mag-
nificently. All is arranged, every last detail, and signed,
too, and I must say he has come down handsomely."

"What is arranged, sir?" she asked, perplexed. "What
have I contrived?"

"Why, to find a husband, child," said her mother, kissing her cheek. "He has been closeted with your papa half
the day, determining settlements and such."

But Alicia had been with Pirate all day! A flicker of
hope arose—had Lord Orford come on his son's behalf?
No, Pirate would surely have said something.

"Wh-who?" she stammered.

"Lord Ransome, my dear. A splendid match, and one
which will save us all from the poorhouse."

"Ransome?" Alicia said, cold tremors quivering up and
down her spine. "But I am not acquainted with a Lord
Ransome!"

Seven

London—1794

Alicia was in no state to appreciate the magnificence of Devonshire House, one of the few great mansions remaining between the Cities of London and Westminster. She spared no thought for the curious receiving line: His Grace, the Duke of Devonshire; his vivacious wife Georgiana, Duchess of Devonshire; and her dear friend, his mistress, Lady Elizabeth Foster—an outwardly amicable *ménage à trois*.

It was all Alicia could do to force a smile and murmur the requisite politenesses as she curtsied.

Pirate was on the look-out for her, fortunately, for she did not think she could bear the chit-chat of friends and acquaintances. After making his bow to her mother, he turned to Alicia.

"May I beg the pleasure of the next dance, Miss Roscoe?" His smile faded to concern as he observed her expression. "Allie, what is the . . . ?"

"Yes, thank you, Mr. Pendragon," Alicia interrupted. Seeing her mother turn away to speak to someone—as always, her father had headed directly for the card room—

she went on in an urgent undertone, "Pirate, may we sit out the dance? I simply *must* talk to you!"

"We shall walk in the garden," he said promptly, offering his arm and placing his hand over hers in a comforting clasp. "It has been decorated with Chinese lanterns, I am told, and is worth viewing."

In the midst of the spreading streets and squares of Mayfair, the Cavendish family had preserved not only Devonshire House but a spacious garden. Now the trees were hung with coloured paper lanterns, glowing in the dusk. The air was scented with stocks and lilac and lily-of-the-valley. Quite a few guests had gone outside to stroll about before the May night grew chilly, so there was no impropriety in Alicia's accepting Pirate's escort.

Not that she cared. She hurried him to a marble bench well away from the main paths.

"I am to be married," she said in a tragic voice.

"What?" He stared at her in dismay. "Dash it, Allie, I'm going to marry you!"

Hope dawned. "Are you?" she asked shyly.

"Of course. Only not quite yet . . ."

"Papa cannot wait, Pirate. He is horridly in debt. He will have to sell the estate if he cannot come about soon."

"No, is it as bad as that?" said Pirate, aghast,

"Yes. So I must be married and then there will be something called settlements, which I do not perfectly understand, and everyone will be comfortable again."

"Except you! But Allie, all I have is an allowance from my father. Though it is quite enough to support you, if we lived with my family, as they would expect, I cannot possibly tow your father from the River Tick."

"Lord Ransome can," Alicia said sadly, "and will, when I marry him."

"Ransome? Good gad, Allie, he is twice your age, if

not three times. Practically a greybeard! I did not know you were even acquainted with the fellow. Do you like him?"

"I scarcely know him. He does not dance. He told Papa he had watched me often and talked to me once or twice, but I had no recollection of him when he dined with us last night. He believes I shall suit him."

"But will he suit you?" cried Pirate, scowling. "And where, may I enquire, is this ardent suitor tonight? Not escorting you!"

"No, and as he could not be here, Papa did not wish us to come, but Mama refused to miss the Devonshires' ball. Lord Ransome has gone into Lincolnshire for ten days to see to setting his house in order for our marriage. It . . . it is to be within the month." Alicia stared down at her clenched hands, blinking back stinging tears.

"Demme if it ain't just like selling you into slavery! Tell them you will not."

"Papa and Mama and Rupert all say it is my duty to the family. I ought to be glad to have caught a viscount, for Papa can marry me to whomever he chooses."

"I daresay," Pirate said disconsolately, "and he would not choose me, if I asked permission to address you, because he is bound to realize that my father would not . . . I say, Allie-oh, I have the most famous notion!"

Breathless as hope burgeoned again, she looked up at his elated face. "I knew you would think of a way to save me," she whispered.

"We shall elope to Gretna Green and be married over the anvil," Pirate proclaimed. "What a splendid jape!"

"But . . ."

"Hush a minute, let me think. Yes, I have it. Now listen, Allie-oh, and do not interrupt."

* * *

They returned to the ballroom, where Alicia stood up for the next two sets with the first two gentlemen to ask her. She did her best to look wan and listless, though she was bubbling with excitement. When her second partner returned her to her mother's side—no easy task, as Lady Roscoe also danced nearly every set—Alicia begged to go home.

"I have the headache, Mama. Truly, I cannot endure any more of this noise and bustle."

Lady Roscoe was irritated but not surprised, since her daughter was ridiculously moped over her betrothal and imminent wedding.

"How tiresome!" she said. "Well, I cannot leave now. I have promised several dances. You will just have to—ah, there is the Pendragon boy. Perhaps I can prevail upon him to escort you. Mr. Pendragon!"

"Ma'am." Pirate bowed over her hand. "I came to ask how Miss Roscoe does. She was not feeling quite the thing earlier, I believe. How do you go on, ma'am?" he enquired, turning to Alicia with a wink.

"She is most unwell," said Lady Roscoe. "She could go home in a chair but I cannot very well send her alone through the streets."

"Allow me to accompany her, ma'am. I shall summon a chair and walk beside to see her safely home."

Her ladyship was all gracious gratitude.

As the chairmen carried her through the dark city, Alicia pulled back the curtain and said to Pirate, "Mama always stays until the very last."

"You are sure she will not come to your chamber to see how you feel?"

"She never has. And her abigail—I have none of my own—will be only too pleased when I tell her I mean to sleep late in the morning, as Mama does."

"Capital! You are sure you can sneak out without being seen, Allie?"

Assuring him that she could escape unseen, she promised not to bring more baggage than a pair of bandboxes, and not to keep him waiting. He went off to pack some clean linen for himself and to fetch his gig.

No one would wonder if he said he was going to stay with a friend for a few days, or even ask exactly where he was going. Alicia envied his freedom. There was certain to be a tremendous hullaballoo when her disappearance was discovered.

Muttering at having her evening interrupted, the abigail helped Alicia take off her ball gown, hung it up, and was dismissed.

Instead of going to bed, Alicia arranged a bolster under the covers, then stuffed a shawl into her nightcap and arranged it on the pillow. As Pirate had instructed, she wrote a brief note, which she hid underneath a book on her bedside table. Then she put on her simplest dress and a warm cloak, packed up several changes of linen, and crept downstairs to the back door.

She heard her uncle's servants talking in the kitchen, and a murmur of voices came from the housekeeper's room, but she saw not a soul. The key was kept hanging on a hook beside the door. Lock and bolts were well oiled. In a trice Alicia was out in the garden.

The tiny square of grass, which rarely saw the sun, had horrified her when first she came to London from the valleys and moors of Cornwall. Now she was glad it took only a few paces to cross it to the door in the wall which led into the mews. The key was kept conveniently on a hook here, too, but in the dark she could not find its hiding place beneath the curtain of Virginia creeper.

She fumbled frantically. Suppose Pirate grew tired of waiting for her and went away! He might decide he did

not want to elope with her after all, and then she would
have to marry Lord . . .

Ah, there was the key. Hard to turn, it grated in the lock.
The noise seemed to Alicia excruciatingly loud, and the
screech of the hinges was louder yet. But no one called out
to her, no one ran down the garden after her. She slipped
out into the lantern-lit mews.

The grooms were all snoozing as they waited for the
carriages to return after bearing their masters and mistresses to and from balls and routs, to clubs or the play.
Unseen by any but a tabby cat crouched by a mousehole,
which stared at her with yellow eyes, Alicia hurried along
the alley to the street corner. A church clock began to
strike the half hour, with others joining in, near and far.
She was right on time.

And as she rounded the corner, a gig drew up.

"That is all you have brought?" asked Pirate, reaching
down for her bag and stowing it under the seat. "Good
girl! My sisters never travel with less than a pair of trunks.
Hop up now, and let us be off."

As a loverlike greeting, a stern critic might have felt
this left something to be desired. Alicia was satisfied with
his praise, and still more with his presence. She took his
outreached hand and hopped up.

Eight

On the Road to Gretna—1794

"This reminds me of running away from Miss Porringe to ride up on the moors with you," Alicia said, as the gig rattled away over the cobbles.

"Lord, yes, what times we used to have!"

Reminiscences kept them going for several miles. The city was left behind, and a bright half-moon lit their way along the turnpike. From recalling their adventures in the dinghy, Pirate moved on to the sloop his naval friend had shown him over. He was in the middle of describing its wonders when they came to a post-house.

"We shall hire a post-chaise here," said Pirate. "I could drive another stage, but you will be more comfortable, especially if it comes on to rain, and we shall go along faster. Not that we are likely to be pursued."

Enjoying the moonlit drive, Alicia had almost managed to forget about pursuit. She glanced back fearfully. "I am perfectly comfortable, but by all means let us go as fast as possible."

He put his arm around her shoulders and gave her a reassuring squeeze. "No one will guess that you are with me, nor where we have gone." He laughed as he turned

into the inn yard. "They will look for you on the road to
Plymouth. You did leave a note to that effect, did you
not?"

"Yes, just as you told me, only I doubt they will believe
it. After all, going home could not save me from Lord
Ransome. Papa would simply fetch me back to London."

"I think he will think that you think . . . oh, this is altogether too convoluted for me! At the very least, it will
delay them."

A groom ran to the horse's head, and a waiter hurried
out of the inn. Ordering one to call a postboy and put a
team to a post-chaise, the other to bring a dish of tea for
the lady and ale for himself, Pirate sprang down from the
gig.

As Alicia wearily prepared to clamber to the ground,
he came around and lifted her down, his hands about her
waist. How strong he was!

"What a little bitty creature you are." He kept his hold
on her for a moment after her feet touched the cobbles,
smiling down at her. "Light as a feather. You will feel
better after a cup of tea."

His touch, his solicitude, and the tea revived her somewhat, driving off the chilly fears of the small hours of the
morning. However, she had slept little the night before,
after learning she was to marry Lord Ransome. In spite
of the chaise's jouncing, she dozed off. Though distantly
aware of a change of horses in the grey dawn, she did not
wake fully until a sunbeam struck her face. She found
herself reclining upon Pirate's chest.

"Oh!" Quickly she sat up, trying to smooth her hair.
"I am so sorry."

"You kept me warm," he said with a grin. "I believe I
am going to enjoy being married."

"I shall try to be a good wife, Pirate, truly."

"The first thing you must learn is that gentlemen appreciate a hearty breakfast. At the next stage, we shall stop long enough to fortify ourselves."

After a good meal, they drove on, talking about how different the countryside was from Cornwall. They agreed that they would prefer to take up residence in Cornwall rather than at any of Lord Orford's other estates. Time passed quickly as the miles disappeared beneath the wheels, and postilion succeeded postilion.

That evening, as darkness fell, they stopped to sup at an inn, and Pirate took two bedchambers. Though nights were short at this time of year, he told the chambermaid to rouse them at dawn.

Alicia slept soundly, if only for a few hours. In the morning she felt quite refreshed. When Pirate proposed that they should drive on through the next night, she was perfectly willing.

Nonetheless, and in spite of having fallen asleep leaning against Pirate again, she was very weary by the time a damp, grey daybreak found them approaching Kendal. The road was in bad shape, the many potholes filled with water by recent rains. Ahead rose the high fells, wreathed in mists. To Alicia, they looked like an insurmountable barrier.

"Must we cross the mountains?" she asked. "Can we not go around?"

"I am not sure," Pirate admitted. "We left in such a hurry, I did not bring a road book."

On top of their travel through the night, this reminder of their hasty departure from London renewed Alicia's fears. She was certain someone must be on their trail by now. When they stopped in Kendal to breakfast and change horses, she kept glancing behind her.

Pirate consulted the postboys. "The other roads north are equally rugged," he reported to Alicia, "and several miles longer."

"Oh, let us take the shortest way!" she cried.

The twenty-eight miles to Penrith took all day and well into the evening. Where the road was steepest, Alicia and Pirate got out of the chaise and walked, to spare the horses. By the time they reached the Gloucester Arms, Alicia was exhausted.

Helping her down from the carriage, Pirate looked at her white face and drooping figure and said firmly, "We shall stay here tonight."

"How much farther is it to the border?"

"I shall find out."

They went into the inn. Alicia sank onto a hard, cushionless settle, while Pirate spoke to an inn servant. He came back to her frowning.

"It's about thirty miles to Gretna Green, an easy road, most of it Roman and straight as a die. So we shall be married tomorrow. But a large party of Scots is staying in the house, and there is only one chamber free. An attic chamber at that, but I have taken it for you. I shall stay in the coffee-room."

"You are as tired as I am, Pirate." She stood up and took both his hands, gazing up at him earnestly. "You will not sleep properly on a chair. And we are to be married tomorrow."

"I shall ask for a pallet and sleep on the floor beside you, then."

Alicia gave him a loving smile and repeated, "We shall be married tomorrow."

Waking in Pirate's arms, Alicia lay quite still so as not to disturb him. Beneath her cheek, his chest rose and fell steadily. She heard the strong beat of his heart.

She had not thought it possible to love him more than she already did.

His body heat kept her warm, although the chamber was chilly. Last night he had forced open the tiny window under the eaves to let fresh air into the small, stuffy room with its low, sloping ceiling. In most of the room, Pirate could not stand upright. He had laughed and said it reminded him of Jerry's sloop, where he had hit his head on a beam, though he was not tall.

Just the perfect height, Alicia thought dreamily, snuggling closer.

Through the open window came the noise of hooves and wheels on the cobbles below, and indistinct voices. The large party of Scots who had taken all the chambers in the inn must be setting out early.

Early? That was not the dim grey light of dawn. It was broad daylight! Jerking upright, Alicia shook Pirate's bare shoulder.

"Pirate, wake up! We have overslept. We must leave at once!"

He was instantly awake, sitting up and gathering her into his arms for a quick kiss before he jumped out of bed, reaching for his breeches.

"The chambermaid must have forgotten to call us, with so many others in the house. You are right, Allie, we must be off at once. While you dress, I shall go down and have the horses put to, and ask them to put up some provisions in a basket, to save time. I am ravenous."

"So am I." Meeting his laughing eyes as his head appeared through the neckhole of his shirt, Alicia blushed.

With a grin, he leant across the wide bed and kissed the tip of her nose. "Don't be long, sweetheart."

"I shall hurry."

"Good girl." He shrugged into his coat, slung his cravat around his neck like a muffler, and dashed out.

Hastily Alicia dabbled her face and hands with the cold water in the ewer on the washstand. Blessing the simple modern fashions, she dug a clean batiste gown out of her bag and slipped it over her head. Crumpled and creased, it was hardly what she had imagined wearing on her wedding day, but after all, the bridegroom was far more important than her clothes, and she had the right bridegroom.

Hurry or not, she must look as pretty as she could for him. She picked up her hairbrush and turned to the small looking-glass hanging over the washstand.

In the mirror, she saw the door latch move. He was back already.

"I shan't be a minute," she called.

The door swung open and Rupert and James strode in, mud-spattered and weary.

The hairbrush dropped with a splash into the basin as Alicia swung round, aghast. "What are you doing here?" she cried inanely.

Head bowed beneath the low ceiling, James crossed to the window, closed it, and perched, half sitting, on the sill. Rupert shut the door and lounged against it.

"Why, Allie," he said, eyebrows raised in a sardonic look, "what sort of a welcome is this, when your brothers have galloped day and night to the rescue?"

"But I do not wish to be rescued! There is nothing to rescue me from."

"Disgrace," said James tersely.

"I shall be married today, and to the son of an earl. That is no disgrace."

"If it were going to happen," Rupert drawled, "perhaps not. But it ain't. Pendragon has just decamped."

Alicia stared at him, uncomprehending.

"The pirate has weighed anchor and spread his sails." He shrugged. "Dash it, Allie, he has ridden off hell-for-leather and abandoned you."

"I don't believe you!" Alicia choked out.

"Come now, my dear," said Rupert cynically, "why the deuce should an eligible gentleman lacking only a fortune wed a girl who has not a penny to her name, but a purse-pinched family lurking in the wings? No, no, all our young friend wanted was to take you to his bed."

Nine

London—1814

"The sets are all made up long since, Mr. Pendragon," said Alicia, recovering her countenance, "and the dance is quite half over."

"I beg your pardon," Pirate said ruefully. "I'm not much accustomed to this sort of affair, though no doubt naval officers attend balls when ashore. You will stand up with me for the next, then? And in the meantime, may I sit down?"

While Alicia was trying to decide what her answers to both questions ought to be, he took the seat vacated by Lady Jersey. She noticed that he moved slightly stiffly.

"You are wounded?"

"Nothing to signify, but I thank you for your concern. The hazards of war, you know."

Alicia seized upon the neutral subject. "You have been a privateer, I understand. I am not precisely certain what a privateer is."

"A privateer is a ship or ship owner who holds a letter of marque," Pirate explained, "which is a licence from the government to attack the enemy's shipping in time of war. That is, to harass, sink, or capture both naval vessels and merchantmen."

"Is that not what our Navy does?"

"Indeed, but they must employ many ships in blockading enemy ports and carrying troops, despatches, and dignitaries, and so forth. The privateer does not have those distractions. Thus the government gains fighting ships without cost."

"Without cost?" Alicia queried. "But the sailors must be paid?"

"Oh, your privateer is in the business for the sake of his pocketbook as much as for patriotism," Pirate said with a grin. "Naturally, he prefers to take merchantmen, and as little damaged as possible. The value of the prize, both the vessel and its contents, is divided between the owner and the crew."

"So it is sort of halfway between being in the Navy and being a pirate? I am glad you attained your childhood goal in the end."

He was suddenly grave. "Yes, but I had no intention . . ."

"I hope you took many rich prizes," Alicia interrupted hastily. Almack's was no place to delve into the painful aspects of the past, if, as she feared, that was what his gravity portended. In fact, on the whole she wished he would just let sleeping dogs lie.

"I have done very well for myself," he replied, cheerful again, but with a determined look which warned her that he did not mean to let the past alone forever.

It also reminded her that he was now a mature man, to be taken seriously, not the harum-scarum boy she had once believed she knew through and through.

"I started out as third mate," he continued, "on the strength of my experience with the *Buccaneer*. We were soon at war with Spain, when the French conquered the country, and the ship I was in had the great good fortune to fall in with a couple of Spanish treasure ships."

Alicia recalled his pirate book. "Galleons full of gold and jewels from the New World?"

"Remember the picture? They have not changed much. Of course, the contents were bound for French coffers. My share gave me a good start. I worked my way up to first mate, and then the owner outfitted a new ship and made me captain. Can you guess what I named her?"

"*Buccaneer II*?" Alicia hazarded. He shook his head, his expression half teasing, half intent, almost anxious. "The *Jolly Roger*?" she guessed again.

"No," he said softly, "I called her *Allie-oh*."

Her breath caught in her throat. "Oh, Pirate!"

He took her hand in both his. He was not wearing gloves, as etiquette required. Alicia recollected that he had always preferred to go without, even when riding or driving. The warmth of his scarred and calloused hands penetrated her thin evening gloves.

"I don't know what they told you in Penrith," he said in an undertone, holding her gaze with the deep sincerity in his green eyes, "but what happened was this. When I went downstairs, they were waiting for me—my two eldest brothers and yours. Before I could utter a single word, they bundled me into a back room, little more than a closet."

"No one came to your aid?"

"They must have paid the innkeeper well, for there was no one about. They flung a coat over my head, so that I could not shout out. Pen and William held me there, while Rupert and James went to fetch you."

"They told me you had deserted me," said Alicia in a low, anguished voice. "That you had taken all you wanted of me and left."

"And you believed them?" Pirate's tone was no less intense for being quiet.

"I did not know what to think! I wanted to trust you . . . but my own brothers . . . and later, you did not come! I kept hoping . . . until I was married and it was too late."

He squeezed her hand, almost painfully. "By then I was far away. While Pen and Will chased us, my father was arranging for the privateer to take me on. It seems he was quite willing for us to wed, but as I had expected, he refused to frank your family. So your father adamantly refused to let you marry me, and insisted that I be removed from the scene until after your wedding to Ransome. There was no scandal?"

"None that reached my ears, or Ransome's."

"Not his, of course, since he married you. I might have come home then, but it was too late to help you, and, to tell the truth, life at sea suited me very well."

"It was what you always wanted," Alicia said soberly. "I am glad you had that. And I would not have you believe that my marriage was excessively unhappy. Ransome was never unkind. Only somehow we never had anything to talk about together. I was often lonely, though he was as good a husband as he knew how to be."

"Had they let us reach Gretna, I would have been as good a husband as I knew how to be, Allie," Pirate assured her, "but looking back upon my callow self, I am certain I am now capable of being a much better husband."

Stunned, Alicia was afraid to believe she had properly understood his meaning. She felt oddly dizzy.

At that moment, the dance she had quite forgotten brought her elder daughter to a spot nearby. Emily left the ranks of the country dance and swooped down upon her mother. She cast a curious glance at Pirate, who hastily dropped Alicia's hand.

"Mama," she said, her green eyes full of concern, "are you all right?"

"Yes . . ." Alicia faltered distractedly, then gathered her tattered composure about her and said more strongly, "Yes, darling, quite all right. Pray return to your partner, Emma—you are treating him abominably, I vow!"

Pirate stared after Emily as the girl hurried back to her set.

"Good Lord, she's mine!" He turned back to Alicia, his face fierce. "Allie, she *is* mine, is she not?"

Thank heaven he had kept his voice down, Alicia thought as she nodded, unable to speak. The secret she had concealed so long in her heart was laid bare. There had never been any question in her mind as to who was Emily's father, from the moment she saw those green eyes.

But the child was born very nearly nine months after her marriage. If her family guessed, they had never referred to the matter, and Ransome remained in ignorance.

Conflicting emotions chased each other across Pirate's expressive features. Alicia had no notion—had never even wondered—how he would feel. She had not expected him ever to discover that he had a daughter.

"Her name is Emma?" he asked at last.

"Emily."

"She must be nineteen. I missed her childhood," he said sadly.

"Unless I miss my guess, she will very soon be betrothed."

Pirate sighed, then demanded, "You let her choose her husband?"

"Yes, of course," said Alicia. "One forced marriage in the family is sufficient. I believe she has made an excellent choice, as has Frederica."

"Ah yes, Spence mentioned you are bringing out two girls. Not twins, I suppose?"

Alicia could not help smiling at his hopeful tone. "No, Freddie came along a year later. They are very close. There she is." She pointed out Frederica.

"A pretty pair," he said approvingly, "almost as pretty as their mama."

"And much better behaved!" Alicia told him, blushing.

"Looking back, you were quite a tomboy, were you not? Such pluck you had, joining in everything we boys did. Have you any more children? I am well-breeched now, you know. I can stand the nonsense for you and any number of children, and do it in style."

That sounded bewilderingly as if he took it for granted they would marry.

Her head spinning, Alicia babbled, "Ransome left me very well to pass, in spite of bailing out my family—my father and mother and brothers I mean. He longed for an heir, but the estate is not entailed—oh, no, we had no more children."

"Then we shall have to have some," said Pirate firmly.

Her cheeks flaming, she whispered, "I am too old."

"Fustian! My dear girl, I know to the day just how old you are, so let us have no more of such gammon. My bosun's wife was just brought to bed at two-and-forty, of a fine, bouncing boy. At any rate," he added, with a glint in his eye which made her cheeks hotter yet, "I have every intention of trying!"

"Pirate, how can you say such . . ."

"Ah, the music has ended." He stood up. "Come along, Allie, it is time for our dance."

"But, Pirate, it is a waltz!" Alicia protested as her daughters came up to them. "Besides, I am a chaperone."

Emily and Frederica looked at each other with the perfect understanding which united them.

"Go along, Mama," Emily said indulgently. "You know

we only waltz with Lord Ames and Mr. Fairweather. We shall be perfectly safe."

"Yes, do, Mama," put in Frederica. Laughing, she added, "I do not suppose, at your august age, you require permission from a patroness to waltz, but if you do, here is Lady Jersey come to give it."

Silence's quick glance surveyed the four of them with avid curiosity, taking in the girls' amusement, the intriguing Mr. Peter Pendragon's determination, and Alicia's blush. Especially the latter. Alicia wondered whether her face would ever feel cool again.

"My dear Lady Ransome," said the patroness, a trifle maliciously, "I believe you must have mislaid your fan. May I lend you mine?"

"Thank you, Lady Jersey," Alicia replied with what dignity she could muster, "I have my own here." She had quite forgotten its existence.

Pirate took it and opened it for her, every move scrutinized by Lady Jersey. He placed the fan in Alicia's hand, took her other hand in his, and turned to the patroness.

"Ma'am?"

"Oh!" Beneath her flibbertigibbet manner, Lady Jersey was not stupid. "Lady Ransome," she said, "may I present Mr. Peter Pendragon to you as a desirable partner for the waltz?"

The music began and, half sure she was dreaming, Alicia moved on Pirate's arm onto the floor.

Where he had learnt to waltz, Alicia could not begin to guess. She only knew she felt completely at home and at peace in his arms.

Until he stopped in the middle of the floor, felt in his pocket, and said, "Deuce take it, I knew I had forgot something. Do you remember, Allie-oh, I once promised you emeralds?"

"Oh, Pirate, when you were a boy!"

"Except under duress, have I ever broken a promise to you? The first Spanish galleon I was at the taking of, I asked for a bag of uncut emeralds as part of my share. I have had them cut and set. I did not bring the whole lot with me tonight—there is a necklace, bracelets, earrings, a hair ornament—ah, here it is!" Triumphantly, he fished a small, velvet-covered box from the pocket. "I brought this, in case I struck lucky and found you first try."

He opened the box to reveal a ring with a large, deep green emerald. Alicia gasped.

"I hope it fits," he said anxiously.

Then right there in the middle of Almack's dance floor, with waltzing couples coming to an astonished halt all around them, he peeled off her left glove and placed the ring upon her fourth finger.

"Oh, Pirate," she said, misty-eyed, "you always did have to do things differently."

"Do you mind?"

"Not a bit."

So he kissed her.

Frederica started the applause. Emily quickly joined in, gamely followed by their partners. It was taken up by those around them, until the greater part of the cream of London Society was cheerfully applauding Pirate and Alicia. And, led by Lady Jersey, even the haughty patronesses lent a hand.

THE ROGUE

by

Valerie King

One

"So this is where the infamous Lord Rotherby resides," Miss Peatling murmured to her charge as the doors closed upon them. "Well! I must say the gabblemongers did not lead me to expect so much elegance, but then, very little I have heard of his lordship has proven true!"

The butler had ushered them reluctantly to the yellow salon, his expression strongly disapproving of their presence in his master's home. He was right, of course. No Lady of Quality or of sense ought to cross such a threshold, for Lord Rotherby's home was reknowned as an iniquitous den of rogues and libertines, where all manner of orgy was said to take place, where wine was consumed to excess, presumably from human skulls, and where it was rumored Cyprians paraded about the halls *en déshabillé.*

Miss Peatling surveyed the chamber she had imagined a hundred times and felt she ought to have shuddered upon such reflections. Alas, Alexandra had very few sensibilities.

"I find this chamber quite lovely," the youthful Miss Burbage observed. "The furniture is of the latest style, and nothing could be more beautiful than the accents of red silk against all this yellow damask. I have a sense that I am in the Orient. Do you not as well, Miss Peatling?"

"I do, indeed. And what a magnificent black lacquer chest, by the fireplace. I wonder if his lordship was at all involved in the arrangement of this chamber, or even the purchasing of the furniture?"

"I was," a masculine voice suddenly boomed from across the room. "I accompanied the chest from China along with the numerous vases and bowls."

Miss Burbage gave a small cry, then covered her lips with her hand, so startled was she at Rotherby's sudden appearance.

Miss Peatling, on the other hand, merely turned toward her host and smiled politely. "How wonderful," she responded evenly. "I cannot imagine a happier excursion."

"On the return trip, we encountered a typhoon off the Bay of Bengal," he said, in dampening accents. "Believe me, there was nothing *happy* about the occasion in the least."

"I beg to differ. You survived, did you not, as did your chest, bowls, and vases?"

His lips twitched as he met her gaze, a puzzled frown between his brows. "By God, you are not in the usual style."

"No, I suppose I am not," she said. "Much to the dismay of my great-aunt, who had the raising of me."

He merely chuckled.

The laughter in his grey eyes was her final undoing. Her heart swelled, creaked, and groaned under the awful weight of a *tendre* which had taken possession of her nigh on five years since. To be in love with a rogue—what foolishness! To have fallen in love with a rogue because she had once *seen* him in Bath—what stupidity!

But there it was. She had formed an attachment to a man she had seen on only one occasion and of whom she had heard truly wretched tales since time out of mind. He might have said she was not in the usual style, but neither was her poor heart.

"You must be Lord Rotherby," she said. He bowed slightly, which encouraged her to continue. "How do you do? I hope you will forgive the intrusion and believe that only the direst of circumstances would have forced me to—er, kidnap your niece in order to seek protection beneath your roof. I am Miss Peatling, governess to your niece, Miss Ernestine Burbage, and I desire above all things to make her known to you." She gestured with an elegant sweep of her hand toward her charge.

She could see that she had stunned him with her speech and was pleased with the manner with which he stared at her, his mouth slightly agape. He found his tongue readily enough, however, as he glanced cursorily at Ernestine.

Shifting his gaze back to Miss Peatling, he addressed her. "You must go," he stated, his eyes suddenly drooping with boredom. "I have no patience with m'sister, Fanny, and no interest whatsoever in her offspring. As for seeking protection beneath my roof, I find the notion laughable. Do you know where you are, madam?"

"Miss," she corrected gently. "Miss Peatling, as I told you before."

"So you did," he remarked quietly. His gaze drifted over her, from the top of her head down the entire length of her to the tips of her half-boots peeping from beneath her round gown of an elegant grey silk. "A spinster, eh?"

Was his remark meant to belittle her? And what nonsense was this to eye her as one might a brood mare one was wishful of purchasing? "Yes," she responded, unruffled.

Again, his lips twitched. "You are deuced pretty—for an ape-leader."

"I have been told as much."

"Then why the devil are you still unwed?"

His question was wretchedly impertinent, but she was of a mind to answer him. "I will confess I have had any number of quite unexceptionable offers. However, and also quite to the dismay of my great-aunt, I am rather particular, having determined since I was quite young to marry only where I loved."

"Your standards are so high, then?"

She nodded.

In return, he scowled. "I daresay a woman with such careful notions would be the bane of any honest English husband."

She smiled faintly. " I would hope any husband of mine would find my faults to be balanced by the high degree of affection in which I would hold him."

He laughed outright. "You do speak plainly. I daresay you send all the high-sticklers in the boughs."

"Yes," she responded evenly. "I have a lamentable lack of sensibility and a dreadful tendency to speak my mind, which was why I did not hesitate to come here. You might have a notorious reputation and you might even have attempted to overset me by your ridiculous leers and bold questions, but I am not such a hen-hearted creature."

He considered this, clasping his hands behind his back, and moving to stand close to the fireplace. "And, it would seem, you are given to breaking the King's law. Kidnapping is a hanging offense. Fanny lives but twenty miles from here. I daresay you have not yet been missed. I suggest you return to Lacey Grove. I have no interest in aiding this—this chit of a girl." He waved his hand dismissively toward Ernestine.

Miss Peatling ignored him and turned to smile warmly upon her charge. "Come. Make your prettiest curtsy for your uncle. Yes, yes, he is a trifle high-handed to be sure, but believe his bark to be much worse than his bite. He has far too much humour in his eyes to be a completely reprehensible character."

"Do not be so sure," Lord Rotherby called out firmly, scowling a little more.

"Nonsense," Miss Peatling said, as Miss Burbage drew close to her. "I have a great deal of experience, especially where irascible people are concerned, and you are not one of them. Generally, such people have a particular ailment which makes them come the crab more frequently than is necessary. You seem perfectly fit." She watched a smile flicker at the corner of his lips. His eyes were dancing. She felt encouraged and continued, "May I present your niece to you?"

"Do I have a choice?" he queried.

She merely smiled in response.

Miss Burbage took this as her cue to drop into a lovely curtsy. When she rose, she said, "I am happy to make your acquaintance, Uncle Phillip. I have heard of you for a long time, though I have refused to believe even half of what is said of you. I do not pay a great deal of heed to the gabblemongers, and I would agree with Miss Peatling—you do have a wonderful smile in your eyes. She was always telling me that the eyes are the windows of the soul."

He scowled even more heavily upon Ernestine, but she held her ground with a gentle smile as she returned his gaze unwaveringly. At last, he grunted and moved swiftly to the bell-pull. "Trying to turn me up sweet, eh? Well, it won't fadge, though you might as well have a little refreshment before you leave."

"I was hoping for a little dinner," Miss Peatling suggested.

"Dinner? Well, that is being forward! Have you no sense of decorum?"

Miss Peatling only shook her head.

"Very well," he said gruffly on a long-suffering sigh.

Miss Burbage began to smile rather broadly. "He is just as you said he would be," she whispered conspiratorially. "And to think I feared he might be an ogre!"

"Miss Ernestine!" Rotherby snapped. "If you intend to remain in my drawing room, then I suggest you cease your whisperings. I think it excessively unbecoming in a young lady."

"Of course, Uncle. You are very right and I do beg your pardon."

He met her gaze once more and a faint frown appeared between his brows. "You favor my father, I think," he said, his tone quieter. "He was quite handsome. You've his light blue eyes, and the shape of your chin and nose is very much like his. Though I must say, you are the nearest thing to angelic I have ever seen, which my father never was. I only wonder—" He broke off as his butler, Norton, appeared in the doorway.

When he had given orders that two more covers were to be laid for dinner, he fell into a brown study. He moved to the fireplace once more where, with one foot on the hearth, he settled his gaze on the flames of the comfortable log fire. "You should not have come here," he stated again, turning toward Miss Peatling once more.

"You are very right, of course. However, the extent of your rather odious reputation makes your home the perfect choice for conducting the kidnapping, since few will believe I would actually come here." She promised to do penance for the whiskers she was telling. "I am trusting that Mrs. Burbage will remain ignorant of her daughter's whereabouts—that is, until I am able to determine precisely what I should do with her."

"You are intent on this kidnapping, then," he stated.

She nodded once, quite firmly.

At that, he lifted a brow and seemed to give pause. In

doing so, he let his gaze drift over her face in a peculiar manner which brought a strong increase to the tempo of her pulse. She repressed a schoolgirl's sigh.

What he might have said went unvoiced as a terrible sound erupted suddenly from the entrance hall.

Miss Peatling exchanged a look with Miss Burbage.

"What the devil?" Rotherby cried.

"I fear it is one of my suitors," Miss Peatling explained hastily. "I had hoped Freddy would show a little sense and remain in Lacey Grove. Alas, I fear he . . . he could not restrain himself." Here she bit her lip slightly, "If you must know, he is a budding poet and favors Byron's rather reckless manners besides his casual style of dress."

"But why, exactly, has he burst into my home?" Rotherby demanded.

"I believe he intends to protect my virtue," she responded.

"To protect your virtue!" he exclaimed, dumbfounded. He stared at her yet again in some astonishment and awaited the entrance of yet another completely unwanted guest.

The doors burst open and Freddy Stanfield appeared, sword in hand. Norton remained behind him, his complexion white, his gaze fixed to the sword, which appeared fully capable of rending Rotherby in two.

Miss Peatling shook her head, for Freddy was a most absurd youth. He had been her protector in his self-proclaimed knightly fashion for the past year and never failed to cut a completely ridiculous figure wherever he went. He was young, and for that reason she had always treated him gently. She might not entirely approve of his conduct toward her, she might even become hotly irritated with him upon occasion, but she knew very well that he was in the throes of his first love, and for the life of her she did not have the heart to reject him out of hand.

He wore a spotted Belcher kerchief tied in a loose knot about his throat. His curls, crafted meticulously in the style known as *à la cherubim,* gave him a terribly romantic aspect made even more youthful by the fact that he was not yet nineteen years of age.

"Rotherby!" he cried, his face turning a dark, reddish hue.

"Yes?" his lordship inquired in just such an affable manner as caused Miss Peatling to tilt her head and regard him wonderingly yet again.

The halfing charged, his sword at full tilt.

Miss Peatling heard Ernestine cry out, but for herself she felt only a mild dismay that poor Freddy would actually assault a man well known to have fought and won several duels, at least two of them with swords.

Rotherby stepped aside swiftly, caught the young man at the nape of the neck, and sent him sprawling. Freddy rammed headfirst into the leg of a solid table near the sofa, and immediately his entire body went limp. His sword clattered harmlessly to the hearth.

Miss Peatling turned to look at Rotherby and saw that he was adjusting his neckcloth a trifle as he regarded Freddy's prostrate form in a rather bored manner.

"Oh . . . my," she drawled beneath her breath. Had she not been undone before, this particular action, performed so effortlessly, must certainly have completed the task.

"And so neatly accomplished," Ernestine whispered, "as though Mr. Stanfield were aught but a leaf."

To Rotherby, Miss Peatling said, "I have never before seen anything like it. You are to be commended, my lord."

He turned for a moment and frowned at the ladies. "Did you actually expect he would run me through?" he snapped. He then crossed the room to bend over the hapless youth. With careful hands, he touched Freddy quite gently in the vicinity of his neck and upper back.

Miss Peatling approached him and offered the use of her vinaigrette. "I trust his neck is not broken."

"I certainly hope not," he stated, staring up at her again with a frown. "You do not mean to swoon, do you?"

"Whatever for?" she replied truthfully.

He narrowed his eyes at her for a full three seconds, as though trying to make her out, before taking the vinaigrette. Withdrawing his attention from her, he popped the lid open, and wafted the pungent fragrance at the tip of Freddy's nose.

The young gallant began to squirm and moan.

Miss Peatling turned to Norton, who was waiting, still shocked, near the doorway. "Will you be so good as to fetch a bowl of cold water and a clean linen? I believe Mr. Stanfield will have some need of it in a moment or two."

"Y-yes, miss," he muttered. After waiting for Rotherby's nod of assent, he left the chamber.

Freddy's eyes opened and he leaned up on his elbows. "What the devil—?"

"Can you move your legs, old chap?" Rotherby queried.

His boots flip-flopped as he waggled his feet. "Yes, but—m'head!"

"You cracked it on my mahogany table. I expect you will be in some discomfort for at least a fortnight."

Freddy blinked and turned to look into Rotherby's face. "Why, you—!" He lifted a hand to the viscount's throat, then suddenly broke off his renewed attack. He grabbed at his head, came to a sitting position, and groaned loudly.

"You had best let me tend to him, my lord," Miss Peatling said. "I have been used to doing so since he arrived in Sussex last year to pay a visit on a neighbour. Unfortunately, he has been in one scrape after another, having taken a fancy to me."

"A fancy!" Freddy cried, looking up at her, deeply offended. " 'Tis no fancy! I *love* you, my dear Miss Peatling! With all my heart, with every depth of honorable sentiment, with——! Oh, *my head!*"

"Yes, yes. There, you see, you should not speak, nor make any more impassioned speeches. Now, try if you can to rise to your feet. Rotherby will assist you. Pray do not, however, attempt to join battle with him again. Time enough once you are recovered, to call him out and face him properly some foggy morning or other. Only I do think you ought to take a few lessons first, or did you not know of your host's reputation?"

"I did not give a fig for his reputation!" Freddy cried grandly, wincing as he slowly rose to his feet. "Only that I must protect your honour. At risk of life and limb, I came to your aid, to do all that I could . . ."

Miss Peatling cut him off. "Well, Freddy, I think it wretchedly unchivalrous of you not to take into account your enemy's skill as a swordsman. Of what use to me would you be, had he killed you? I would have been left to fend for myself." She heard a choking sound nearby, but she refrained from meeting Rotherby's gaze.

Freddy stared at her, wavering on his feet. He appeared horrified yet again. "I had not thought of it in that light!" he cried.

"Well, you ought to have. For all your professions of love and wishing to defend me, you have not precisely proven yourself to be at all reliable. Only look! The very man whom you meant to slay is even now supporting your right arm."

Freddy appeared entirely disconcerted as he glanced at Rotherby. "My head aches," he said at last, in a very small voice, as Rotherby and Miss Peatling guided him carefully to the sofa. Once there, she saw him propped up on several pillows. Norton arrived and she immediately dipped the linen in the cool water, wrung it out, and laid it across his brow.

"Please lie quietly for a time," she said.

When she attempted to move away, he caught her wrist. "Sit with me," he said, his eyes droopy with love.

She cast him a reproving glare, and he immediately released her wrist. "Much better. And now I have business to attend to with our host."

She addressed Rotherby in a whisper. "Is there another chamber to which we might remove? I feel I ought to acquaint you with the particulars of your niece's unhappy plight."

"Yes, of course," he said, his expression somewhat bewildered as he gestured to the doorway. Guiding her across the chamber, he queried, "Only tell me, am I to expect more of your suitors? Ought I to inform Norton?"

Miss Peatling thought for a moment. She could see that her host was being facetious; however, she felt obliged to tell him the truth. "Yes," she stated baldly. "I am not certain how it came about, but Freddy may undoubtedly be the first of many, for I made the supreme mistake of telling my maid of my destination. It was rather badly done, for she is of a volatile disposition, though quite extraordinarily skilled with a pair of curling tongs, and took it into her head that I would be in some danger were I to venture into your domicile. She, in turn, informed our dear vicar, who has been forever trying to marry me off to his friend, Mr. Cropston. Unfortunately, he sought out Mr. Cropston at the Bell and Eel Inn, and proclaimed my intentions to all the inhabitants of the tavern. Sir Marcus Flintham, also a suitor, was there, along with Lord Ravenstone."

"The Earl of Ravenstone?" he queried, pausing at the door. "Also a suitor?"

"Yes, I fear it is true."

At that, he burst out laughing. "He is sixty, if a day."

Miss Peatling stiffened her spine in an entirely playful manner. "Yes, but he is excessively devoted to me besides being quite wealthy."

He met her gaze fully at that, his face still lit with laughter. She looked into eyes she could only describe as being the colour of a dove's wing. How odd for a rogue to have eyes the colour of a dove. She felt in terrible danger at that moment, not of being seduced by any means, but of something more profound, more dangerous by far, surely, for she felt certain that she might never reclaim her heart.

He said, "My original estimation of you has only been confirmed—you are not in the usual style."

He led her across the hall and into what was a small antechamber decorated charmingly in soft shades of violet, green, and beige. "How lovely!" she cried ingenuously. "Is this your handiwork as well?"

He left the doors wide, for propriety's sake.

"Not by half," he said, giving his head a shake. "A most excellent friend of mine, Mrs. Lealand, took it into her head that a garden room was just what was needed and I permitted her free rein. You see, it overlooks a particularly charming aspect of my southerly gardens." He gestured to the tall windows, through which a spring sun was shining. The windows opened onto a small terrace which spilled into an exquisite garden below.

She moved to the windows and sighed. "Your friend has excellent taste. I vow I would spend every afternoon just here, though perhaps not in summer for I suspect that the room might become a trifle warm, but in every other season, surely. The gardens are laid out so prettily. At your instigation?"

"No," he said, joining her by the window. "My grandfather's. After his obligatory tour of the Continent when he was twenty, he could not resist fashioning at least part of his extensive grounds in the European tradition. His father encouraged his involvement in the estate."

Alexandra heard the faint disgruntlement and turned toward him. She wondered two things—whether Mrs. Lealand was more than just a friend and what dissatisfaction was presently tasking his thoughts. She might have begun a gentle probing of these curiosities had he not looked at her suddenly and said, "You do not give a fig for Ravenstone's wealth, do you?"

"No, why should I? After all, I am mistress of my own fortune."

"I beg your pardon?"

"I am mistress of my own fortune. I have been since I gained my majority six years ago."

"I do not understand in the least. Why the devil are you yet a governess?"

Miss Peatling glanced across the hall. She noted that Ernestine was at present arranging a pillow for Freddy beneath his left elbow. "I could not leave her," she said somberly. "Even after I gained my majority."

"How and why did you ever become her governess in the first place, if your future was already so hopeful?"

She smiled sadly. "When I was eighteen, I quarreled with my great-aunt, with whom I resided. At the time, she was adamant that I should wed a man of her choosing. I refused, and because she was a lady who did not take kindly to having her will thwarted, made the proposed marriage an ultimatum—either marry or forfeit her patronage. For me, there was no choice, not really, for as I told you before, when I marry, I shall marry a man who pleases me. Hence, I became a governess, which I preferred vastly to waiting on her every whim or, as I have said before, to marrying where I did not love. She forgave me in time, but by then I had served as Ernestine's governess for a year and was not inclined to return to my aunt, fearing that we would quarrel yet again."

"But you must have come into your fortune a year or two later, yet you say you could not leave Ernestine. I profess I am utterly mystified. I should have thought you would have been anxious to remove to London, to live before the world in a fashion that might have brought the best of tonnish society to your feet. I have little doubt you would have been pursued by a great many suitors, even more than you apparently possess in Sussex."

She saw the laughter in his eyes and once more was charmed by him. Oh, how much she had hoped that once she finally met the notorious Rogue Rotherby, she would have been able to set aside her ridiculous *tendre* in order that she might be able to accept another man's hand in marriage. She was fully convinced that her incomprehensible attachment to Rotherby had made any other love an impossibility and at seven and twenty, she had reached just such an age that she desired more than anything to marry, to set up her nursery, to grow old beneath the loving kindness of her husband as her children flowered and matured in her care, to one day shower her grandchildren with all manner of affection and gifts.

Yet, here he was, as charming, as accomplished, as elegant as she had supposed he would be given her encounter with him in Bath. She realized that she had been sincerely hoping that he was in fact the ogre all the gabblemongers had insisted he was. Then she would have had no difficulty at all in relinquishing her schoolgirlish dreams about him.

Alas, with so much good-humour in his eyes, she feared her sentiments for him were deepening with each minute she remained in his presence.

Repressing a sigh, she explained why she had not gone to London, or anywhere else. "I know it must sound quite odd in me, but I have come to love your niece as I would love a daughter. I never expected to feel such a closeness to my charge. But there it is. And"—here she hesitated—"though I risk giving offense, I could not bear the thought of leaving Ernestine in the care of her mother."

"You need not spare my feelings where my sister is concerned, for I have none on the subject. Fanny is a vain, silly woman with whom I have had nothing to do since I was in my salad days. But tell me, who was it your great-aunt wished you to wed?"

She smiled. "Ravenstone."

At that, Rotherby started. "And he still pursues you?"

"I believe it has become a habit with him. I cannot explain his interest otherwise."

"You continue to underestimate your charms."

She shook her head. "On no account," she argued. "I believe he presses his suit because he is certain of a refusal. He is perfectly safe in my company and well he knows it. I promise you that were I to suddenly accept his hand, he would go off in a fit of apoplexy."

He barked his laughter once more, after which he smiled rather broadly, revealing a display of even, white teeth. She loved his smile in particular, for she had seen him smile that day in Bath, his expression warm and tender as he looked at the young lady beside him. There had been something in the exchange, so full of mutual affection and devotion, that had quite stolen her heart. She had at first believed she was his wife, though rather young, but she had learned afterward that she was his natural daughter by a woman who had died of consumption some years earlier.

"What is it, Miss Peatling?" he inquired softly. "You have a very odd expression on your face at the moment."

She turned away from him and began a slow progress toward the far wall, upon which hung a landscape which featured his home in the very center. "Have you ever been in love with a dream?" she queried.

"No, I do not think so," he responded, following along beside her. "Have you?"

"Yes, I have, for some time now. Only I wish very much to be rid of the dream that I might live my life more fully, but I do not know how to manage it, precisely."

"Were you to relinquish this dream, would you likely marry, perhaps even one of your suitors?"

"I think so," she said, moving to stand in front of the painting. "You know, your home is quite lovely, prettier than I imagined."

"Your incredulity tells me you expected to find me living in my barn with the horse stalls for drawing rooms. Admit it is so."

She chuckled. "I thought no such thing. I will confess, however, that though I made every effort to treat all the gossip I heard about you with disdain, I still could not quite dispel in my mind the numerous descriptions I heard of your home having been decorated in the manner of a brothel."

He chuckled. "All your sources are greatly mistaken. I only transformed the London town house in that manner, making use of a great deal of brocade and velvet and a quite gaudy purple silk woven with gold threads."

She could not prevent laughing even though she knew such a conversation was quite beyond the pale. Somehow she could not be offended by the man before her.

"You are not shocked? Not even a little?"

She shook her head. "As I told you before—"

"Yes, yes. You lack a fitting degree of sensibility."

"Scarcely any."

A silence, very gentle and companionable, fell between them. She knew she should speak to him of Ernestine's present difficulty, but of the moment she had no thoughts but of the inescapable truth that there seemed to be no way of detaching her stricken heart from the man beside her.

"This dream," he began slowly, "how long has it possessed you?"

"Several years," she stated easily.

"And it involves a man?"

"The dream of a man, yes."

"A gentleman?"

She smiled. "I believe so."

He chuckled. "But you are not certain?"

"If you will recall, I am quite particular, and I am not sufficiently acquainted with the man to call him a gentleman. However, he has proven himself in many respects to deserve the appellation."

"Ah. Has he ever kissed you?" he asked teasingly.

"No," she responded.

"That is a great deal too bad, for I daresay were he to kiss you, he might seem a little less like a dream and more like a man. You might even find you wished to marry *him*."

"Perhaps." The very thought of kissing Rotherby made her face warm and her heart beat wildly in her breast.

"I have embarrassed you. I do beg your pardon."

She chuckled. "I am not embarrassed."

"Your cheeks are quite pink."

She turned toward him. " I am not embarrassed, I promise you."

He regarded her strangely for a long moment, his eyes locked with hers. "Have I ever met you before? In this moment, you suddenly seem quite familiar to me."

She drew in a long, quiet breath and confessed the truth, or at least part of it. "I saw you once, in Bath, at the Pump Room, some five years past. The season was winter, just before Christmas. I would not expect you to remember, precisely, but the encounter might perhaps explain your impression of knowing me." She felt breathless, both at the memory of the brief encounter as well as at the hope he would know her after all.

He cocked his head slightly. "By all that's wonderful!" he cried. "That day! Yes, five years ago. I remember you most particularly and am stunned that I have only now fitted the memory, and your presence before me now, together. You wore a cherry-red bonnet and snowflakes dotted the dark blue woolen cape covering your shoulders. I recall it as though it were yesterday. You met my gaze quite boldly, just as you do now. I was stunned by the circumstance because generally ladies of quality were wont to give me the cut direct. I recall feeling as though you had peered into my soul, and your smile was as soft as winter's light. By God, it is you!"

"Yes," she stated serenely, a tremendous joy flooding her heart. So, he not only remembered the moment but had taken some apparent delight in it as well, just as she had.

He moved closer to her so that he was barely a foot away. "Would I offend you if I told you I returned to the Pump Room every afternoon for a full fortnight afterwards in hopes of seeing you again?"

Her heart took flight. "In what manner could that ever be offensive to me or to any lady?" she asked, meeting his gaze fully.

"Because I am not considered a proper sort of man. But that's right—you do not have a great deal of sensibility."

She merely smiled.

"Why did you not come back to the Pump Room? I spent hours in that wretched place hoping to catch another glimpse of you."

"I returned to Sussex early the next day."

"Would you have come back otherwise—that is, if you had remained in Bath?"

She nodded. "Of course."

His expression was full of wonderment. "What would have happened, I wonder? Would you have permitted me to address you?"

"Yes, most certainly." She wanted to tell him how much she had admired him in that moment, but she felt that such a revelation would have been wholly improper.

"My God," he murmured. "Yet, you knew then of my reputation and you still would have come to me?"

"Of course."

"How easily you say that. I believe you are speaking humbug or trying to turn me up sweet again."

"Now I am offended. Is there anything I have said to you today that would lead you to believe I am in the habit of telling whiskers or of employing feminine artifice in the hopes of achieving my objectives?"

"No, but then, you are presently kidnapping my niece, so I ought to be allowed to doubt your character at least a trifle."

"Well, there is that, to be sure," she said, giggling.

"Where have you been all these years?" His voice was nearly a whisper.

"In Sussex—looking after your niece."

"Good God. Are you telling me that all these years, had I been more nearly involved with my family, I might have had occasion to meet you again?"

"Undoubtedly," she breathed. "Indeed, I hoped for it season after season. Alas, you were fixed in your disinterest in your sister."

"Then I have wasted a great many years."

He took a step closer, and his hand touched the sleeve of her gown. His gaze was still locked tightly to hers. She felt very light-headed, almost as though she might faint, yet she had never swooned in her entire existence. Oh, to kiss Rotherby! Was that what he desired in this moment?

"I would kiss you," he whispered, as though answering her unvoiced question. His right arm slipped about her waist, and he caught her chin in his hand. "I have waited so many years to do so. Do I have your permission?"

"Yes," she whispered.

His lips touched hers in a light kiss that seemed suspended in time and in the past of so much waiting. She trembled, and he held her more tightly. His lips moved over hers and her arm crept about his neck. His tongue touched her lips, and a terrible weakness assailed her. She clung to him and he supported her with the strength of his arm about her waist. He kissed her very deeply, and her mind became full of stars and of a dark night sky. She was dreaming. Surely, she was dreaming!

The stars began to disappear one by one. Her mind was filling with a blackness. Somewhere deep within her soul, she knew she was about to swoon. Oh, what madness! To swoon from a rogue's kiss!

She was jerked suddenly from her faint by shouting which originated from across the hall.

She opened her eyes and blinked. Feeling returned to her feet, and her mind began to clear.

"What the devil?" Rotherby cried, still holding her firmly, as though unwilling to let her go.

She bit her lip. "Oh, dear. Mr. Cropston has arrived." She paused and listened. "With Ravenstone, I think."

Rotherby's arm slid away from her. "More of your suitors have arrived?"

"I fear it is true."

She started to move away, but he stayed her. "Wait. Miss Peatling, why did you let me kiss you so easily?"

She smiled falteringly. "Because you are the dream I

am trying to dispel, and you were right. You seem much more like a man to me now than just a dream."

He seemed utterly astonished as she turned to make her way back to the yellow salon.

Two

When Alexandra arrived on the threshold of the drawing room, she found that Mr. Cropston had picked up poor Freddy's sword and was brandishing it in front of Lord Ravenstone. Lord Ravenstone, on the other hand, squinted at him, for he could not see at all well.

"You have a sword in hand!" his lordship cried at last. "Whatever for? I vow, you are the silliest fellow that ever lived."

"I shall run you through, Rupert! I never liked you. Never! Always boasting about your hunters as though no one else on earth knows how to breed good stock. I do not know why you are here! I told you not to come, you and—and Flintham."

"You did not tell Freddy to stay away," his lordship stated petulantly.

"Freddy is a child!"

Freddy sat up quickly. "I am not! I am nearly nineteen and shall be at university next term! Oh, my head!" He lay back down and closed his eyes.

Ernestine, who was tending him, laid the cloth once more upon his forehead.

"Mr. Cropston!" Miss Peatling called out. "Pray put Freddy's sword back on the hearth and cease harassing

Lord Ravenstone. You could not do battle with him anyway, for I daresay he forgot to bring his spectacles, did you not, my lord?"

Lord Ravenstone squinted in her direction and began patting every pocket on his person until he announced, "So I did! How well you know me, my dear Miss Peatling." He moved toward her, a hand outstretched. She did not hesitate to place her hand in his, whereupon he lifted her fingers to his lips and placed a gentle kiss on them.

"Is your rheumatism bothering you at all?" she queried gently, for, indeed, she had a fondness for the old gentleman. "There are a great many clouds in the north, and I daresay we shall have a fine rain by evening."

"I am perfectly well. Only tell me what persuaded you to cross Rotherby's threshold?"

"My lord," she said hastily, "May I present our host, Lord Rotherby? Are you known to him? Shall I make the introductions?"

Lord Ravenstone stared up at the man beside her and squinted hard at his face. "Rotherby, eh? Met you years ago in Tunbridge Wells. Remember the day quite clearly, for you had just jumped down from your High Flyer and your father presented you. He was half foxed and you were impertinent. No, no, do not apologize, for I've heard excellent things of you in recent years and the rest I set down to an erratic upbringing, so I do not intend to scold you now. Presently, however, and I do not mean to offend you, I cannot like Miss Peatling or Miss Burbage being here. A bachelor's house, you know."

"I told Miss Peatling as much when she arrived an hour ago, but she refused to leave. Do you wish to stay to dinner? I should be happy to instruct my man to lay covers for you, for all of you."

"Only for me," he stated quickly. "Cropston is just leaving and Freddy Stanfield should seek a physician's care at once. It is my opinion the child should be bled, having received such a blow to the head. He will develop a brain fever otherwise, as children are wont to do."

"I am not a child!" Freddy cried hotly yet again. "I am nearly . . . oh, my head. Miss Burbage, pray dip the linen in the cool water again."

"And *I* have no intention of leaving!" Mr. Cropston exclaimed with equal indignation. "I did not chase your dust these past four hours merely to take my leave because you have chosen to be uncivil. Though why you must—"

"Mr. Cropston," Miss Peatling interjected hastily. "Are you known to Lord Rotherby as well?"

Mr. Cropston bethought himself and made his bow. "I am. We were formally introduced at the Leicester hunt two years past."

"I remember it well," the viscount said evenly, his eyes dancing.

"You were riding the finest stallion I'd seen since time out of mind. Well, well, since I am here, I shouldn't mind having a look at your stables a little later, if you would permit me to do so."

"My head groom would be delighted to show you about."

"Thank you. Only"—here he realized he had allowed himself to be deterred from his objective, for he suddenly turned toward Miss Peatling—"I nearly forgot. I . . . I meant to take you away, as swiftly as possible. My carriage awaits you, and Miss Burbage, of course. You poor things! You cannot like being under the roof of such a man as our host? Come, let me take you back to Lacey Grove. I daresay Mrs. Burbage is frantic with worry, and—and we can sort it all out once you are under her protection. And mine." He smiled hopefully.

Miss Peatling folded her hands in front of her. "Mr.

Cropston," she began firmly, as one chastising a school-boy, "I beg you will offer your apologies at once to Lord Rotherby for your speech, lest he call you out for so wretched an insult."

"Oh, I say!" Mr. Cropston cried suddenly, glancing at Rotherby. "I meant no disparagement, m'lord, only I am quite of a mind with Ravenstone—neither of these dear ladies should be here."

Lord Rotherby appeared quite amused. "I could not agree with you more. However, I promised to feed them both before turning them out of my house, so we will all simply have to endure the trials of the situation. Do you care to dine with us?"

"Well, yes, of course I shall," he cried enthusiastically, "since it seems quite settled that the ladies must remain, for it is well known you set one of the finest tables in all of Surrey." He turned back to Miss Peatling. "And I shall remain by your side until this terrible ordeal has been brought to a just and honourable conclusion. You may depend upon it!"

Miss Peatling repressed a long-suffering sigh, and though Mr. Cropston was being quite solicitous by offering his arm to her and suggesting she rest herself by taking up a seat by the fire, she refused him gently. Turning to her charge, she queried, "Ernestine, will you come with me for a moment?"

"Of course," Miss Burbage said, leaving her station beside Freddy. She dropped the linen summarily into the bowl, which was cradled on Freddy's stomach. The water splashed onto his face.

"Eh?" Freddy cried, dabbing at his chin and staring after Ernestine's retreating back.

Miss Peatling withheld a smile, for it was evident to her that the action was purposeful on Ernestine's part. Her young charge was quite enamored of Mr. Stanfield, who was not even aware of her existence.

To her assembled suitors, Alexandra stated, "Pray excuse us for a few moments. I must have a word with Rotherby concerning a pressing family matter. Pray, do try not to kill one another while I am gone."

The gentlemen eyed one another warily as she hooked Ernestine's arm with her own and quit the chamber. Rotherby followed behind.

Once in the hallway, she turned to him. "Where might the three of us have a comfortable cose, away from the yellow salon? I daresay my—er, suitors are sufficiently calm now and we should be able to converse with ease, at least for a few minutes."

"Shall I send Norton in with a decanter of sherry? Do you think that would aid the gentlemen in their lovesick agitation?"

Miss Peatling chuckled. "Yes, I believe it an excellent notion."

He took the ladies to the formal drawing room near the front of the house, which was happily separated from the yellow salon by several antechambers. Once there, he excused himself to perform his errand and returned a few moments later with the happy news that Norton had already foreseen the need for a little refreshment and was even now serving the gentlemen.

"You have a most superior butler," she stated.

He eyed her askance. "Flattery again," he said with a smile. "I only wonder what manner of nuisance you mean to thrust upon me. Only tell me why you found it necessary to kidnap my niece."

"Uncle, may I explain the unusual nature of our call today? If you must know, Miss Peatling has not exactly kidnapped me, since I was more than willing to come with her."

Lord Rotherby turned to Ernestine, whose beauty once more reminded him of heavenly beings. She was a lovely young woman, and not just because of the excellent lines of her face. She carried herself with great elegance and dignity, much as Miss Peatling did. She had a great deal of countenance, which was more than could be said for most schoolroom chits, and she was not in the least awed by his rank or the magnificence of his home. He realized, much to his amazement, that he approved of Fanny's daughter, quite thoroughly.

"Yes," he responded to her query, "if you please."

"As it happens, my mother arranged for me to marry, and I disliked her choice exceedingly, even from the beginning. I cannot, I will not marry the man she has chosen for me, for he is quite despicable!"

Lord Rotherby smiled in a tolerant fashion. "Arranged marriages are quite usual in your circumstances, my dear," he said kindly. "You have no fortune."

"I understand fully the nature of my situation," she responded reasonably. "But I am just sixteen and have not even had a come-out ball. I was hoping that in a year or so I might go to London in order to take part in the Season and see if, even though I am quite impoverished, I might find a gentleman in possession of some degree of fortune, who would be desirous of marrying me and yet who would not give me so great a disgust as—as the man Mama has chosen for me."

He eyed her with growing respect. "Your plan seems sensible enough. Did you not discuss it with your mother before she arranged your betrothal?"

"She would not listen to me, nor to Miss Peatling. From the first she has been determined that I wed Mr. Gilmorton."

"Gilmorton!" he cried, shocked in spite of himself.

"But he is older than even Ravenstone, with a reputation as vile as . . . well, never mind that."

"Everything you have just said is quite true," Ernestine stated mournfully. "However, he possesses one quality which Mama could not resist, for he is nearly as wealthy as Golden Ball Hughes. He saw me in Brighton summer last and insists he formed an attachment on the instant, though how he could have done so when he never spoke even a single word to me, I cannot imagine, but there it is! He is as determined to wed me as Mama is that I wed him! I am doomed without your help. Grandmama was unable to assist me at all."

Thoughts of his mother sobered him. "What does your grandmother think of this match?"

"She despises it, but Mama will not heed her warnings, even though Grandmama tried to explain how she was herself similarly circumstanced at very nearly the same age as I am now, and how unhappy she was. Will *you* help me, Uncle Phillip? Surely you would be able to dissuade my mother against this marriage."

At that moment, another noise was heard in the direction of the entrance hall. "What now?" he cried.

Alexandra listened intently and believed she knew who, indeed, had just arrived. She fell silent. How was she to explain what next she had done? She believed Rotherby would be furious when he learned the identity of his latest guest.

A moment later, Norton arrived, quite out of breath, and said, "Your mother, m'lord."

"My mother?" Rotherby queried, stunned. He had not seen her since the day of his father's funeral.

"Yes. She is presently ensconced in the blue antechamber."

"I suppose that will have to do. Only, whatever is she doing here?" He turned slowly toward Alexandra and eyed her narrowly for a long moment. "Miss Peatling, are you by any chance acquainted with Lady Rotherby?"

She blinked up at the ceiling several times. "Only a very little, m'lord."

"How little?" he queried in a voice that tended to boom when he was displeased.

Alexandra heaved a sigh and turned fully toward him. "We have been rather faithful correspondents for the past . . . four years."

"Four years! The devil you say! Then did you . . . that is, you summoned her here!"

She nodded. "Yes, my lord. I felt, under the circumstances, it would be best."

"But whatever prompted you to bring her here? What can you have hoped to achieve by doing so?"

"I believe you must know by now what I have been hoping to accomplish. Your mother knew quite well she could not sway her daughter to release Ernestine from the betrothal."

"And she thought I could?"

"I believe she did. However, that was not precisely—"

He did not let her finish. "And that is why she is here? To convince me that I must dissuade Fanny from this course?"

Miss Peatling bit her lip, for she felt this was the only weakness in her entire scheme. "Well, no. As I was trying to tell you, she is here because I felt it was time you spoke with her . . . after all these years."

"What!" he shouted.

"You need not come the crab, my lord," she stated quietly.

For a long moment, he could not speak. Finally, he said, "Ernestine, I believe it would be best if you quit the room for a time. I have something very particular I must say to *your governess.*"

Ernestine drew very close to Miss Peatling. "I will not," she stated emphatically. "Not when it is evident you are in a temper!"

"Go," he commanded her, flinging his arm dramatically toward the door. "At once!"

Miss Peatling turned to her and spoke in an affable manner. "Please leave us, Ernestine, but do not fret! Remember, he is a gentleman. What can he do but bluster for a time?"

Ernestine looked up at her and smiled. "You always amaze me," she said, tears fluttering on her lashes. "See how I am trembling?"

"Well, what a goosecap you are when from the first he has treated you with nothing but kindness. Now, do as your uncle bids. I shall be perfectly well, I promise you."

Ernestine straightened her shoulders and addressed Rotherby with a firm lift of her chin. "You look just like my mother in this moment, Uncle." With that, she quit the chamber.

Rotherby stared after her, obviously horrified at having been compared to his sister. When he turned back to Miss Peatling, he, too, saw that she was completely unperturbed and not in the least distressed by his display of temper. Something about her composure struck him as quite amusing and it was all he could do to keep from smiling.

However, when he thought of his mother awaiting him in a nearby room, and all because Miss Peatling had chosen to interfere in his affairs, his amusement faded.

"I do not know precisely where to begin in telling you how angry I am that you have brought this wretched situation down on my head without so much as a by-your-leave. First, you burst into my home and hold me hostage, for that is what I call this—this barrage of suitors. And now my mother. I suppose next Fanny will arrive."

"Yes," she admitted baldly. "With Mr. Gilmorton in tow, if I do not much mistake the matter."

He blinked and raised his hand, lowered his hand, splayed his fingers, opened his mouth, closed his mouth, stared up at the ceiling, all the while remaining mute. At last he queried, "What have I ever done to you, Miss Peatling, to have deserved this wretched treatment?"

"You make too much of it, my lord, surely! Think of your house as being full of guests for a few hours. We will all be gone soon enough."

"And I am supposed to merely smile and greet everyone politely until the storm has blown through?"

"What an excellent notion. You know, I have always ascribed to the proverb, 'Best to get over rough ground lightly.' Besides, I do think it a small thing I have done to have begged for your assistance in this manner. Do you truly wish for Ernestine to be wed to Mr. Gilmorton? Or do you not believe that such a marriage would be as hard for Ernestine as your mother's marriage was for her? Or did you not know that she had been given in marriage to a drunkard and a libertine at the age of sixteen?"

Her words sobered him. "Of course I did."

Miss Peatling watched him carefully for a long moment. "Your mother awaits you," she said at last.

Rotherby cast her a scathing glance, but chose to quit the chamber.

A moment later, he stood on the threshold of the blue antechamber, unable to credit that his mother was actually in his house. She had never graced this room before. The only chamber in the house which she had ever been in was the yellow salon, and that only twice in his entire existence. He did not know the woman before him, but he was struck immediately that after all these years, she was still quite beautiful. Time had been kind to her.

"Miss Peatling has managed the entire business quite

badly," he stated coldly, entering the chamber in his forthright manner. "You have been summoned to no purpose,
for I have not the smallest intention of involving myself
in Fanny's affairs, much less her daughter's."

"Hallo, Phillip," she said quietly. She was seated in a
wing chair of blue-and-white striped silk. Her gown was
a lovely shade of amethyst and about her neck were three
strings of matched pearls. Her complexion was quite pale,
however, as she removed kid gloves of a delicate shade
of lavender.

He frowned slightly. "You are trembling. Are you cold?
Do you wish a fire lit in the grate? I understand the clouds
are piling up in the north. While you are here, you may
as well be comfortable."

"Thank you. But if I tremble, it is not because of the
temperature. You just . . . look so much . . . like your father. The resemblance is quite astonishing."

At that he barked a laugh. "I look nothing at all like
him, though I must say Ernestine does."

She smiled, rather sadly. "You mean Rotherby. I believe
she does. She is grown quite beautiful, particularly in the
past three years, though for the last year I have had only
reports of her. She resembles her grandfather a great deal,
and whatever he might have been in character, he was
certainly the handsomest man ever born."

He did not know what to say. She seemed a trifle addled.
Both he and Ernestine could not resemble his father.
"Your granddaughter is quite angelic."

"With a temperament equally sweet, would you not
agree? Or have you not been in company with her long
enough to divine her nature?"

He found his attitude softening toward her. "Sufficiently to have concluded that you should be well pleased
with her. I am happy to say there is not the least simpering
in her manners. She is quite forthright and converses with

intelligence. I would congratulate Fanny on her daughter's progress, but I know perfectly well the accolades must go to her governess."

"A most exceptional creature with a great deal of spirit. I admire her excessively, for she had the good sense to take up a profession before she was forced down a path not of her own choosing. I only wish I had had enough courage to resist those who arranged my marriage to . . . to Rotherby."

Lord Rotherby did not know what to say. In the course of his life he had not exchanged but a half-dozen sentences with the lady before him. She had lived an estranged existence from both himself and his father, and later even from Fanny. Her choice to ignore her children was something he doubted he could ever forgive. Indeed, he had no desire to converse with her even now and found himself agitated that Miss Peatling had forced him down this unwelcome path. Blast all governesses! he thought uncharitably.

He regarded the lady before him curiously. "Tell me what you hoped to achieve by presenting yourself here this evening. Surely Miss Peatling is unaware that we are not precisely friends, you and I."

"Miss Peatling is the reason I am here," she said.

He glanced down at her lap and saw that her hands were clenched tightly together as she held her lavender gloves. He could see that she was becoming increasingly overset. Indeed, as he glanced at her face, he saw that there were tears in her eyes. Whatever was the matter with her? Or did she expect that after all these years he would welcome her with open arms?

"I realize you have come on a fool's errand, but I trust you will stay to dinner," he offered. Then, on a sardonic note, he added, "Everyone else is."

She looked up at him. "Everyone else?"

"Yes. Ernestine, Miss Peatling, and several of Miss Peatling's suitors, of which apparently there are sufficient number to form a brigade. I expect at any moment to be inundated with at least a score more."

"Dear Alexandra," her ladyship murmured, between a laugh and a sob. Suddenly, she was weeping.

"Lady Rotherby . . . that is, Mama. Please do not cry." He moved toward her and quickly retrieved his handkerchief from the pocket of his coat and handed it to her.

She took it gratefully. "Thank you," she murmured between sniffs. "I did not mean to become a watering pot, only you put me so much in mind of your father—"

"You keep saying that, but I vow I am not at all in his likeness. If you recall, he was very fair and in his youth possessed curly blond hair. Mine is nearly the shade of a raven's wing and my eyes are nothing like his in either shape or colour. His were a light blue, as I recall, and mine are this odd grey which cannot even be said to resemble yours because yours . . . are very brown." He searched his mother's face and realized she was watching him quite steadfastly. He saw a message in her eyes and suddenly he understood. "Good God. Rotherby was not my father, was he?"

She met his gaze and shook her head. "No, he was not, though I have no intention now or ever of revealing who your father was. Once I was known to be increasing, and Rotherby had been in London for six months, he would only acknowledge my offspring were I to live separately from him forever and to promise never to see the child— that is, never to see *you*."

Rotherby felt as though his world had simply turned upside down upon this shocking revelation. So much was explained about his life in these few, blunt words. "You certainly kept your promise to him," he stated coldly.

"I was very young when I married, and I was in great

despair. I know it was all very wicked of me, yet I have only one true regret—that I did not have the raising of you, that I must sit here now, looking at you and seeing naught but a stranger before me. You cannot imagine the pain it gives me."

"When my father—when Rotherby died, why did you not come to me then, for that was fully ten years past?"

"I wrote to you and received in return a very curt . . . a very nasty refusal."

He turned away from her." I remember now. I was in a dark time. I daresay I was fully in my cups when I answered your letter, for even now I can scarcely bring it to mind."

"Are you happier now, Phillip? Is your life better? I have followed your career all these years and saw where your father's influence had led you. I never ceased hoping that one day you might come to comprehend everything, to live a more sensible, a more meaningful life, that you might come to understand and to forgive me. And from everything I have heard of you, I believe you have come to terms with at least some of the despair of your childhood. Is that not so?"

He watched her closely, but was reluctant to give her an answer. "What of Fanny?" he asked instead. "Even Ernestine favors Rotherby."

"Fanny was Rotherby's daughter. I had attempted a reconciliation when you were three in hopes that I might be a mother to you, but I had no idea how cruel he could be. Fanny was the result of my effort in that regard, but once she was born, Rotherby took great delight in giving me yet another choice of exposure and divorce, or complete separation from both my children. Perhaps I should have been stronger. Perhaps I should have permitted him to divorce me even if it involved dragging all our lives through the rigors of Parliamentary procedure, in order that I could be a mother to you. But my circumstances were truly wretched. I would have been penniless, and my own mother made it clear that she would disown me were I to disgrace the family in such a manner. But even now, I wish I had been as strong as Miss Peatling." Tears spilled over her lashes once more.

His thoughts were drawn to the governess quite suddenly. "She is an unusual female."

"Very. Not at all in the usual style."

"That is precisely what I said to her when she first arrived today. Later, she mentioned you had been correspondents for several years."

"Yes, she has kept me abreast of Ernestine's progress, and I must say, Fanny's child is quite exceptional. She speaks Italian and French and has a real proficiency in mathematics. Her watercolours are unparalleled. I have one of them hanging in my chambers." She rose to her feet. "I should like very much to stay to dinner, Phillip, if you will permit it."

"Of course," he said gently. "I am glad you've come today, Mama, for it would seem there is much to say."

He moved to stand by the bell-pull, and because the door was ajar he noticed that Miss Peatling was waiting in the hall. He excused himself and quit the room. "What the devil are you doing here?" he barked in a harsh whisper.

Miss Peatling motioned for him to follow her. "I have just heard another carriage in the drive. Fanny is come with Gilmorton, just as I suspected she would. Rotherby, I beg you will do something, intervene. Pray do not permit this tragedy to take place."

"You know very well I have no intention of lifting a finger."

"As you wish," she stated in her calm manner.

Three

Rotherby escorted Miss Peatling to the entrance hall, a rumble of thunder heralding the change in weather, just as she had predicted. He murmured, "Rain. Did you direct the thunderstorm to my door as well?"

"Now who is being ridiculous?"

When he reached the arch below the lofty staircase, he bade her pause in order to observe his sister and Mr. Gilmorton battling their wet outer garments. He was amused, for it would seem his sister could not refrain from fussing like a mother hen over her daughter's betrothed.

"My dear Mr. Gilmorton!" she cried, dabbing at his face with her kerchief. "I am shocked, for you are nearly wet through. You will become quite ill. I vow it is so!"

"Undoubtedly you are right, Mrs. Burbage." He relinquished his sopping cape to Norton, who already held Fanny's pelisse. He then permitted Fanny to complete the removal of rainwater from his face. Afterward, Fanny began untying the ribbons of her own dripping bonnet.

Gilmorton addressed Norton. "I shall require a bowl of rum punch," he snapped. "See to it at once!"

"Indeed," Fanny added soothingly. "He must have a bowl of rum punch else the ague will completely overtake him."

"Very good, madam," Norton responded politely, his expression strained. "You may follow me to the yellow salon."

Fanny fell into step beside Mr. Gilmorton. "If only that terrible female had not forced us to venture forth—oh!" She chanced to spy Rotherby and Miss Peatling. "Rotherby! And *you,* you, you . . . ! Oh, of all the wicked governesses I have ever had to endure, Miss Peatling, you are by far the worst! Kidnapping my daughter! Oh, that I had never hired you, for you have filled her head full of the most useless nonsense, like history and mathematics and—and *Italian*—when you should have been instructing her on her duty to her mother! And though I do enjoy her watercolours very much, I shall turn you off even now . . . and that without a reference, though you hardly need one what with the fortune you possess!" These last words quite took the wind out of her harangue.

"Hallo, Fanny!" Rotherby called out congenially moving forward to welcome his new guests. "What? No greeting for your brother?"

Mrs. Burbage merely pulled a face, making her appear even younger than Ernestine in that moment.

"You will want to join the others, I am certain," he added.

"The others?" she said, pulling off her damp gloves. "Who else is here besides my daughter? Do not tell me you have a house full of rakes and libertines, though I do not doubt it in the least!"

"As to that, I cannot say for certain," he responded with a twitch of his lips. "Only Miss Peatling will be able to answer your question, for it is a number of her suitors, who arrived before you." He turned to Miss Peatling and queried, "Are your suitors indeed a collection of rakes and libertines? Surely not Freddy, for he is far too young, and Ravenstone cannot see, which would certainly dampen his ability to pursue the delights of Aphrodite with any degree of proficiency. As for Mr. Cropston, I have no knowledge of him other than his interest in my stables. Perhaps you could enlighten us all with regard to the estimable Mr. Cropston."

Miss Peatling apparently did not feel in the least inclined to respond to this ridiculous sally.

Fanny rolled her eyes. Mr. Gilmorton had apparently ignored his speech entirely, his gaze having drifted to Miss Peatling. His expression became rather lecherous as he cast his eyes over her. "Ah, yes, the infamous suitors," he said. "Always underfoot at Lacey Grove—all four of them. Quite a nuisance."

Rotherby stole a glance at Miss Peatling and saw that she had grown rather stiff in the spine, though her expression had scarcely changed a mite as she met Gilmorton's impertinent stare. He now understood precisely what trials Miss Peatling had endured over the past few months. Fanny lifted her chin to her brother and her daughter's former governess as she directed Norton to lead her to the yellow salon. She began instructing him with great precision as to the ingredients necessary for the punch Mr. Gilmorton favored.

Gilmorton, however, did not seem inclined to follow immediately in Fanny's wake. When he attempted to draw near Miss Peatling, his gaze still fixed intently upon her, Rotherby quickly stepped between her and the old rogue.

Gilmorton merely chuckled. "Playing the knight, Rotherby? An odd role for you." He took the viscount's rebuff in good humour and passed into the hallway, following behind his future mama-in-law, his corsets creaking audibly.

Miss Peatling would have turned as well, but Rotherby stayed her with a gentle hand on her arm.

"Has he *insulted* you, even once?" he queried.

Alexandra looked into grey eyes that had grown quite flinty. Her heart fluttered like a wild bird in her breast, and her mind was drawn swiftly back to the kiss he had placed on her lips just a short time ago. She wished madly that he would kiss her again, even though she knew she should be satisfied with one kiss. But just now, when his expression was so intense, she longed more than anything to be ravished. He had known her little more than an hour and already he disliked excessively the notion of Mr. Gilmorton taking advantage of her.

He swallowed visibly and his gaze fell to her lips. "Though of the moment, I am not certain I could blame him. I vow you are the most kissable female I have ever met."

"Then kiss me again," she responded in a whisper. Oh, how brazen she was being, yet she understood clearly that Rotherby would never pursue her, and if she was to make the smallest dent in his rogue's heart, she must certainly cast all caution to the wind.

"Faith, but I am tempted." He leaned toward her. Yes, certainly he was leaning toward her.

She lifted her face to him, but he shook his head. "Nothing can come of this," he murmured and released her suddenly. "Only tell me that Gilmorton has not accosted you."

"He would not dare," she responded evenly. Her heart sank with disappointment that he had not touched her lips again. She adjusted her thoughts once more and ordered her senses to be calm.

He narrowed his eyes. "But he has gone beyond the pale, and more than once, I vow. No, no, you need not deny it is so, for I see the truth in your eyes."

She sighed. "I confess that I have more than once wished I was a man that I might draw his cork."

He threw his head back and laughed. "What manner of governess speaks boxing cant?"

"Only in your company would I dare to do so, my lord. Besides, there are no proper words with which to describe my repugnance of that man. He has no shame, none whatsoever!"

"No, that he does not."

"You know him well? Do not tell me he is one of your bosom bows for I will not believe it."

"Not in the least. Let us just say that I have been acquainted with him for some time. He was one of my father's cronies."

"Then you can surely comprehend my desire to keep Ernestine out of his clutches. I will not permit her to be sacrificed to such a . . . a blackguard. Are you certain there is nothing I can do or say to persuade you to lend us your assistance?"

Rotherby looked down into lovely, imploring eyes and for the first time felt his determination waver. He had been struck from the first by Miss Peatling's beauty, but in this moment, with her heart in her eyes as she pleaded for her charge's happiness, he felt rather overwhelmed.

Her eyes were a luminous green, a shade which reminded him of the finest of summer days. Her hair was a dark, lustrous color, almost a chestnut, and very thick. She wore it piled atop her head which had the good fortune of emphasizing her long neck and beautifully sloped shoulders. She wore an elegant gown of a pale grey silk caught up high at the waist in the current Empire mode. A lovely fichu of lace covered the décolleté of the gown. She was beautiful, elegant, and with a jolt he realized she was what he had always wanted in a wife—sensible, not easily shocked by the world, and in every sense a lovely, darling creature.

Of course, he could never take such an innocent to wife.

At the same time, he still felt disinclined to lift a hand where Ernestine was concerned. He had for so long a time lived out his existence apart from a family which had been utterly indifferent to him that he could not bring himself to any pretence of familial feeling. He had no desire to acquiesce to Miss Peatling's plea.

"No, my dear," he said gently. "I fear you have come to the wrong house if you are hoping that I might suddenly become stricken with a strong sense of loyalty to a family I have never known."

Alexandra saw the sincerity in his eyes and would have been discouraged had she not had a genuine confidence that somehow the situation would right itself. She had but to set her mind to the difficulty before her and something, somehow, at some moment would present itself to resolve her difficulties. For now, she merely smiled. "Very well," she said. "Shall we collect your mama and take her to the yellow salon?"

He frowned for a moment before saying, "I wish for a word with her, if you do not mind."

"Of course not."

He nodded, still frowning. "Would you please see to my sister and Mr. Gilmorton? I shall bring my mother along directly."

"As you wish."

When Alexandra arrived on the threshold of the yellow salon, she saw that Fanny had settled Mr. Gilmorton into a chair by the fire and was bringing him a glass of sherry. She had no intention of arguing with either of them about Ernestine, who was at present playing backgammon with Mr. Cropston. She would have joined them, but Freddy immediately sat up and addressed her. "Miss Peatling, I beg you will tell Ravenstone to stop pestering me with his insistence that I should be bled."

Lord Ravenstone lifted a sharp penknife for her inspection. "I could do the job myself if someone would bring me a suitable bowl!"

Alexandra bit her lip and approached his lordship. "Come, come! Cease teasing poor Freddy."

Ravenstone smiled broadly. "You understand me then?"

"I believe I understand you too well," she said affably. "Perhaps I ought to accept your hand in marriage after all. We seem quite suited to one another and I do enjoy your wit exceedingly . . ." She let her words trail off, since poor Ravenstone had paled to the colour of gaslight. She feared suddenly that he might swoon. "On the other hand," she continued, patting his arm, "I dislike the notion of disrupting our wonderful friendship at a church altar."

He breathed a visible sigh of relief.

Rotherby entered the blue antechamber with a polite smile. "Do you care to join the others in the yellow salon? I daresay we shall be dining in a few minutes and I am certain that not only will Ernestine desire to see you but Fanny as well, for she has just arrived with Gilmorton."

"I should be delighted," she said. "Rotherby, please tell me you will not permit this marriage?" she asked, her expression pleading.

"I do not see on what basis I can alter its course. I am not Ernestine's legal guardian. I have no authority in the matter, none whatsoever. Knowing Fanny, were I to even attempt to interfere, she would murder me in my bed."

"You know very well you have but to offer a threat or two with either your sword or your pistol and Gilmorton will flee to the Continent without so much as a backward glance." She smiled as she spoke these words. So she had been versed in his activities all these years as well.

"I have not engaged in a duel for nigh on eight years, and I have no intention of doing so now."

"Of course not. I was merely teasing."

She rose in her elegant manner, and he naturally offered his arm to her. She was very tall and stately. He tried to picture her as a young girl of Ernestine's age and presented with the horror of having to wed a drunkard and a libertine by parents as indifferent to her happiness as they were avaricious—just like Fanny. He saw in her demeanour the long-suffering history of her life, and he felt sorry for her suddenly, as one who comes across a wounded animal in a field.

He gently placed his hand over hers, but did not lead her towards the door. He felt there was something he should say to her first. "I must apologize for my letter of ten years ago. I beg you will forgive me for any cruelties I might have spoken at the time. As I said before, I was caught in a very dark time, and the truth is I cannot recall even a word of what I wrote to you."

"Well, that would explain a great deal," she said. She slipped her arm from about his and, opening her reticule, withdrew a missive. She tossed it into the fire. "I kept it all these years. I had intended to discuss each point with you, hoping to refute your blame. However, seeing you now, hearing the kindness in your voice, I see no need. I only hope, dear Phillip, that I might now have a place in your life, if nothing greater than the chance to correspond once or twice a year, to hear of your comings and goings, or perhaps to send you a present at Christmas, for it is become quite fashionable of late to do so . . . for those one loves."

He looked into her eyes and saw them shimmering with ancient tears. "Of course," he murmured. His own throat began to ache in a devastating and surprising manner.

"You will always be welcome in my home and . . . and I am sorry you have had to endure so much sadness."

He again offered his arm and she took it up once more. He escorted her towards the door.

"I hope you will not begin pitying me," she said. "I have known much joy in my life as well, for I do live before the world in complete luxury. What a fool I would be to hold what has been given to me so cheaply merely because I was denied certain choices in my life."

"You cannot have always believed yourself so fortunate."

"No," she said, chuckling. "Only time and years can give such wisdom. But I want you to know that there was not a day that passed in which you failed to be in my thoughts, in my heart, and in my prayers. I realize I am a complete stranger to you, but I feel as though I have known you all my life, for you have lived *here* for thirty-eight years." She pressed her fist to her bosom.

A sense of wonder filled him suddenly, like a spring sky suddenly alive with birds. He understood by her words and this simple gesture what it would have been like to have known his mother all his life, for her gentle and loving disposition was clear to him, and for that reason much of the pain he had endured in the past drifted away.

When he arrived at the threshold of the yellow salon, his eye was drawn immediately to the presence of a new member of their strange tribal group—a man, perhaps in his mid-thirties, who was talking in a very intimate manner with Miss Peatling. Rotherby felt the hairs bristle on his neck as he watched the manner in which this unknown gentleman slid his hand beneath her arm.

"What the devil—" he murmured. "Do you know who that fellow is?"

Lady Rotherby scanned the assemblage. "Which man?

I fear I am unknown to all of them except the man standing so closely to Miss Peatling."

"That is the man. Who is he?"

"Sir Marcus Flintham. A very great man in London, quite fawned over by all the leading hostesses. A friend of Wellington's and one of Prinny's advisors. I would not be surprised if one day he was Prime Minister."

"Indeed." Regardless of his many virtues, he had no business touching Miss Peatling in that husbandly fashion.

"Mama!" Fanny cried. "Phillip did not tell me you were here! What brings you to—? Do not tell me that—that wretched female requested you to come to Surrey?"

"If you refer to Miss Peatling, as it happens, she did."

"I cannot imagine why you bothered. You have no rights in this situation."

"Of course I do not," she said. "I believe Miss Peatling desired that I should spend a little time with my son."

"Oh," Fanny responded, deflated.

Rotherby ignored his sister's venom. Indeed, he scarcely heard the exchange between mother and daughter. For some inexplicable reason, his attention was fixed entirely on Sir Marcus's hand which had just touched Miss Peatling's elbow in a wholly possessive manner which he found irritating in the extreme.

"Miss Peatling!" he called out abruptly. Whatever the conversation, she jerked her attention away from her most promising suitor.

"Yes, my lord?"

"Will you do me the honour of introducing me to our latest arrival?"

"Of course. I should be delighted." Alexandra saw at once that Rotherby wore his flinty expression again as he eyed Sir Marcus. She might have been delighted by this second display of canine incisors, but of all her suitors, Sir Marcus was the only one who could properly challenge

Rotherby on a field of battle, whether the drawing room or the dueling ground at twenty paces.

She quailed slightly as she regarded the two men. She felt obligated to temper the situation if possible.

When the introductions had been performed, she was not surprised when Rotherby edged between herself and Sir Marcus. The viscount regarded his quarry intently. "Have you seen my stables?" he asked. "Cropston here has been anxious to view several of my hunters, a stallion in particular which has blood lines two centuries long. I suggest you take the opportunity and accompany Cropston. The walk might afford a calming perspective. The gardens, even at night and when it is raining, are quite lovely. Although there is an underground passage if you are timid of the rain."

He then withdrew his snuffbox from the pocket of his coat. "Snuff?" he queried, popping the box open rather abruptly, so that some of the powdery grains fluffed onto the sleeve of Sir Marcus's coat. "Oh, I do beg your pardon."

Sir Marcus glared at Rotherby. "I have not the smallest interest in your stables, though I trust I do not give you offence in saying so."

"Not in the least," he responded with feigned affability.

Sir Marcus appeared to war within himself before adding, "I also beg you will forgive this intrusion into your home." He bowed with great politeness, his neck quite stiff.

Rotherby eyed him narrowly. "It isn't necessary to offer your apologies. No one else has. Why should you?"

Alexandra rolled her eyes. This was hardly a congenial response. Sir Marcus ground his teeth. Alexandra bit her lip slightly. She did not want the men to come to cuffs and said hastily, "Sir Marcus was just telling me that he admired your home exceedingly, did you not?"

"Yes, I was saying something to that effect."

"Indeed," Rotherby cried, his voice acquiring that booming sound once more. "And which of my chambers do you admire the most?"

Flintham turned to face him more squarely. "The one which Miss Peatling inhabits, of course."

Rotherby's eyes turned a deep charcoal in colour. His jaw became set in a manner which truly frightened Alexandra. "Yes, but you have failed to tell me why, precisely, you are here."

Flintham continued, "As it happens, I felt obligated to come and will not offer you the insult of explaining just why."

"No? All the others did. Apparently not a one of you trusted Miss Peatling's virtue farther than the lintel above my front door."

Again, there was no response Sir Marcus could offer which would do anything except provoke a duel. Alexandra realized that the entire chamber had fallen silent. Tension filled the air, as palpable as the snuffbox still open in Rotherby's stiff hand.

She sought frantically in her mind for a subject she might introduce which would break the challenge imminent between the two men, but nothing rose to mind, not one single word which could end the stalemate. She felt her lip quiver with fear. This was not at all what she had envisioned happening tonight.

Suddenly, Norton appeared in the doorway with a bowl of rum punch, and Gilmorton's voice rent the air. "Took the fellow long enough," he complained loudly to Fanny.

"Oh, look!" Alexandra cried, taking Rotherby roughly by the arm. "The punch has arrived!" She knew she sounded hysterical, but she did not care. The jerk of Rotherby's arm caused the snuff to spill on the carpet. Sir Mar-

We'd Like to Invite You to Subscribe to Zebra's Regency Romance Book Club and Give You a Gift of 4 Free Books as Your Introduction! (Worth $19.96!)

If you're a Regency lover, imagine the joy of getting **4 FREE Zebra Regency Romances** and then the chance to have the lovely stories delivered to your home each month at the lowest prices available! Well, that's our offer to you and here's how you benefit by becoming a Regency Romance subscriber:

- **4 FREE Introductory Regency Romances are delivered to your doorstep**
- **4 BRAND NEW Regencies are then delivered each month (usually before they're available in bookstores)**
- **Subscribers save almost $4.00 every month**
- **Home delivery is always FREE**
- **You also receive a FREE monthly newsletter, *Zebra/Pinnacle Romance News* which features author profiles, contests, subscriber benefits, book previews and more**
- **No risks or obligations...in other words you can cancel whenever you wish with no questions asked**

Join the thousands of readers who enjoy the savings and convenience offered to Regency Romance subscribers. After your initial introductory shipment, you receive 4 brand-new Zebra Regency Romances each month to examine for 10 days. Then, if you decide to keep the books, you'll pay the preferred subscriber's price of just $4.00 per title. That's only $16.00 for all 4 books and there's never an extra charge for shipping and handling.

It's a no-lose proposition, so return the FREE BOOK CERTIFICATE today!

Say Yes to 4 Free Books!
Complete and return the order card to receive this $19.96 value, ABSOLUTELY FREE!

If the certificate is missing below, write to:
Zebra Home Subscription Service, Inc.,
P.O. Box 5214, Clifton, New Jersey 07015-5214
or call TOLL-FREE 1-888-345-BOOK
Visit our website at www.kensingtonbooks.com.

FREE BOOK CERTIFICATE

YES! Please rush me 4 Zebra Regency Romances without cost or obligation. I understand that each month thereafter I will be able to preview 4 brand-new Regency Romances FREE for 10 days. Then, if I should decide to keep them, I will pay the money-saving preferred subscriber's price of just $16.00 for all 4...that's a savings of almost $4 off the publisher's price with no additional charge for shipping and handling. I may return any shipment within 10 days and owe nothing, and I may cancel this subscription at any time. My 4 FREE books will be mine to keep in any case.

Name _____

Address _____ Apt. _____

City _____ State _____ Zip _____

Telephone ( ) _____

Signature _____
(If under 18, parent or guardian must sign.)

RN060A

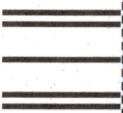

Ilbdollmdldddddddddddddddlllld

REGENCY ROMANCE BOOK CLUB
Zebra Home Subscription Service, Inc.
P.O. Box 5214
Clifton NJ 07015-5214

PLACE
STAMP
HERE

cus backed away, the tips of his boots covered with the fine, yellowish powder.

As she moved Rotherby toward the punch, he leaned down to her and whispered, "You need not have worried. I would not have called him out."

She turned to glance at him sharply. "That much I do believe. However, Sir Marcus might have been inclined otherwise. He shot a man on Hounslow Heath, three weeks past."

Rotherby, quite infuriatingly, merely lifted a brow. "Indeed?" he queried, as though making the lightest of conversation. "And did he shoot his mark dead?"

"Of course not. He is an expert marksman and merely wounded him in the wrist."

Rotherby chuckled. "Then I must thank you for rescuing me as you did. I daresay that had it come to a challenge, I might have been entombed with my father quite sooner than I had expected."

"Or Flintham," she stated somberly, trying to bring him to a sense of the nearness he had come to another duel.

"Flintham?" he queried softly, as he took a cup of punch from Norton and handed it to Fanny, who was anxious to take the spirits to her future son-in-law. "Why would Flintham be entombed with my father?"

At that, she burst out laughing. "You are odious!" she cried. "A truly wretched, incorrigible creature. I should never have come here."

He handed a cup to Cropston and bade him take it to Freddy. Cropston pouted as he moved away. "Are you truly sorry you have come?" he asked, oversetting her anew.

"Of course not," she responded. "Only do not call Flintham out. I should dislike it excessively."

"Are you in love with him?"

She felt a blush mount suddenly on her cheeks. "Yes. No. Oh, I do not know."

He smiled. "Your answer pleases me, your blush even more so."

"Oh, Rotherby, please do not say such things to me, unless you wish me to stay."

At that she looked at him, quite forcefully. He accepted the challenge with a serious expression that undid her heart yet another notch. She realized that for all his absurdity of the past few minutes, he was actually considering what she had said.

Ravenstone, arriving to stand at Alexandra's elbow, said, "I will have a cup. Smells to heaven! Gilmorton's receipt? The best in the kingdom. Ah!" He took the cup between both hands and walked away smiling. The rain had brought a chill to the chamber. Rotherby directed Norton to have the fire built up.

"I should take a cup to your mother," she said at last and left his side.

When Gilmorton, having imbibed two cups, suddenly sought out Ernestine, Alexandra was careful to take up a seat next to her.

"Forever playing the chaperone," he murmured, his eyes holding a now half-foxed leer. "Well, well, there is little you can do, after all. The contracts have been signed and you know very well Fan—that is, Mrs. Burbage—will not relent." He took another sip of his punch and smiled at Ernestine. "You may as well accustom yourself to the fact you will very soon become my wife. With the banns posted three weeks past, we have only a sennight remaining before the wedding. You shall return home with us, of course. As for you, Miss Peatling, you may remain here as well as anywhere." With that, he laughed and moved away.

Alexandra was a woman with few sensibilities. However, in this moment she felt very close to setting up a caterwaul.

Never in her existence had a man been able to raise her ire more quickly than Mr. Gilmorton.

"I detest him so," Ernestine murmured, a catch in her throat. She slid her hand into Alexandra's, who held it tightly.

"Never fear," she responded quietly. "I shall contrive something, even if I must kidnap you a second time. After all, I am quite wealthy, and if nothing else will serve, we could embark on a trip round the globe."

"We could, indeed!" Ernestine cried, turning to stare in wonder at her governess. "I should like that above all things, for then I might truly be educated."

"What is it you should like to do?" Sir Marcus inquired, having moved close once more.

"To travel, quite extensively. You have been to the Colonies, have you not, Sir Marcus?"

"Indeed. A rather wild place, but there is much to admire in the Indians. One can find them even on the streets of Boston."

Ernestine released a very deep sigh. "I should love to see Boston and a real tobacco plantation."

"When you travel, I cannot recommend the summertime, at least not for the southernmost states. You will find more insects flying about than birds over a recently plowed field."

"How wretched," she responded, holding her hand to her lips.

Alexandra's gaze drifted toward the door. Rotherby was speaking with his mother and she was smiling, a warmly affectionate expression on her face. She could not help but feel a deep sense of satisfaction, for she had long hoped that a reconciliation might occur between them. Ever since she had had the occasion to observe Rotherby in Bath, to witness his ability to be truly devoted, she had been longing for the Viscountess of Rotherby to be reconciled to her son. Though her ladyship had never openly expressed her desires in that regard, more than once in her numerous letters had the hint of her disappointment made its way to the tip of her pen.

The most recent words came back to her. *I have heard many fine things of Rotherby this season. Apparently he has become a philanthropist after all these years. I am very proud of him.*

A philanthropist. How did a rake become a philanthropist unless he possessed such a heart all along? Only, how to awaken that heart to the possibilities of love?

She truly did not know if it was possible. Indeed, so slim were the chances of any such awakening this evening, that she withheld a very profound sigh and returned her attention to Sir Marcus's further anecdotes about his journey to America of two years past.

Four

The miracle of the entire evening to Alexandra was the sumptuous feast Lord Rotherby's cook had been able to contrive at what would for any kitchen have been the eleventh hour. The first remove contained a fine assortment of broiled fowls with mushrooms, roast beef served with boiled potatoes, mulligatawny soup, cauliflower, and eel. The second remove heralded an excellent pigeon pie, thinly sliced ham, lobster patties, green peas, fried sole in a delicate oyster sauce, salad, pears, and an old-fashioned trifle.

Scarcely a person present did not compliment Rotherby on his excellent table, though Cropston, having imbibed four glasses of claret, besides more than his share of Gilmorton's rum punch, shocked everyone by saying in a sly manner, "Perfectly understandable, since I daresay you have always had a large society of exotic birds to keep well fed over the years." He waggled his eyebrows in a meaningful manner.

Alexandra saw that the thinly veiled reference to ladybirds was not lost on anyone, not even upon young Ernestine, who barely withheld a gasp. Rotherby glared at him coldly, but Cropston was in fine fettle and immediately reported that he meant to make his way to the stables once he had enjoyed a glass of port following dinner and was Mrs. Burbage of a mind to accompany him? Again he waggled his ridiculous eyebrows.

Alexandra glanced at Fanny, whose attention was fixed on Mr. Gilmorton, seated beside her. "Yes, yes, Mr. Cropston, whatever would please you," she responded absently. "Only pray do not tip your wine on me again. You have already ruined the sleeve of my blue silk besides my gloves."

"What? I say. So sorry! The stables then? After you've had your tea?"

"The stables?" she cried. "Whyever would I wish to go to the stables? I had rather walk about in the rain for an hour than be subjected to the smell of damp horse dung!"

"You'd succumb to an inflammation of the lungs were you to march about in the rain," he argued.

"I would not. I have very strong lungs. Only ask Mr. Gilmorton, for he has heard me swell my voice in song many a time. Have you not, Mr. Gilmorton?"

"Miss Peatling has a very fine voice," Mr. Gilmorton observed, staring at her from above the rim of his wineglass. "I have seen her swell her voice in song many a time. I should like to hear *her* sing, after she has had *her* tea."

Alexandra ignored him. Seated beside Rotherby, she turned toward him and spoke in a low voice, "I fear the punch has gone to too many of the heads present."

"I believe you may be right," he responded.

She sighed, catching sight of Ernestine's wide-eyed stare as she glanced from one half-foxed countenance to another. Oh, dear. This was by far too much of an education for her young charge.

Freddy blurted out suddenly, "My head still hurts."

Lord Ravenstone, seated opposite him, looked up at

that. "Silly coxcomb!" he cried. "Of course it hurts. You struck it on mahogany. Scarcely a harder wood than mahogany. Still think you should be bled. I could use my dinner knife and have the job performed in a trice, if you will allow it." He held up the silver-handled implement and smiled upon Freddy as one from Bedlam.

"I say!" he cried. "On no account!"

"Gudgeon!" Lord Ravenstone retorted, his small, aging eyes dancing with glee.

Gilmorton addressed Rotherby. "So, tell me, do you mean to lift a hand against my marriage to your niece, or not? Your sister is quite terrified by the prospect, though I have been assuring her for the past two hours that you don't give a fig for her offspring and never shall."

"Of course I shan't object," Rotherby responded easily. "I am neither her parent nor her guardian. I have no legal claim in the matter whatsoever."

"But you disapprove?"

"Disapproval is too strong a word. I merely believe you would do better to take a more mature lady to wife, someone more interested in sustaining your health than fleeing from your embraces." When he glanced meaningfully at his own sister, Fanny had the good grace to blush rather fiercely.

Gilmorton merely laughed, then took another deep draught of wine.

Sir Marcus cleared his throat. "I believe we would all do well to remember that we have a young lady present," he stated in depressing accents.

At that, both Cropston and Ravenstone begged pardon. Freddy said nothing, but appeared to be feeling miserable. Gilmorton, however, merely contented himself to leer at Ernestine while Fanny took to rubbing the wine stains on her glove.

Alexandra found suddenly that she had grown quite

weary. The exigencies of the day's travel, the absurdities of at least three of her suitors, Flintham's somber, disapproving countenance, Mrs. Burbage's fawning all over the most infamous rogue in England, even her own sentiments concerning Rotherby, whom she feared she would never see again after tonight, had all served to depress her energies quite severely.

Chancing to catch Gilmorton gazing lecherously at Ernestine yet again, she came to a full and sudden awareness that she would have to kidnap Ernestine again, probably before morning's light. So that was that.

Very well. She would take her to the home she had recently purchased in Berkshire, a very fine cottage made of a rosy brick, covered in ivy and climbing roses and containing five principal receiving rooms and eleven bedchambers. She would secrete Ernestine in the house, hiding her away indefinitely—or at least until she came of age in five years! She would pretend to be a widow, a Mrs. Mary Smythe, perhaps, and Ernestine her own daughter, whom she would call . . . Rachel. Mary and Rachel Smythe. Yes, very plain names to attract little notice. She might even take up cloth-weaving or tatting.

She took a sip of Madeira, the remnants of ham, lobster, and sole growing cold on her plate. She repressed a second sigh, which she was certain would have resounded from the tips of her gray half-boots had she let it pass her lips. She did not wish to be closeted away in Berkshire, weaving cloth and pretending to be a widow. She wished intensely to begin her own life, to marry, to have her own children, to make annual pilgrimages to London, even to Paris and Rome. She wanted a husband, a companion, a father for her children.

Her thoughts forced her to cast her gaze to Sir Marcus, who was presently engaged in conversation with Lady Rotherby, who in turn seemed quite animated in his company. And what lady would not, for he was everything that was polite and courteous. Indeed, he was everything a lady ought to desire in a husband, and more than once she had truly contemplated the notion of accepting his hand in marriage.

Throughout the past two years, he had been the most intelligent, the kindest, the most sensible of all her suitors. His conversation was always witty and elegant. He dressed, if not with a great sense of style, at least with no small degree of precision. He was a tolerable dance partner on the ballroom floor, and she knew he would make a most excellent spouse.

Still, her heart had been so full of Rotherby for the past five years that she had never allowed herself to become intrigued by Flintham. Now, however, with the prospect of living out the next five years of her life in Berkshire, in great secrecy as the Widow Smythe, she wondered if she was making a mistake by not accepting his hand. After all, he had promised he would do everything in his power to keep Ernestine out of Gilmorton's clutches. He had a great many connections, not least of which was his association with the Prince Regent. A single official letter, demanding Gilmorton's presence in Brighton or at Carlton House in London, would remove the old rogue from Lacey Grove as quick as the cat could lick her ear. Gilmorton had been attempting to ingratiate himself with the Regent since time out of mind. He would no more pass up the opportunity than he would cease wearing his ridiculous Cumberland corset!

All she had to do was accept Sir Marcus's hand in marriage.

"You have grown oddly quiet, Miss Peatling," Lord Rotherby said, his voice a warm sound against Ravenstone's loud chatter about a bet he had won recently at White's.

She glanced up at him and smiled falteringly. "I am contemplating what next I ought to do," she murmured. "I fear I am at a crossroads of no small moment. I wonder what you might think of my wedding Sir Marcus Flintham?"

She watched him carefully and thought she saw a dagger enter his eye, but she was not certain. "A fine choice," he responded at last, his gaze shifting to his wineglass. "Certainly he would make a more suitable spouse than either Ravenstone or Stanfield."

"One does not need to be in possession of profound mental abilities to draw that particular conclusion. Only, do you believe we should suit?"

He met her gaze. "I do not know. How could I, for I have just met you today, and of Sir Marcus I know equally little. I believe I would have to know each of you a great deal better before making a proper judge of the matter."

Alexandra drew in a deep breath, for there was something in his expression that had caused her heart to pause, an intensity which plucked strongly at her heartstrings. She felt that he was pondering her, perhaps even what it would be like to be married to her. She said, "I wonder, for I believe I understood you from the first moment I saw you."

A faint frown split his brow. "But how could you?"

"I saw you smile at your daughter, remember? And in that smile was everything you possessed. I could never have been mistaken in that."

"You must have been. Are you forgetting my reputation? For even though you might not listen to half of what the gabblemongers say, the other half must certainly hold some credence."

"I did not say that I believed you a complete innocent," she responded.

At that, he laughed. "I am not an innocent."

"You spent many unfortunate years under the tutelage of a less than honourable man. We, none of us, may choose our parent. Tell me I am wrong that you have made your life over."

He held her gaze for a long, long moment. "You are not mistaken. Yet, I believe one cannot undo the past."

"But one can untangle it, and I believe you have."

He grew disquietened suddenly. "You do not know me," he stated harshly.

She laughed at that, for she could see very well he meant to dispute the point and she had no desire whatsoever to do so. "There is no sense arguing," she stated easily, "and I see that the ladies are ready for their tea, though I hope the port bottle will not be passed around too liberally. Mr. Cropston can scarcely keep his eyes open as it is, and it seems Mr. Gilmorton has now taken to eyeing even your mother in a truly wretched fashion."

Rotherby glanced sharply at the old rake. "You were right about him. He is utterly shameless." In a commanding voice, he addressed his mother, "Mama, will you lead the ladies to the yellow salon? I shall have tea sent in directly."

"I should be delighted."

Everyone rose, and in a matter of a scant few minutes, the ladies were moving in the direction of the drawing room, where they were soon settled.

After the tea had arrived and was passed round, Alexandra carried her cup and saucer to the window. The rain had ceased, but the ever-present clouds created a blanket of night over the landscape. The vista, now in deep shadows, was merely the reflection of the candlelit windows of the house, arrayed on shrubberies, groomed flowerbeds, and neatly scythed lawns. Already she was half in love with Rotherby's home and rather thought that were she to live here, she would build a temple on the far hill, a wonderful, charming folly to which she might retreat when her dozen or so children became too noisy. Perhaps Rotherby might occasionally accompany her.

Would she ever stop dreaming?

She knew she could not hurry her life, nor love, nor Rotherby. Yet the impasse at which she had arrived weighed on her heart mightily. Rotherby might never see her as the sort of woman he could or even wanted to wed. Perhaps even now he was courting the daughter of an earl, marquess, or duke, a lady who had been raised in a great house and who would know instinctively how to be the wife of a lord.

Yet, she knew he was not courting anyone. She had made it her business to know of his comings and goings since that day in Bath. She had many acquaintances all over the island, including a dear friend of Rotherby's— Mrs. Lealand, the very one who had decorated the garden room. Her mother had been a friend of Mrs. Lealand's, and that lady had taken a particular interest in her from the day of her mother's death so many years ago. She smiled and sipped her tea. Mrs. Lealand had proved to be one of her greatest resources. Yes, she had loved Rotherby for a long time, and she had known his true character for an even longer period.

As though conjured up by her own reveries, Mrs. Lealand suddenly appeared in the doorway. "Miss Peatling!" she cried. "You are here at last!"

"Mrs. Lealand! How odd, for I was just thinking of you. But how did you know I was here—or did you?"

The newcomer advanced on Alexandra, beaming, her gloved hands outstretched to her. Her expression was entirely conspiratorial. "Norton, of course," she said. "For several years now, I have made this house my particular interest, just as I am certain by now that you have guessed as much."

Alexandra smiled, placing her hands in Mrs. Lealand's. "The garden room is particularly lovely."

Mrs. Lealand burst into a trill of laughter. "I do not believe a man was ever more bowled over than Rotherby when I told him that not only did I mean to become his dearest friend, but also that I fully intended to design his room, which previously had been filled with all manner of armory. It was an absolute horror!"

"Well, it is truly lovely now," Alexandra said, then added, "I have long wanted to thank you in person for all your kind letters."

"And you proved such a faithful correspondent." She searched her face. "Do you know, the older you become, the more you resemble your mother. How well I recall her. Did I never tell you that she cut quite a dash in London in her day? We were all powdered and trussed up like Christmas geese in our exacting gowns, yet none shone as she did. I only wish you had given up your absurd employment when you turned one and twenty, that I might have presented you. I daresay you would have gathered as many beaux about you as your mother did. Now you are aught but a spinster, though quite beautiful, but it would not do at all, at this late hour, to rig you out in white satin and present you to the Queen like a chit just out of the schoolroom."

Alexandra could only laugh, for the picture was as lively as it was ridiculous. Besides, she had long given up any notion of being presented at court.

Finally, Mrs. Lealand released Alexandra's hands, but not without a firm squeeze of all of her fingers.

"How do you find Rotherby?" she asked, her blue eyes dancing with great merriment.

"All that I expected him to be. A gentleman, a trifle coarse, even blunt at times. I must say his home is a tribute to him."

"And how does he find you?" Expectation was wild in her eyes.

"I cannot say. I believe there might be some interest, but my greater concern is for Ernestine."

"Is she here?" Mrs. Lealand queried, then glanced around quickly. "Of course she is. Pray, introduce me. I daresay that is her mother, the one who has fallen asleep in the chair."

"None other." Alexandra observed Fanny's bent posture and wondered how her neck could support her at such an angle. Lady Rotherby was presently engaged in speaking with her granddaughter.

Alexandra made the introductions, but found that Lady Rotherby and Mrs. Lealand were well and quite fondly known to one another, a circumstance which both surprised her and made her a trifle suspicious.

"How happy I am to see you here this evening," Mrs. Lealand said. "And is Rotherby in a way to speaking to you, as a son ought?"

Lady Rotherby nodded. "We have made an excellent beginning."

"There!" Mrs. Lealand exclaimed with a clap of her hands. "Did I not tell you that Miss Peatling would see everything settled in a trice? Now we have but to see her settled and I vow we shall all be one quite large and happy family."

Lady Rotherby glanced at Alexandra, who could feel the warmth rising on her cheeks for she of course had never mentioned her interest in Rotherby to either of the ladies.

"Oh, do not appear so conscious, my dear," Mrs. Lealand said, taking her by the arm. "We have both known you to be in love with him forever. Well, at least since you saw him in Bath."

The warmth in Alexandra's cheeks extended to her

neck. "I daresay you think me quite foolish, since I have known him but a scant few hours."

Ernestine chimed in. "You are in love with Uncle Phillip? Do you mean I might one day be able to call you aunt? Oh, but this is too wonderful!"

"You are far too hasty!" Alexandra cried, horrified that the subject had taken such swift turns. "All of you!"

"Of course she will marry Rotherby," Mrs. Lealand said. "Goodness, Miss Peatling. I had thought you long past the age of blushes."

"You ought not to say such things," she chided gently. "Only, how did you know of my sentiments? I was so careful . . ."

Lady Rotherby replied, "Your letters betrayed you, or have you forgotten all that you have written to me over the years? You spoke of my son so frequently that I began to wonder if you were not attached to him. I also think that your sentiments encouraged me to come here today. I owe you a great deal of gratitude."

"I am so happy for you," Alexandra returned, tears starting in her eyes.

"I destroyed the letter," Lady Rotherby added, "the one I told you about."

"The one Rotherby wrote ten years ago?"

"Yes. I could not let him read it. He said he had no recollection of what was written within, for he believed he had been in his altitudes when he composed the missive. I burned it in the grate. He spoke of a dark time."

"What child does not suffer such a time, when deprived of a parent's love?" Alexandra could not keep from glancing in Fanny's direction, for even though Ernestine had resided with her mother her entire life, there had been little of love in the relationship. Fanny was now snoring.

"Have you been able to persuade Rotherby to exert his influence?" Mrs. Lealand asked.

Alexandra shook her head. "Unfortunately, I have not."

"What will you do?" Lady Rotherby queried.

"Do you think if you spoke with your daughter—?" Even as the question passed her lips, she knew it was hopeless. Fanny had no interest in her mother, much less her opinions.

"I have never succeeded in winning my daughter's trust, or her respect. I broached the subject once, a month past, and she very coldly told me to go to the devil." She chuckled. "Now I have shocked you. No, she did not use those words precisely, but she might as well have. Oh, dear, what a coil! Oh. Sir Marcus has joined us . . . alone. Miss Peatling, I believe he is trying to gain your attention."

Alexandra turned and saw that he was waving in her direction. She went to him at once, wondering if perhaps Lord Ravenstone had fulfilled his intention of sticking Freddy with his knife. "Is anything amiss?" she queried.

"No—that is, may I have a word with you... in private? Please?"

"Of course," Alexandra responded. She bade the ladies excuse her for a few minutes, then directed Sir Marcus to the blue antechamber.

So the moment of truth had come. Only, what would she tell him? she wondered. Could she wed him?

Once alone with her, Sir Marcus did not hesitate to state his purpose. "I wish you to marry me, Miss Peatling. I love you more than life itself, and have for these two years past. I desire more than anything to make you my wife, to take you from this house, from the taint of Rotherby's reputation. I believe, as well, that I can set your mind at ease about Miss Burbage, to whom you have shown incredible dedication of purpose and resolve."

Her heart began beating swiftly upon hearing this last part. "You have heard from the Prince Regent then?" she queried.

He nodded, a warm smile suffusing his face. "I have a letter stating that he is desirous of intervening and will do what he can. Unfortunately, he is at present on the Isle of Wight. But when he returns in a fortnight, he will make every effort—"

She interrupted him. "He shall be a fortnight too late, for the nuptials are scheduled to take place Wednesday next. No, no, pray do not look so chagrined. You have done all that you could, and for that I will always be exceedingly grateful."

"I am so very sorry. Perhaps I could warn Gilmorton away with threats of the Prince's involvement. If both you and Miss Burbage were to accompany me tonight, to London, I would happily bear any of Gilmorton's reprisals—one and all! Only, do say you will come with me." He quickly and quite suddenly possessed himself of her hands and placed an impassioned kiss on her fingers. "I would do anything for the woman I love. Anything. You know that. You must know that by now."

She had never before realized of what a romantic turn Sir Marcus truly was, besides being a man of great chivalry and honour. She tried to imagine loving him, being in love with him. She ordered her heart to respond in kind to the baronet's enamored expression and to his utter willingness to act the gallant with her.

Alas, her poor heart would not respond, not even a mite, even though it ought to have, for Sir Marcus Flintham was a perfect man in every respect.

She slowly withdrew her hands from his grasp. "You have been a very great friend to me over the past two years, and I shall always be deeply appreciative of your steadfast devotion and attention to me, in particular of the manner in which you strove to aid me where Miss Burbage was concerned. But, dear Sir Marcus, I cannot marry you. Indeed, I ought to have told you sooner, yet I suppose I continued to hope beyond hope that my sentiments would deepen sufficiently to call you more than friend. But they have not."

He was silent for a long moment as he stared into her eyes. At last he spoke, albeit quite solemnly. "I feared this was how it would be. I feared it from the first, for somehow you were always a little distant in our discourse, as though your heart was not present to be won. Is this how it has always been? Was your heart never truly present to be won?"

"I believe you have the right of it."

He glanced about the chamber. "I never expected to see so much elegance here in this house. So you are in love with Rotherby?"

She said nothing in response, though she wondered how he had guessed.

"I see. Well, I shall leave now, so long as you tell me that you are indeed content and . . . safe."

She chuckled. "You know very well I am."

He smiled ruefully. "Yes, damme, so you are. Whatever *he* might have been in the past, there is none of that scapegrace here tonight."

"No, there is not."

He sighed heavily, his features drawn. He had indeed loved her. "Good-bye, Miss Peatling, and may God bless you."

She offered her hand to him and he shook it gently, then turned on his heel and quit the chamber. She heard his steps veer off in the direction of the entrance hall and knew that within a few minutes he would be gone.

She remained in the drawing room, standing where he had left her, staring at the empty doorway. So, she had ended all possibility of marrying the only one of her suitors who might have been in the least suitable had she not tumbled in love with Rotherby so many years ago. She felt oddly empty, yet at the same time exhilarated. She had cut herself loose from her moorings, at least from one of them, and thought it was now time for the tide to take her in whatever direction it chose.

The tide chose to begin with a great deal of shouting!

Five

The tumult came from the direction of the hallway, near the dining room. Alexandra's feet moved swiftly as she picked up her grey silk skirts and ran towards the sound of the chaos. She heard Freddy's voice first.

"Damme, I love Miss Peatling, which is more than either of you can say! I mean to marry her, tonight! We shall elope to Gretna——if she will but listen to reason!"

"I should have bled you when I had the chance!" Ravenstone shouted in response.

Cropston's slurred voice chimed in, "I mean to take her to the stables!"

"Stubble it, Cropston!" Ravenstone and Freddy cried in unison.

"I say!" Cropston cried, considerably taken aback.

The moment her suitors spied Alexandra, a sudden and fierce cackling ensued as each began pressing his suit. The cacophony only made her smile, for it was as ridiculous as it was incomprehensible.

Rotherby appeared from the dining room, his grey eyes lit with laughter. She exchanged a glance with him and in that moment decided she must dash all their hopes once and for all.

"Do hush," she said firmly and the gentlemen, by long

habit of waiting upon her, responded promptly to her command. "I would not be surprised if all the servants came running at so much caterwauling, fearing that the house had caught fire!"

"It is all Ravenstone's fault" Freddy bawled.

But before Ravenstone could counter this remark, she lifted a hand and said, "I cannot marry any of you. It is time I confessed the truth. Though I am ashamed to admit it is so, the fact is"—and here she met Rotherby's gaze, willing him to comprehend her meaning—"I have been betrothed to your host nigh on five years now." This was not entirely an untruth, for her heart had indeed been thusly engaged.

Her suitors stared at her with three mouths agape, like little birds begging for their dinner.

"B-but you cannot be engaged to Rotherby!" Freddy exclaimed, as though struck down by Zeus himself.

"Oh, but she is," Rotherby announced suddenly. "You will offer your congratulations, Mr. Stanfield, if you please."

Freddy stiffened, from his toes to his neck. "I had rather not. You, my lord, are entirely unworthy of her, and I do not hesitate to say as much to your face. Although I daresay now that I have said as much, you will wish to name your seconds."

"Are you calling me out?" Rotherby queried.

"N-no. But I assumed, since I offered you an insult—"

"What insult?" he asked, passing by Mr. Stanfield. "You spoke nothing but the truth. I am unworthy of Miss Peatling." He approached Alexandra wearing a wonderfully warm smile which served to weaken her knees. Did he know how his smiles affected her? He continued, "Even so, she consented some time ago to become my wife, though for reasons I shall not endeavor to explain, she requested a long engagement. A very long engagement."

Alexandra took on a perfectly demure expression.

Three pairs of puzzled brows met her blank gaze.

"So that's it, then?" Ravenstone murmured, blinking several times. "Ah, I believe I begin to understand." To Rotherby, he said, "I had heard a number of rumors to the effect that you'd mended your ways, what with the orphanages you have established and other things. Heard recently your estate was one of the most profitable in England, that even Coke of Norfolk was known to advise you. Must say, I thought it all humbug at the time. Now that I've been here, I begin to believe it's all true. So, you gave up a rogue's life for Miss Peatling. Well, I suppose any of us might have done so. Except Freddy here, who has scarcely begun to live . . ."

"I am nearly nineteen!" he cried hotly.

"You behave as though you are scarcely out of leading strings. Come! Make your bow to Miss Peatling. We have intruded long enough upon what appears to be her betrothal party."

"But I love her!"

"No matter now, halfling. She's to be wed."

Freddy's shoulders slumped. "I shall give myself to writing poetry, for there is nothing else left to me."

"There, that's the fellow. Dash off a couple of sonnets that would make Byron weep and dedicate one to Miss Peatling. Now, make your bow." Ravenstone's voice was full of fatherly kindness.

Freddy took Miss Peatling's hand in his and with a face longer than that of a dog without a bone, bowed low over her fingers. He then lifted his head nobly and after nodding curtly to Rotherby, turned to follow in Ravenstone's wake.

Cropston appeared confused. "Where the deuce are they going? The stables?"

Rotherby said, "To Lacey Grove. You are to go with them. Miss Peatling will be staying here."

"What?" he queried, his eyes rolling unevenly in his head. "Oh. Pity, but then you are to wed Rotherby."

"Yes, I am," she stated with some finality.

"See your stables another time," he said, inclining his head to the viscount. "My best wishes for your every happiness," he slurred to Alexandra.

Rotherby did not guide Alexandra back to the yellow salon as she supposed he would. Instead, he insisted there was something of some moment he wished to show her in the library, which, as it turned out, was some distance from the yellow salon, arrived at only through a great number of charming antechambers.

Not a single taper was lit in the lofty room; only a small fire burned in the grate. He guided her towards the fireplace and gently took up her hands. "So, we are to be wed," he stated, his eyes dancing wickedly.

"I hope you did not mind my telling such a whisker, but of the moment I felt I ought to end this ridiculous situation."

His arm slipped quite easily about her waist, and she found she had no desire whatsoever to reproach him. He said, "I do not mind in the least, though you should have been warned that I always exact a forfeit when I am required to feign a betrothal, particularly one which arrived so suddenly."

"Ravenstone was very wrong about you," she said, teasingly. "You have not mended your ways in the least."

He chuckled low as his other arm snaked about her. Still, she did not protest. "Of course I have not," he said, "particularly where a beautiful woman is concerned."

She lifted her face to him and her stomach drew up into a tight, excited knot.

His lips settled on hers as gently as they had before. She did not know when it happened, precisely, but before very long her arms were about his neck and she was clinging to him in a wholly wanton manner. His tongue pressed inside her mouth, and she could no longer feel her knees, not in the least. A series of soft whimpers sounded in her throat as she gave herself fully to the rogue's embrace.

She had imagined his kisses a thousand times, and she had always felt she had been quite clever in determining just what it would feel like to have Rotherby assault her. The truth was, however, that nothing in her daydreams could have predicted the difference between an imagined kiss and a real one.

She felt as though she had been transported to a different world entirely, one in which night was day and day was night, in which the ceiling was the floor and the floor the ceiling. With her eyes closed, she felt as though she were floating and could not have told anyone whether she was right side up or upside down.

"Oh, Rotherby," she murmured against his lips.

"Alexandra," he whispered in return, once more slanting a kiss across her lips.

She felt wild and uncontrolled, as she held him more tightly still. His arms were feverish about her as he kept trying to draw her closer to him. He kissed her in rapid bursts, then settled in for a long, wicked exploration of her mouth. She felt devoured and yet so unsatisfied. She wanted to be in a place where he would never stop kissing her.

After some time, the length of which she found impossible to gauge, he drew back. His eyes were nearly black in the shadowy chamber. She could not release him entirely. Her hands clung to his arms. She did not wish to let him go. She was even afraid to do so. The charm of the moment would be gone. His common sense would return, she had little doubt of that, and in a few hours she would be gone.

Breathing hard, he said hoarsely, "Would to God you were my wife."

"Rotherby," she whispered earnestly. "Marry me."

He closed his eyes, then smiled and chuckled. " I cannot, you know I cannot. I would not do anything so cruel to you, for already you have become quite dear to me."

"The only cruelty you could possibly heap upon my head in this moment is to refuse my proposal."

"A lady cannot beg a man to wed her."

"I do not give a fig for propriety at present. I . . ." She paused, yet once more threw caution to the wind. "I have loved you for so long a time. Indeed, I came here desirous not of finding myself in your arms precisely, even though I wished for it, but rather in hopes of ending my ridiculous *tendre* for a man I once saw in Bath. Only, dear Rotherby, you but spoke a dozen words to me and my heart fell farther still. I even rejected Flintham's suit, once and for all."

"Oh, my dear, you should not have." All this while, he had been petting her hair, and kissing her face and her neck. "He will renew his addresses, I have little doubt, once you explain you erred." He somehow flattened these words by gently sucking her neck just below her ear. She thought she might go mad.

There was only one thing she could do. "I suppose you are right," she said. Then she turned her head, found his lips, and kissed him quite forcefully, sinking her fingers into his hair and opening once more to the length of his tongue.

She felt his breath in a long sigh against her mouth. "Now you torture me."

"I know I am of an age when I should marry," she said. "I desire more than anything to set up my nursery, but I wish for my children to resemble you and no one else."

He clung to her and kissed her cheek. "Why did you have to come here and say things to me that can never be?"

She rubbed her cheek against his and breathed in the smell of him. "I am leaving tonight, with Ernestine. I have purchased a house in Berkshire. Your mother knows where it is, no one else. I intend to reside there as the Widow Smythe until Ernestine comes of age."

"You will marry Flintham."

"No," she said with a smile. "Not unless I grow very, very lonely, though I doubt that I will. I am able to find a great deal of pleasure wherever I am circumstanced and besides, once my loyalties are given, I do not easily relinquish them."

"You have proven that quality in your care of Ernestine. She will continue to shine under your guidance."

She felt she was losing him and for that reason buried her face in his shoulder that he might not see the sudden tears which started to her eyes. She sensed there was nothing more she could say to him.

He released her at last. "Do you wish to return to the others?"

She nodded. "But only long enough to pretend to bid good night to Ernestine. I must tell her what our plans are. We shall not be staying much longer. I trust you will keep our secret?"

"Of course," he murmured, his expression quite somber. "But let me order the carriage. I shall have a basket of food prepared for your journey. Berkshire is not far. If you leave around midnight, you will undoubtedly arrive sometime in the morning."

"Yes, we should." She took a moment to memorize his

face. She had no portrait of him, no miniature she could at times remove from her reticule in order to recall his features exactly. She wondered if it would be another five years before she saw him again.

Later, well past midnight, he escorted them both to the carriage house. He handed Ernestine up into the travelling coach but did not immediately assist Alexandra in boarding. Instead, he drew her apart and gathered her once more into his arms. "This must be good-bye," he said.

She held him tightly, the lantern light casting his features in strong relief. She touched his face with her gloved hand and placed a gentle kiss on his lips. "Good-bye, Phillip," she said with a smile.

"Good-bye, dear Alexandra."

One last, long look, and she pulled from his arms, climbing deftly into the carriage without his assistance. He shut the door and bade the postillion to ease slowly from the drive so that the departure of the ladies would not be noticed.

The postillion gave a nod and quietly set the lead horse in motion.

Lord Rotherby stood at the end of the gravel drive watching the lantern light sway with the motion of the carriage as it moved away from the stables. He remained in the same place long after the coach had disappeared at the end of the lane.

In the morning, breakfast was conducted in a leisurely manner. The sideboard was laden with at least a dozen dishes from which his guests could partake once they arrived in the morning room. Neither Mrs. Lealand nor his mother had yet made her way from her bedchambers.

Fanny wore a distraught expression while Rotherby stared, utterly bored, into the red-faced countenance of Mr. Gilmorton. He was ranting and raving about how he had been tricked yet again by Miss Peatling.

Rotherby stifled a yawn. "Your eggs are growing cold," he said.

"I do not give a fig for my eggs!" he exclaimed.

Fanny interjected. "Mr. Gilmorton, perhaps you would care for something else to eat. I requested apricot tartlets of Norton last night, and I daresay Cook has them prepared by now."

Gilmorton turned to Fanny. "Is this so? Why, yes, I would like it above all things. You are very good to me."

Fanny smiled—quite sadly, Rotherby thought. "Also, if you care for it, there is Norton with a little brandy. Do you wish for a drop or two in your coffee? I believe it might be beneficial after the shock you have received of learning Miss Peatling has once again kidnapped my daughter." She regarded him hopefully.

Rotherby thought Gilmorton might be irritated by so much motherly meddling. Instead, the old rogue laid his feathers at once. He nodded for Norton to do the honours. A moment more and he was sipping his coffee with something akin to pleasure.

Rotherby found himself surprised. It seemed to him that Fanny's coddling was having a profoundly happy effect upon Gilmorton.

After a time, when Mr. Gilmorton had left his eggs and taken up a seat near the fireplace, Fanny also rose. Leaning over Rotherby's shoulder, she addressed him. "If you know where my daughter is," she whispered, a catch in her voice, "I beg you will say nothing." She then gave his shoulder a squeeze and moved to adjust a pillow behind Gilmorton's back.

He watched her with some interest, this sibling with

whom he had been so rarely in company. She met his gaze, and an understanding peculiar perhaps to brother and sister passed between them. He understood her. Fanny was in love with Mr. Gilmorton—quite deeply it seemed.

He smiled at her and she smiled in response. Were there actually tears in her eyes?

At that moment, his mother entered the chamber, gowned charmingly in a white patterned-silk gown, trimmed with gold lace. Pearls were draped about her throat. She carried herself with great elegance, much as Miss Peatling—*Alexandra*—was wont to do. She glanced about the chamber and approached Rotherby. "I do not see either Miss Peatling or Miss Burbage. Are they still abed?"

He shook his head. "They are gone. My head groom informs me that they departed some time around one o'clock this morning."

"I see. Miss Peatling was desirous of leaving?"

He paused before responding. "She wished to remove your granddaughter from my house."

Lady Rotherby pursed her lips then said, "Rotherby, will you not make a push to set this situation to rights?"

"There is nothing which needs to be done. Miss Peatling has it all arranged."

"She will marry," she said concernedly. "You do understand as much, do you not?"

"Of course. Of course she will marry. Flintham, undoubtedly, or if not him, then someone equally . . . *worthy*. She is desirous of having a family. She made that much clear to me last night."

Last night. How dreadfully he had been haunted by memories of having kissed her last night. It was a great absurdity, of course. He scarcely knew the chit. Only she was not a chit, she was seven and twenty. She was a woman, with a woman's mind and heart, and she loved him, not Flintham or anyone else, but *him!*

He did not want her to marry anyone else. He wanted her in his bed, forever, curled up beside him, her stomach swollen with his child, not anyone else's.

"Rotherby!"

He snapped his attention to his mother. "I beg your pardon?"

She was smiling. "I addressed you three times, but you did not attend me. I wished to know if she was very sad upon leaving—Miss Peatling I mean."

"I suppose so. Yes, a little."

"I do not wonder at it, when she is so very much in love with you."

He started and stared at her. How did his mother know?

At that moment, Mrs. Lealand arrived on the threshold, adjusting the sleeves of her amber calico gown. "Rotherby, is it true?" she cried. "Did you actually permit Miss Peatling and Miss Burbage to escape your house last night?"

"I *permitted* nothing," he responded easily.

"Ah, breakfast is ready. How perfect, for I am famished! Do you think Miss Peatling will wed Flintham, after all?" She headed directly for the sideboard and began loading her plate. "Oh, I know she sent him away yesterday, but it is an awfully good match, do you not think so, Rotherby?"

He grunted his response. Why was it ladies were always anxious to see their friends married off?

"Rotherby," Mrs. Lealand called out. "Why do you scowl so? Are the eggs not to your liking? I find them perfectly cooked, turned just as I like them."

"The eggs are well enough," he muttered.

Mrs. Lealand spoke over her shoulder to Lady Rotherby. "I saw Miss Peatling talking with Sir Marcus last night.

Her expression was full of fondness. I believe she could grow to love him . . . given time."

"Indeed, I know you are right. There is not a kinder, more considerate man in the entire kingdom than Sir Marcus Flintham. I personally know of no hostess who has ever removed him from her guest list."

"He is well respected at White's." She moved to the table and seated herself next to Lord Rotherby. "Mr. Lealand was telling me so just the other day. His opinion is sought after everywhere. She would be a perfect wife for him, as composed and elegant as she is. She will be a very great hostess one day, mark my words. Rotherby, do pass the pepper, if you please. Ah, thank you very much. For myself, I mean to encourage the match as often as I am able. If you do the same, I daresay we will see them wed by Michaelmas."

"I believe you may be right."

Rotherby could bear it no more. "Confound it!" he exclaimed. "Must you both prattle on in this absurd fashion! I am sick to death of hearing of Flintham as though he were a god!"

The ladies merely smiled. His mother said, "Of course we shan't say another word if talk of Sir Marcus distresses you."

"Not another word," Mrs. Lealand agreed, but with just such an expression on her face as indicated her true opinion on the subject.

He glanced from one countenance to the other. He glared at each lady in turn. He saw both of them open their mouths to speak, but Gilmorton was before them. "Come, Rotherby, I believe it is time to admit we've both been beaten hollow." He reached over and took Fanny's hand in his and kissed her fingers passionately. "I have decided to break off the engagement with Miss Burbage. It would seem that my affections are engaged elsewhere.

Knowing Fanny's daughter to be in excellent hands, I mean to take a trip to Gretna, if Mrs. Burbage will do me the honour of accompanying me."

Fanny regarded him with tears in her eyes. "I wish it more than anything, Mr. Gilmorton."

Gilmorton smiled softly upon her. "Imagine, all these years, tumbling in love." He then turned to Rotherby. "You had best follow after her. I know the ladies were teasing you to a purpose, but Miss Peatling will not wait. She held Mrs. Wharton's baby for two hours a sennight past. She will not be content until she has babes of her own. Not her, even if she has persuaded herself otherwise for the time being."

Rotherby felt more apprehensive than he could remember.

His mother rose at once and came to his side. "You must forget the past."

He looked up at her, wondering how she could have read his mind. "I do not deserve her, nor any lady of quality."

"Nonsense," she said softly, touching his cheek lightly. "Now who is speaking absurdities? Go to her. Mr. Gilmorton is right. I believe she might tarry a twelvemonth, but no longer. She deserves to have the family of her heart and so do you. You have single-handedly saved thousands of children. Now take a precious few for your own."

Only one thought truly rose to his mind as he searched his mother's eyes—that he had, for some incredible reason, actually fallen head over ears in love with a lady he had seen once in Bath, and who had stormed his home a mere sixteen hours past. He wanted her more than life itself, and so it was for that reason he rose suddenly and bade his guests adieu.

* * *

"I remember it being far prettier when I was here last," Alexandra said. "But then it was late summer and the roses covered nearly the entire front of the house." A spattering of raindrops struck the roof of the carriage.

Ernestine slipped her hand into Alexandra's. "You have been so very sad, Miss Peatling. I doubt that even a thousand roses could lighten your heart at present."

"You have come to know me far too well," she said, "for you have described my spirits precisely."

In the distance, she noticed a man standing by the front door of her house.

Ernestine leaned her head against her shoulder. "Who is that, I wonder, on the steps? He seems to be waiting for us, but he is not dressed at all as a merchant or a servant. His hat is far too fashionable and set at what my friend Jenny always described as a 'rakish' angle. Perhaps he is one of our new neighbours."

"He might be a solicitor." The rain began to pour, and the image of the man became blurred. "I believe I have a few papers yet to sign where the property is concerned."

Alexandra watched the faint image grow larger, the closer the coach drew to the front steps. She could not imagine who might be awaiting her in such dismal weather. The man smiled, however, and sudden recognition gave her a severe jolt.

"Whatever is the matter!" Ernestine cried. "You have given me such a fright!"

"Oh, I do beg your pardon," Alexandra responded. "But for just a moment I thought . . ." Her heart began beating furiously in her chest as though it knew the identity of the person now walking down the three shallow steps.

The coach followed the curve of the drive, and in a moment, her disbelief was completely overturned as Rotherby's face came into view in the side window.

"Why, it is Uncle Phillip!" Ernestine cried. "However did he know where we were?"

"His mother, I suppose, for she was the only one who knew my direction. Only, what is he doing here?" Her voice was but a whisper, and her throat had become choked with tears.

The door opened. "Hallo, Miss Peatling, Ernestine," the rogue said in an irritatingly nonchalant manner. He tipped his dripping hat to both the ladies.

"Hallo, Rotherby," Alexandra returned, as one in a dream.

"Uncle Phillip!" Ernestine cried, accepting his hand as she began making her descent. "You came! But how? Why? And how did you possibly arrive before us?"

"I harnessed four horses to the curricle and had them changed several times en route. I took at least three short-cuts, and here I am. As to why I have come, that is simple. I mean to accept Miss Peatling's hand in marriage. I know it must be shocking to you to hear it, but she asked me to marry her last night and I have decided I would be a perfect nodcock not to agree to it."

"Why, yes you would!" Ernestine cried enthusiastically. "For there is no finer person in all of England than my governess."

"I would have to agree," he said, glancing from his niece to Alexandra.

She, in turn, could not see Rotherby precisely, for her eyes had misted over in the strangest way. Nor had she heard every word of the exchange between him and Ernestine, since for some reason she felt as though her ears had become stuffed with cotton. Despite all of her sudden physical infirmities, however, she had been able to comprehend that Rotherby would be her husband after all. For that reason, tears poured from her eyes and her handkerchief was practically wet through.

"Pray do not weep, Miss Peatling, or you will be accused of an excess of sensibility," he said, as he extended his hand to her.

"I *am* weeping!" she cried, stunned. "How extraordinary!"

Her gaze, now sufficiently clear, landed upon Rotherby's outstretched hand. He was to be her husband, at long last. Was she dreaming? She took his hand and squeezed it very hard. "You are real, are you not?" she asked, lifting her gaze to his. "I will not awaken in a moment, having just arrived at my home, only to discover you were but a ghost who had been passing through my dreams for a time?"

"I am not a ghost, Miss Peatling. Only, are you very certain you wish to take a rogue to husband?"

She drew very near and placed a kiss on his lips. Water from his dripping brim splashed onto her chin, but she did not care. "More than life itself," she murmured.

"Then come into the house and we shall begin settling the details of our marriage agreement right away, for I do not intend to delay our wedding very long. Indeed, if I can procure a special license, I shall do so, even if I must travel to Canterbury in the morning."

"Kent is not so very far. We shall journey together, if you like."

"And set all the tabbies to gabblemongering?"

"I do not care what the gossips may think of me or of you. Not one whit."

She descended the carriage and saw to her considerable dismay that Ernestine was standing in the rain watching them.

"Whatever are you doing?" Alexandra cried. "Pray go into the house at once!"

"I am so happy!" she exclaimed, "for you are to be my aunt and I shall know you my entire life!"

"You will not be so happy should you suddenly develop an inflammation of the lungs." She moved toward Ernestine and propelled her firmly towards the door.

Ernestine obeyed her and moved quickly into the house. Once they were all inside, she whirled on Alexandra quite suddenly. "I have just thought! I shall miss you excessively once you are wed . . ." Her voice trailed off in despair.

"Whatever do you mean?" Alexandra queried.

"I can see now that I will have to leave you both."

"What nonsense is this!" Rotherby cried. "You will remain under my roof until you are of age, or until you marry, or until you desire to leave. Besides, I daresay Gilmorton will not want you underfoot or distracting his wife from her duties. He is quite particular and will expect her to tend to him most especially, although she seems perfectly reconciled to serving his every whim as it is."

He smiled crookedly.

"I find your speech utterly incomprehensible," Alexandra exclaimed. "What are you talking about?"

Ernestine moved to stand close to her. "If I am not to be his wife, then who is?" she queried.

"Mr. Gilmorton has decided to elope. He is more anxious for a bride than I would have thought possible. He has probably already left my home—with my sister. When last I saw him, he was planning a several-day holiday in Scotland . . . with Fanny."

Alexandra could not credit what he was saying. "Do you mean to tell me he is taking her to . . . to Gretna Green?" she cried.

He nodded.

"Oh, but this is too wonderful!" Ernestine exclaimed. "Mama is to marry Mr. Gilmorton?"

"Yes, indeed, but the most amazing thing is that I believe it to be a love match."

"Mrs. Burbage, actually in love with Gilmorton?" Alexandra cried.

"My mother loves Mr. Gilmorton? How is that possible?"

"Love is a mystery," he murmured, glancing at Alexandra, his eyes full of affection and wonder. "In the meantime, you will remain with us."

Ernestine took a step toward Rotherby. "But is this indeed what you wish for, Uncle? I would not for a moment intrude on your life. Perhaps Mama will want me, once she is wed . . ." Her face became pinched, like a drying fig.

He moved close to her and placed a kiss on her cheek, then hugged her. "I desire you to live in my home as my daughter, very, very much." He then smiled ruefully, a warm, teasing light in his grey eyes. "Of course you realize that even were I of a different mind, I know Miss Peatling well enough to comprehend her feelings fully upon the subject. If I did not agree to your remaining beneath my roof until you were married, she would either demand that such a promise be placed in our marriage documents or she would kidnap you yet again and I would see neither hide nor hair of either of you for five years and that thought I find utterly intolerable."

Alexandra chuckled. "You do understand me, then," she said.

Rotherby looked at her, an intense longing in his grey eyes. "I do," he responded softly.

Ernestine suddenly announced that since it was all settled, she meant to seek out the housekeeper that she might learn which of the bedchambers would belong to her. Alexandra did not prevent her from leaving. Nor did Rotherby.

When she was gone, Rotherby divested Alexandra quickly of her bonnet and pelisse and gathered her up in his arms. The kiss he placed on her lips was full of summer's promise.

"What are you thinking?" he queried, petting her hair and kissing her cheek as he cradled her in his arms.

"That day in Bath, when I first saw you." She lifted a hand to stroke his face tenderly. "I never truly believed that we would one day be together even though I wished it so."

"Nor I, though you lived in my dreams."

"I did?" she queried, surprised.

He nodded. "I used to have long conversations with you," he confessed. "Ravenstone was not entirely wrong. I may not have been betrothed to you, but the dream of you prompted me to mend my ways. I never thought myself worthy, however. I still do not."

"Love is not about worthiness," she said, "but about fitting together properly. I could never have been happy with Sir Marcus. He is far too *proper* for my tastes."

"Are you saying only a rogue would do for you?"

She shook her head. "No, I am saying only *you* would do for me."

He grew very solemn. "I do love you Alexandra Peatling."

"And I you, Phillip Rotherby."

THE RAKE

by

Isobel Linton

One

Castle Leighton was home to a duke and a rake; it was an estate so extensive and imposing that it could be taken for nothing else, save perhaps for a palace. No visitor could come to the Castle without spending some time in amazement at its impressive stone façade. A grand formal staircase was its centerpiece, leading up a whole graceful flight of steps from the wide cobblestone courtyard.

To either side of the central building were tall, grim, twin stone towers which were once part of a surrounding fortress and now marked the beginning of the East and West wings, respectively. From there, the enormous building seemed to stretch out endlessly to either side.

Two dark-haired gentlemen were looking down from the stone parapets of the West Wing of Castle Leighton just as the party of ladies from Norwood, Lower Barchester, drew up. They watched with mild interest as two modishly appointed lady guests were being handed down from their carriage by several footmen dressed in the silver and blue livery of the Rylands.

The shorter of the two brothers turned away and re-entered the great house, while the taller, a handsome, well-dressed gentleman, remained a moment longer before disappearing from view.

Glimpsing the last figure just before he disappeared, Miss Huntington whispered excitedly to her chaperone, "Is that the duke? He is a very well-looking man!"

"Hush, Serena," ordered Lady Clayburgh, rather more sharply than she had intended. "Do stop staring! Gawking as you do is most unsuitable! Be a good girl, heed my words, and watch your step, lest you create for your intended a lasting first impression of his bride-to-be tumbling onto the dirty cobblestones. Is that how you wish to make your entrance? Of course you do not. Now pick up your skirts, and watch what you're doing. Let the servant assist you, take his hand. Slowly, slowly—the steps are very fine and springy. There you are. Watch where you step in those slippers. Even a duke's courtyard requires that a lady be on the lookout to avoid the frequent natural—ah, hazards, shall we say."

Miss Serena Huntington, a tall beauty with claret-red hair, carefully stepped out of the post-chaise his grace had kindly sent to fetch her, and allowed herself to be handed down by the livened servant, placing her feet gingerly upon the steps, just as her aunt had bade her do.

It took all of her inner strength to prevent herself from looking up once again to see the handsome face of the gentleman she had briefly glimpsed on the parapet, Alastair, Duke of Leighton, who was quite soon to ask Miss Huntington to become his wife and his duchess.

It had all been arranged.

By the kindness of Lady Clayburgh, Miss Huntington's fond aunt, and through the knowledgeable intervention of Edwina, Countess of Shelburne, acting on behalf of the duke, a very promising match was as good as made for her.

It was a fairy tale coming true. She, Serena Huntington, daughter of a mere gentleman, would become a rich woman. She would become a powerful woman. Most importantly of all, she would finally be in a position to assist the rest of her family.

Then, God willing, if fortune shone on her, as she devoutly hoped it would, she might even be a happy woman as well—for she trusted her Aunt Gillian to act in her very best interests. It was all terribly exciting, really, and had come about with such apparent ease, and with such swiftness! One minute she had been in her father's study, looking over the bills and wondering how she would ever find the funds to pay them, and the next thing she knew, Lady Clayburgh had sent her a letter saying that Lady Shelburne had as good as completed the nuptial arrangements. Serena's heart beat hard in her chest, as she perceived the realization of her hope of overcoming all her difficulties, all at one stroke.

Yes, she thought, this whole uncommon enterprise seems to be working out for the best!

The Duke of Leighton, a dark, heavily built man, motioned to Lord Jack Ryland, who followed his brother from the vine-covered stone balcony through a door into his outer privy chamber. The room had been the privy chamber of their father, and his father before him, since the time when the old inner court of Castle Leighton had been built.

Three tall windows draped in thick golden damask opened out to the splendid southern view of the formal front courtyard, and the grounds beyond. There one might enjoy the sight of great, rolling lawns, dotted with sheep, and ornamented by several huge old chestnut trees spreading their shade; nestled within was lovely Silver Lake, past which guests and visitors might drive, following a sinuous path.

The interior of Leighton Castle was as splendid and well

conceived as its exterior. The Ryland family's wealth was unparalleled in the county of Haworth, and a series of excellent stewards had ensured that with each generation the resources of the family were augmented, never squandered. To any visitor, the sheer number of rooms and servants to keep them seemed overwhelming; but every visitor to the Castle remarked on the fact that despite its size and grandeur, the house always was kept just as one would wish.

The duke's private apartments were, if anything, even more meticulously kept than the rest of the house, and the duke's privy chamber, his inner sanctum, the most meticulously kept of all. There was to be found a large, priceless mahogany desk, polished to perfection, which dominated the room. It boasted intricate carvings including the ducal crest; it was a treasure in itself designed by a previous duke, sent out to the Orient to be made, and shipped back in the 1700's.

High shelves displayed leather-bound books, collected by various members of the family over many generations. A large gilt-framed mirror hung over a carved, white-marble mantel. Beneath it was a huge fireplace in which wood was stacked high, ready to be lit at the touch of a bell. There were many oriental carpets, and a few leather chairs, shined to perfection.

The two brothers stood in front of the fireplace, talking. The elder was not really a stout fellow, but seemed heavier than he was due to his choice in clothing; the duke was dressed in a courtly, almost ornate manner similar to that of His Royal Highness the Prince Regent. His waistcoat was made of Chinese brocade done up in a peony design; the pure white tie at his neck had, unusually, a bit of Mechlin lace on it, giving it the quality of a previous era. His jacket, although expertly cut, had had its shoulders padded, and his pantaloons were cut a bit too snugly to suit his figure.

The younger brother's attire, on the other hand, was cut from an altogether different cloth—his was the simple style of Beau Brummell, with a white cravat tied in an impeccable knot, dark-green coat cut by Weston, beige breeches, and well-polished top-boots.

Lord Jack had a strong, almost rough face: a strong jaw, distinctive aristocratic nose, and high cheekbones. The duke's features had a softer mien altogether, as if softened by pleasure, or perhaps by a lifetime of having had his own way. The duke's demeanor spoke of privilege and satisfaction of desires, while Lord Jack Ryland's spoke of resolve, character, and will.

The duke walked to the window, moved the drape, peered down toward the front court, and let the drape fall again.

"I cannot see her. She must have gone within. Really, I had promised myself I would not look. What did you think of her, Jack? A splendid specimen, is she? I asked that she be a diamond of the first water, of course. One could do no less, in my position, could one?"

"She was tall, carried herself well enough," replied Lord Jack. "I could not make out her face; she was wearing a bonnet, after all. Do you mean to say you have not seen her? Not even a miniature?"

"No, and I shall not until tomorrow night," pronounced the duke, smiling. "It is part of my plan for marital happiness."

"That being 'ignorance is bliss,' I presume?" asked Lord Jack wryly.

"Sheath your savage wit, I pray you, Jack. I thought it quite amusing that Aunt Edwina would arrange for me to wed an unknown bride. You have no idea how much the very thought of marriage plagues me. My first principle is this—out of sight, out of mind. My second principle is that I beg Aunt Edwina handle everything about matrimony, right down to choosing the doilies. I don't want to see the girl at all until the very last moment that I must."

"You are a queer fish, Alastair. *You* know you are—but does she? In her utter ignorance, this girl is promised to you, all the same?"

"Indeed. It is all done but the asking, as it were. Aunt Edwina is in complete command of all the details, has met the girl, knows the family, has apprised her and her people of my very precise needs and wants and expectations, and these are, I am told, very acceptable to her."

"Are they?" drawled Lord Jack, unimpressed.

"Well, mock me if you must, Jack, but it is my marriage and it is my wish that Aunt Edwina should act for me in this manner. I can tell you that I really am most grateful to her. Unlike you, my dear, wild brother, I have never had much taste for the ladies and regard this whole area of my life with some trepidation. Aunt Edwina assures me it is a wildly successful match for the girl—as it would be, of course, even *I* know that I am a fine catch—and a very unexceptional match for me. It offers the important qualification that it can be achieved at long distance, without my having to engage in any tiresome games of courtship. She brings to the match an old lineage and good blood. Superior provenance, all in all."

"Sounds as if you're buying a mare, not making a marriage, Alastair. I wonder that you can be quite so hard-headed in matters of matrimony."

"I wonder you can be so softheaded, my dear brother, in matters of the heart! Recall that long dance Idelle Mountjoy led you on, throughout our childhood. I had thought that she had quite ruined you for the ladies. Dear Lady Idelle, unkind girl, adored the very ground you walked upon, or she did until she grew old enough to appreciate that you were not the heir. Then she deserted you quite completely, as I recall, dropping you like a hot stone."

Lord Jack Ryland's face darkened. "Oh, I shall never again be taken in by any female as I was by Idelle. She was my first and final error in the petticoat line. I now participate wholeheartedly and exclusively in the sweet yet temporary physical pleasures of love."

The duke shuddered, removed his lace handkerchief and waved it around in no particular direction.

"I wish you well of it. I suppose there must always be one amongst any noble family whose behaviour is a blot on the name, and that is, of course, the part you seem to have chosen for yourself. As head of the family, I suppose I really *should* be talking you out of it, or remonstrating about your lack of morals, your love of wenches, of gambling, and of general waywardness."

"Should you, Alastair?"

"Well, I somehow feel that I ought to, that society expects it of me. On the other hand, that would be *so* tedious, don't you think?"

"I do indeed. Besides, I think the name and fashion of 'Rake Ryland' suits me rather well. Do you not agree?"

"I do. All in all, Jack, I think it suits you very well indeed. You may be sure that however much *other* tongues wag about your scandalous affairs, you shall not hear a word of censure from me."

Lord Jack's lips turned up in a sly smile. He replied, "You are becoming magnanimous, Alastair."

"Am I, indeed? That is very good of you to say. I would wish to be magnanimous. Not that I am entirely sure what that *is,* but who cares?"

"Just so. I must take my leave of you and remove my things from the inn, where I spent a very jolly evening last night. You should visit it, my brother—but I forgot. You do not approve of such low places and persons, do you? In any case, I wish you well in this *engagement* of yours, though I confess that I can't help but wonder, Alastair, whyever did you not offer for Idelle? You must know how much she would like to become a duchess, even *your* duchess."

His Grace of Leighton thought for a moment.

"There is that, isn't there? Remarkable oversight on my part. You know, it simply did not occur to me. I might have offered for her. She'd do just as well as this girl, and she is, of course, a known quantity. That itself, might have been the problem! Idelle can be so—well, interfering. One does not want one's wife to be interfering, does one? One wants one's wife to be biddable. One wants one's wife to be—retiring. One wants one's wife to be lovely and malleable, content to remain safely in the background like an heirloom set of china, brought out on special occasions to grace a table or two. Idelle is *not* so biddable. Furthermore, she is hardly like bone china. More like one of those dreadful porcelain Pekinese dogs," he said firmly, waving his handkerchief again.

"I wish you all the best, then."

"Thank you, brother. I appreciate your coming out to the house to celebrate this occasion. Everyone who is anyone is arriving for the ball that will celebrate our engagement. I know you do not generally enjoy such events, for balls attended by young ladies of quality are not in your usual line."

"Don't mention it, Alastair. I'm sure I will find some lovely lass among them who will provide me with some momentary amusement. There is always someone, I have found."

"There is always someone when Rake Ryland is around, at any case."

"That, my dear brother, I must readily admit! It is the one occupation for which I am uniquely talented—that of winning female hearts. One must have something to do with one's life, mustn't one?"

"Must one?" drawled the duke vaguely. "Must one, really? I confess I had never thought of doing anything, ever, at all."

"Well, of course not," said his brother. "You are a duke."

"Ah, yes. To be sure. I am! Yes, exactly!"

Two

Poor Mary White was nearly in tears. Tall, red-headed, impulsive Miss Huntington was throwing gown after gown from her large leather trunk onto the floor, paying no mind to Mary's pleading that she let the abigail try to find the lost Pomona green walking dress.

"It's from Paris, Mary, and it's worth a small fortune," cried Serena. "I am sorry to be so bad, but I really must find it, at once!"

"Go into the next room, Miss, and I'll find it directly. Please, see what mischief you are doing to that lovely jonquil gown you like so much! I'll never get those wrinkles out, Miss! Please! Go next door! Visit your aunt!"

Abruptly, Serena laid down the gowns, with a guilty look on her face. She tried to smooth out the fabric, then stood up.

"I am sorry, Mary. I was quite wrong. I will stop interfering at once."

Mary gave her charge a skeptical glance.

"Don't be telling me that taradiddle, Miss Serena. The day you stop interfering is the day you stop drawing breath, and well we all know it. I wonder, does this Duke know it? Did your aunt let him know, when she was bragging about all your charms?" she said acerbically.

"Mary, how can you say such a thing! Of course, she could not have said that I am impulsive and interfering, for who would want such a care-for-nothing bride? I expect she said that I am—um, spirited and curious. Which is nothing other than the truth."

"Impulsive and interfering will do for me, Miss Serena. You know I don't approve of this whole business, just because of that. You shouldn't have jumped into this mad marriage with a fellow you haven't even seen yet, and may as well have six heads as one, leaving beside the point that one of them has a coronet with strawberry leaves on it. Second, you shouldn't be plaguing me trying to find you a walking dress when I need to be unpacking all of your belongings in a proper, settled way. You shouldn't be going out walking at all. You'll ruin your shoes, you'll ruin your pretty Parisian dress, and more than that, you're sure to get lost, wandering about in a county you have no notion of. It's mad, not that you haven't done a slew of mad things in your young life, you scamp."

Mary shook her head and gave her young mistress a fond chuck under the chin.

"It's right here, the green dress! Lovely thing it is. You shouldn't be wearing it, and you shouldn't be walking out in it as yet. You've just got here!"

"Mary," her mistress admonished.

"Well, if you must have your walk, you madcap miss, be sure you take a manservant with you!"

"No! I am not so craven!"

"This estate is the size of a small city, you goose. I have a good mind to call for your Aunt Gillian. She won't stand for this nonsense, and well you know it!"

"Noo-oo!" wailed Miss Huntington. "I've been

cooped up in that post-chaise for three days, and if I don't get some fresh air, I'm going to wither away and die, I tell you. I have to get out, to strike out on my own. Besides, I'm beside myself with excitement. I need a walk to compose myself to calm down and prepare to face my future. Surely you can understand."

Mary's face darkened.

"Pshaw. You know what I think of you gettin' shut up in the parson's pound like this, Miss Serena. No way to be goin' about it. People should marry them as they knows, not them as they don't know."

"I haven't said I'm going to marry him. Not yet, anyway."

"Well, he's spent a pretty penny on that post-chaise, bringing you down here to meet him, then."

Miss Huntington considered this argument, then shrugged her shoulders as she allowed Mary to help her on with the handsome apple-green gown, saying, "He's a duke. He can afford it. He should have sent his coach!"

This brought another dark look from her abigail, who asked, "Is this my pretty, good Serena, talking about money as if it were pouring down out of the trees? It makes me want to weep, it does. What your mother would say about this, I can't think."

Serena's face grew solemn.

"You think that she would not approve, Mary?"

"Are you daft, child? Your mother, bless her heart, who gave up her health and her position for the love of your dear father, you think she would think well on her eldest girl selling herself for a title? Pshaw! Think again, young miss."

Serena blushed till the colour of her cheeks nearly matched that of her titian hair.

"Selling myself? Is that what you think I am doing?"

Mary nodded grimly as she buttoned up the walking dress. She helped her mistress on with a jacket, and with her half-boots, and then helped tie a Coburg bonnet on her head.

"That's just not so, Mary, and I'll thank you not to say such a thing, nor to think such a thing! The idea!"

"I'm not one to put on a happy face at a funeral, Miss Serena, and all you'll ever get from me is the truth. For all your family's troubles, there's no need for you to put aside what you know to be right."

"Don't say that."

Mary shrugged, and said nothing.

Serena frowned, and looked in the mirror. The bonnet looked very well indeed, but she herself looked careworn, and so she felt. She pinched her cheeks, trying to bring color to them, and but their stubborn, pale color only reminded her more and more of her papa, and this thought, in turn, brought tears to her eyes that she could not hide from Mary's steady gaze.

"There, there, child, things can't be that bad for you. You don't have to do this. You can say no to the man anytime you want, and you should do it, too, if he don't meet your expectations in a husband."

"Aunt Gillian said I must marry him. Everything's been arranged."

"You're throwing away your whole life," Mary pointed out. "On a man you've never met."

"I've seen him, Mary! I saw him just an hour ago. From a distance. He looks perfectly decent, perfectly attractive, even more than that! He's a duke, after all, just how bad could he be?" said Serena with forced gaiety.

Mary rolled her eyes and made something between a laugh and a snort of derision, adding, "You're too young to know some of the tales told below-stairs, of the strange doings of those they call my betters. Who knows, indeed? I just want you to make sure you know this duke, and know his character, before you start making any vows."

"I will, I will, I promise," said Miss Huntington, a little unhappily. "Is the bonnet well tied? May I go now?"

Lady Clayburgh came in to the room, and Mary excused herself, giving Serena a speaking glance before she left, which Serena returned, motioning to Mary to keep her plan to go walking to herself.

"You're looking very well, Serena. That dress was an excellent choice. Wise of you to begin trying on your wardrobe. At these country houses, one cannot dress in too much splendor. In your position, it will have to become a daily necessity, really." Lady Clayburgh, a handsome woman with blue eyes and grey-gold hair, paused and surveyed her niece. "Now, my dear, that Mary's not been scaring you with her upcountry talk, has she? I know she objects to your marriage, not that it's any business of hers."

"Just a little."

"I should get rid of that woman. She thinks she may interfere in what is none of her concern, taking it on just because she loved your mother. As if that gave her the right, which it does not. No one has the right to frighten you, Serena."

"Am I doing the right thing, Auntie?"

"I believe so, dear. Yours is rather a desperate case, and this is rather a desperate solution, but it is hardly anything out of the ordinary. Great marriages are not usually made by the actual persons involved, but according to the needs of time, or of blood, or lineage, or joining of estates. It isn't meant to be a personal decision—it's a *mariage de convenance*. You'll do very well, my dear. You'll be a great lady," pointed out Lady Clayburgh, giving her a small hug.

"I don't want to be a great lady, I just want to do what is best for my family. I want Papa to get better. If he doesn't have to worry so much about what is going to happen to all of his children, he must get better! I know he will! I want James to be able to afford a commission in the army so he can marry Miss Mills. I want Frank to have a proper education, and I want Maria and Sybil to have a proper dowry so that they, at least, can marry whomever they want. Is that so bad?"

"No, my dear. You are being very, very brave, and very dutiful, indeed. I'm sure your dear father, if he knew about your sacrifice, would be so very proud of you!"

She hugged her niece. "As would your sainted mother, too."

"I miss her so much, Aunt Gillian," whispered Serena.

"We all do. Very well, dear. I am still fatigued from the journey. I shall lie down for the rest of the afternoon, I think. You shall continue trying on your wardrobe."

"Well, yes. I shall try out this dress first," Serena said carefully.

"What a good idea. I will see you at dinner, then."

They kissed, and Lady Clayburgh withdrew. Serena found her parasol, one her mother had given her, dutifully put on her gloves, and walked down the stairs to the front entrance.

She crossed down the main staircase and over the cobblestoned court, and strode out over the grassy grounds, raising the parasol and thinking of her dear mother. Thus it was with real tears in her eyes, and a

real need for solitude and contemplation, that Miss
Huntington, daughter of Charles Huntington of Norwood, Upper Barchester, slipped out all alone, to ex-
plore the countryside, wearing her lovely Coburg
bonnet and her Pomona-green walking gown.

Three

Miss Huntington was quite lost, and worse yet, she was quite, quite late. Serena looked at the sun's place in the sky and decided it must be far onto three o'clock. She had started out at ten! What she had meant to be a cheerful excursion to reach the Norman Tower of Leighton Castle had turned out to be an utter disaster, her situation worse than even the disapproving Mary White could have predicted.

She could not have been more lost had she been set upon by kidnappers and thrown out along a highway.

Serena stopped at a rough rail fence and leaned against it. She cursed herself for being a stubborn fool and removed first her gloves, then her fine half-boot, noting with unhappiness a large red blister that had broken, making it impossible to put her shoe back on, for all the pain of it.

She was tired, she was hot, she was lost, and she was alone.

How could a simple walk turn out so badly? She certainly should have taken a servant with her, as Mary had urged her. She shouldn't have gone far away. She shouldn't have been so dreadfully impulsive, thinking that she could make her way in completely new territory. It was pride, it was madness, and now she was, quite rightly, being punished for having given in once again to her besetting sin.

She removed her other slipper, only to find a matching blister of equal size and fury to the first. Serena put both boots in her left hand, hiked up the skirt of her lovely walking dress in her right, a dress now quite ruined, splattered with mud and with grime, while she tried to take a fix on her whereabouts.

Serena felt sure that the ducal manor would show itself just over the next hill—but she had had that hope dashed time and again, for several small hills now. The whole trip had been an extremely lowering experience, especially for someone who previously had prided herself on her excellent abilities as a cross-country walker.

No matter. Sooner or later someone would come along, and assist her, or sooner or later she would come upon some landmark by which she could assay where she was. How could she miss a forty-foot Norman Tower, after all? How could she manage not to come across some knowledgeable denizen of the area?

It was ridiculous, she thought, that no one had come down the muddy little lane along which she had been trudging for three-quarters of an hour! She had come out of a long patch through a winding old forest that must have been some part of the duke's preserve. Shouldn't there at least be a gamekeeper running about, taking care of the duke's lands, who could help her find her way?

There should, she thought, but there was not.

Another whole hour must have passed, with Miss Huntington walking steadily toward what she devoutly hoped might be Duke's Minster, before at last a farmer came by driving a little haycart, and took pity upon the poor young lady. He was kind enough to agree to take Miss Huntington on the back and drop her at an inn at the nearest crossroads.

Although the cart was dusty and rough riding, Serena put on her gloves again and raised her parasol, desperately afraid she was going to receive both a sunburn and a scold. She was very glad to at least be making her way somewhere with certainty, and felt sure that her luck was turning, and that she could make her way back to the Castle without too much more time lost.

Miss Huntington had no money to pay the man, of course, but she dutifully noted his name, Farmer Willis, spoke with him politely, favored him with a smile, and promised to reward him when she could. She thought it a bit ominous when the farmer gave a hearty wink at her words about reward, but then thought no more of it.

She was in Duke's Minster at last, and she recognized the inn at the centre of town as the Duck and Crossroads. Everything would now turn out for the best, for their party had stopped briefly at this very inn on the way to the Castle. Miss Huntington felt she could now regard the whole afternoon as having been nothing more than a lark, a pleasant misadventure.

She removed her Coburg bonnet, her little gloves, now quite sullied, and wiped some perspiration from her brow. She would be able to put her dress together at the inn, she reasoned, and make herself look a bit more respectable, once she'd brushed the straw and dirt off her walking dress.

Her troubles were over, she was certain, for at the inn she would surely be able to find someone to take her back to the Castle and, with any luck at all, she might still arrive in time not to sustain too severe a scolding from Aunt Gillian.

On the other hand, when she saw what had become

of her mistress's fine clothing, her abigail was sure to read her the Riot Act. Lady Clayburgh was one thing, but from the wrath of Mary, her maid, there would be no escaping.

Four

The Duck and Crossroads Inn was loud and crowded, and Serena had considerable difficulty making her way through a packed mass of people. She felt very uncomfortable, squeezing past this strange man and that strange man, trying to find the innkeeper, when suddenly a tall man spun her around from behind by her shoulders, tipped her back over his left arm, and planted a long, lingering kiss upon her lips.

"Welcome back, Nell, my dear," he said upon releasing her. "I've missed you! We've all missed you."

Miss Huntington staggered to her feet, put a hand to the lips he had crushed against her, and had her small bare fist raised, about to deal the insolent cur a fine slap, when she recognized her attacker.

She gasped instead of striking, and put her hand to her mouth. It was the tall man she had seen at the Castle!

It was the duke!

She had just been accosted by the man to whom she was all but promised!

How could this be happening? Was it really her intended, the Duke of Leighton, carrying on in a common tavern, treating her as if she were a common bar wench?

At first, Serena did not know whether feelings of shock

or of disgust were uppermost in her heart. These feelings were swiftly succeeded by surprise at realizing how very pleasant and secure it felt to be taken up in a handsome gentleman's strong arms!

The tall man at once recognized his error, unhanded her, and swept her suddenly a complete and courtly bow. He took her hand and raised it to his lips, his dark eyes surveying her deeply all the time, so that Miss Huntington could not help blushing.

Said he, "I do beg your pardon, madam. I beg you will forgive my—my truly unforgivable impertinence. I took you for Red Nell, who is employed here, and with whom I am, for some time, acquainted. A thousand apologies. I meant to steal a kiss from her, but not from you, whom I now perceive to be a young lady of quality. You do possess Nell's colour hair, you see, and share many of her—other admirable attributes, as it were. Forgive my error. It is unusual to meet a young lady of quality, you must admit, unaccompanied, in the bustle of a country inn."

Serena blushed again, "To be sure, to be sure, sir."

She wished she had not been so headstrong as to go out on her own, without at least a lady's maid or a footman. Lady Clayburgh and Mary White had been quite right about that; how could she have been so foolish? The duke must think her very hoydenish indeed!

Her worst fears were realized with the handsome gentleman's very next words.

"It is not quite the usual thing, you must admit," he pointed out, smiling at her in a way she found utterly charming, "For a young lady of quality to go about unchaperoned, you know. In fact, I feel sure that you do know that. The question must occur: why would such a lovely, well-bred young lady have cause to flout the strictures of polite Society? In general, those females who move freely about these small rooms are of quite a dif-

ferent persuasion, so to speak, and freer with their favours."

Just when Miss Huntington should have become most
ashamed by her own behaviour, the duke's words set her
back up. A flash of temper passed over her face, and she
bristled. She responded pertly, challenging him, "You
seem to know a great deal about the ways of barmaids
and other female persons, sir. Am I to gather that you
have had considerable experience in such affairs?"

Lord Jack laughed, then smiled brilliantly at Miss Huntington, saying, "You are a plain speaker, I see. I like that."

Miss Huntington smiled as well. " 'Plain speaker', am
I? Rash, impulsive, tactless, undiplomatic—those are
words more generally applied to me, I confess. I should
not have said what I did just now. It was uncivil of me,
and I am sorry for it. I have a bit of temper as well, I am
sorry to say."

"Have you, now? Then, in that generous spirit of honesty, I will confess that I do have a reputation as a rake,
my dear young lady, if that's what you were implying. I
hope that will not give you a disgust of me."

*A strange thing for a man to reveal to a young lady at
their first meeting* Miss Huntington thought to herself.
*Who is this fellow? What can he mean by it? Is it merely
that his rank makes him so powerful that he can do just
as he pleases, and speak just as he pleases? Calling himself a rake? It is more than passing strange. A stranger
thing for a man to reveal to a young lady he intends to
wed! Does he recognize me, or does he not? If he does
know who I am, is he trying to warn me off? Is he trying
to test my mettle? I shall let him know that I am no milk-
and-water miss, but a lady with some spirit!*

Miss Huntington gave him a sly, flirtatious look and said,
"Oh, dear! A rake, are you? Thank you for warning me. I
must admit I have never met an actual rake before, though

of course I have heard of them and of their exploits, though not in great detail. That being the case, sir, I shall take great care to protect my heart."

At this, Lord Jack laughed out loud.

"You, my dear, may be a beautiful young lady of quality, but you are also a minx. You shall not charm me with your wiles, however. Now that I know who you are not, I shall treat you with the deference and circumspection that are due to your rank and position. I cannot deny my past misdeeds, but I hope you will allow me in the present to make amends for my want of recent conduct with respect to you. A gentleman should not treat a lady so— unless and until she is his wife."

At this, Serena blushed charmingly. This was all going very well. He must know her! He must be playing with her, teasing her! He was courting her, flattering her, flirting with her, and it was all so deeply charming that she found it difficult not to throw herself directly into his arms. He was the kind of man with whom it was deeply pleasurable just to converse, and whose presence itself was captivating. The fast beating of her heart was proof of this.

Lord Jack gave her a penetrating glance, adding, "No, a gentleman must not do as I did and merely take a young lady into his arms, embracing her as I did you—unless, of course, he cannot help himself being quite overcome by her beauty."

He was looking at Serena in an amused, yet contemplative manner. "You are a very handsome young woman. Has anyone ever told you that?"

Serena shook her head, shyly.

"It is very true, and I have a great deal of experience in these matters. Yes, you are a remarkably pretty young woman, you know, the more so when you blush in that particularly attractive fashion."

"Thank you, sir."

"So, tell me—are you here to visit the Castle?"

Is he joking? Can it be the duke has no idea who I am? That would provide a different picture of the man, indeed. "Tell me, young lady, have we ever met? Who are you? You fascinate me, I must confess. How came you to be so bold as to come out to the Duck and Crossroads all alone, but so modest that you blush and stammer when addressed directly by a gentleman?"

He does not know me! No, it seems that His Grace of Leighton has propensities that have been withheld from me by Aunt Gillian. It is clear that this man is a rake, just as he himself admitted!

I suppose I should be angry with them for not telling me, Serena thought to herself but the truth is that he is the most charming man I have ever met in my life! The thought of marrying him is now not only pleasant, it seems a godsend! Will he give up his light o' loves when he is married I wonder? How shall I know? Who can tell a rake's heart?

"I am not bold, sir." Serena replied. "I was out walking, having come from the Castle, and I became lost. I asked a farmer driving a haycart for a ride into town, and he said I could find a ride to the castle here. It was perfectly simple. Perhaps I should not have walked out quite so far."

"I see. What is your destination now?" he asked.

"I must return to Castle Leighton," she said.

"You have come to attend the celebration, perhaps?"

Miss Huntington nodded, saying, "Yes, I have."

"I would be honoured if you would permit me to escort you back to Castle Leighton."

Truly, unless he is playing me false, it seems that he does not know who I am, she thought to herself. *Perhaps he was too far away to catch a glimpse of me correctly, though certainly he will recognize my name, if I give it him.*

Dare I conceal my identity? I think I must. If he is flirting in this outrageous way with a mere stranger, then he is a rake, indeed. I should know the true character of the man I am to marry, to know if my husband-to-be has a roving eye when it comes to the ladies. Shall I deceive him, or not?

"May I know your name?" he inquired.

I shall do it! she thought mischievously. *After all what harm could ever come of it? We are as good as betrothed already!*

"I am Miss—Norwood," said Miss Huntington, bobbing a slight curtsey.

"How do you do?" said the gentleman, bowing to her in his turn. "I should like to make myself known to you, Miss Norwood, without more formal introduction, if you do not object, of course."

"Oh, no! You need not, sir! I know who you are," said Serena lightly.

Lord Jack looked somewhat taken aback.

Serena explained at once, "My aunt pointed you out to me when we arrived at Castle Leighton. You were on the balcony, watching the guests arrive. I'm sure you will recall it."

"I do recall being there, but I do not specifically recall seeing you or your aunt. Many guests arrived this morning. I do not know whether I have had the pleasure of your aunt's acquaintance. Her name is—?"

Serena panicked for a moment, caught in the consequence of her own lie. What was she to do? Answer truthfully? Falsely? "Oh, what a tangled web we weave, when first we practice to deceive"—her mother's words came back to her.

"My aunt is—Lady Clayburgh."

"No, I have not had the honour to know her."

That was a bit of luck, Serena thought to herself She had expected him to recognize Lady Clayburgh's name, from all the wedding arrangements that had been conducted, but perhaps the women and the settlement lawyers had mainly been involved. Her husband-to-be was not merely a rake, he appeared to be rather uninterested in his own affairs. An odd combination, to be sure. She began to wonder if the duke's desire to marry was guided mostly by duty, or by convenience. It was beginning to appear to be the latter.

Five

What am I to do now that the extremely charming Miss Norwood has entered my life? A dalliance with her, upon any terms, would be worth enduring the company of my popinjay brother and his useless friends from among the Upper Ten Thousand, Lord Jack thought to himself handing the lovely young lady up into his phaeton. He held her hand steadily till she had her balance and was well seated, and she rewarded him with another of her dazzling smiles.

Remarkable-looking girl. Exceptional.

Lord Jack, who had had the pleasure of the company of many a good-looking female during his rakish career, found he could not quite put his finger on what it was about her that held him so in thrall. It was almost like a physical intoxication, if one believed in such things. In all, he could not recall having felt so very strongly drawn to a female ever before in his adult life.

It was an odd and a worrying thing, really.

If she were merely some wayward wife of a peer, or if she were merely a wanton, he could allow his tendencies their full rein—seduce her and abandon her, and be done with her. That was Rake Ryland's reputation, and it was a reputation that was very well deserved. After Idelle, there had been a bevy of females, of one class or another, each one a diamond of the first water in her own way, and each one kept carefully at arm's length by Lord Jack, who had sworn never to become entangled by a female, ever again.

However, the more he eluded women, the more women set their caps at him. Thus, Lord Jack Ryland became known round London as a rake—a breaker of hearts.

He had his limits, however, and tried as best he could to avoid young ladies of quality, thinking it would be cruel to attract love where he could not return it. It had never before presented a difficulty. His attractions were passing and confined to the lower classes, as a general rule, as with Red Nell and her ilk.

Miss Norwood, and more specifically, the feelings she was inspiring in him, were presenting a difficulty. Being moved by real feelings of appreciative desire toward a young lady of quality—that was quite out of Rake Ryland's line, or at least it had been, until today.

What a novel and pleasant experience! He began to be glad he had accepted the invitation of that fool of a brother of his to come out from London and disport himself at the ancestral mansion.

Should he dally with her? Would he do so? It remained, for Lord Jack, an open question.

He might see what came of it. He might as well, really, seize the time! If he did, who knew where a dalliance with this shockingly lovely young lady might lead?

"I trust that riding in a high-perch phaeton won't distress you too much," said Lord Jack, urging his horses to pull smartly out of the inn. "Some ladies say they find them very frightening, being so high above the ground, although for myself I cannot see it and have no idea why they should feel that way. Do you?"

"N-no," replied Serena, clinging to the side of the carriage, desperate to maintain a solid hold on her seat. Despite her terror, she had to admire how well the duke handled the reins of the phaeton as he swerved and turned, negotiating the crowded cobblestoned streets of Duke's Minster, the small town that was nearest to the Castle. She hung on with white-knuckled hands, a little dismayed by the speed and the bouncing. Miss Huntington started to relax a little when they reached the hedge-lined lane that began just outside the town. He eased the pair into an extended trot, and Serena was able to settle back and enjoy the ride in the country.

Her driver began to relax as well, enough to begin to converse with his passenger, remarking, "I prefer a curricle myself for driving in general, but I found this gathering dust in the stable, and I had an urge to give it a spin. I hope it does not displease you."

"It is very n-nice," said Serena.

Lord Jack seemed to be satisfied with this minimal response, and the two continued on their way for a few minutes in perfect amity. At this point, the phaeton made a sharp turn to the right and headed onto a bumpy, disused cartway, a happening that made no impression at all upon the driver, but caused Serena to cling to the sides of her seat until her knuckles paled.

"As you are new to the neighborhood, Miss Norwood, how do you like our part of the world?" inquired Lord Jack. "Does the county please you so far?"

Miss Huntington was relieved to have something to think about other than whether or not she was going to tumble from her seat to the ground, and she replied brightly, "Well, the Castle is, of course, magnificent, almost overwhelming to me. I'm sure you will think me quite a bumpkin when I admit that I have never been anywhere quite like it, not in the whole of my life."

"It is an extraordinary place."

"It is like living in a piece of history, or in a museum! Everything is inexpressibly well chosen and well cared for. Words fail me; all that I can say is the merest commonplace. The grounds are beautiful, the landscape in beautiful; the architecture is beautiful—how many times can one say that, or think that?"

"True," he admitted.

"Exploring it, I walked through the park over from the South Lawn, and it seemed as if it would go on forever. I had it in mind to try to reach the Norman Tower, which I had read about in a guide book, and that is when I became so hopelessly lost."

"The Norman Tower? I see how you became lost, then! You will be pleased to learn that even locals need guidance to find it. Would you care to see it now?"

"I think my aunt will be looking for me, but it is very tempting. Is it very far out of our way?"

"Not at all. My horses are fresh, and I don't think the detour will add more than a half an hour to our journey. We will certainly be back in time to dress for dinner. What is your wish?"

"My dress at the moment is an embarrassment to both of us, but I assume the Tower won't mind. If you can forgive my *déshabillé*, then I should very much like to see it. It would be very kind of you to take me."

Serena thought him to be very courteous and accommodating for a duke, and very polite and attentive for a gentleman in the petticoat line.

She was pleased that she had thought to conceal her identity. It was much better to spend some time making his acquaintance in a situation such as this, rather than having to make small talk during a quadrille, whilst also being weighed and inspected by the full fury of the ton. *I can see who he is*, she thought, *and learn of what he is made.*

Lord Jack Ryland, on his part was finding himself still shocked, traveling in uncharted waters. He still could not quite put his mind to the particular reason he found this girl so very attractive, but it was increasingly clear that this was so.

Perhaps it was the brightness of her emerald-green eyes, or the easy, relaxed way with which she carried herself, perhaps it was the charming musical sound she made when she laughed, or the fact that she seemed so preternaturally gay.

He thought of how Lady Idelle, his calf-love, might have behaved after an unpleasant ordeal such as this girl had been through—there would have been tears, tantrums, recriminations, fury. She would have stormed back to the Castle, finding someone to blame for her misfortune.

Not this Miss Norwood. This girl was cut from quite another cloth, and the thing of it was, he found that, somehow, mere exposure to her gentle presence aroused his passion.

The thought struck him forcefully just as the Norman Tower came into sight, and he turned the horses up into the stony path that led to it. Yes, all things considered, it was true. Just as surely as the sun was beginning to set in the sky, he was becoming enamoured of this girl.

Enamored? Rake Ryland? Impossible! Whatever might that lead to? Becoming leg-shackled? Now, that was a gruesome thought. Lord Jack shuddered and discarded the idea as he shook the reins to help the horses climb the last incline to the Tower a little faster. It was not to be considered.

Their pleasant conversation ceased, as did his internal speculations, as Lord Jack had to concentrate, helping the pair negotiate the rocky, rutted way. At last he drew the horses to a halt, tied them, and helped the young lady down.

"No wonder I could not find it," she remarked. "It is a very long way off. I was completely mistaken."

"One really must know the way. We ought to repair the road, though. It has become almost impassable, and that's a pity. Time was when the Tower was quite the spot for picnics and afternoon outings. These days hardly anyone visits it, except for the occasional couple looking for a place to be private."

Serena flashed him a look of surprise.

"Don't be alarmed, Miss Norwood. I shall exert my utmost will so as not to be once again overcome by your beauty, though the presence of such charm in a place known to be a trysting site for lovers does make for a powerful combination. In fact, it is almost overwhelming. However, I am doing my best to restrain myself, I assure you."

"You have a sweet way with words, sir."

"I am a rake, my dear. It could not be otherwise."

She laughed at this, and he took her hand, and the two of them climbed the round staircase that was within the stone tower. After a few minutes, they arrived at the top and emerged onto its round stone battlement.

To one side was Duke's Minster, a spider web of lanes leading toward it, and a warren of houses and shops; to the other side was Castle Leighton, its wide grounds, and its famous silver lake. Farther off was a wide quilt of farmlands, separated by hedgerows and patches of woods, with a river winding leisurely through them.

"Magnificent view! Now I know what I think of your county! It is glorious!" she remarked. "I thank you so much for bringing me here!"

Lord Jack seemed as well absorbed in the glories of the countryside, to the eye of the unobservant, when in fact he was paying far less attention to the qualities of the countryside than he was to those physical attributes of his companion.

She was so very close to him. He could smell the rose fragrance of her skin, and if he moved his hand just a bit, he could touch her hair. He could feel the warmth of her body. He had feasted his eyes on her and listened to the sound of her melodious laughter. If his natural ardour overcame his good intentions, who could blame him?

Taking her to the Norman Tower could be seen as a golden opportunity for someone like Rake Ryland. The girl was very young and was unchaperoned, a rare occasion for a young lady of the ton.

Of course, I could make love to her here and now, but ought I to do so? Lord Jack wondered. *On the other hand, if I do not make love to her here and now, whenever will I get another chance?*

He wanted to touch her, to pursue her, to capture her for himself alone. At the very least, he wished to cover her in kisses. If he took advantage of his opportunity now, when she was alone, inexperienced in matters of the heart, she might well fall in love with him. That would be a good thing—or would it?

He could smell the fragrance of her hair. He could feel her warmth as she stood close to him, trusting him. What if he were to wind that stray auburn ringlet about his finger? What if he were to pull her toward him once again and press his lips to hers? What if he allowed her presence to ignite his passion?

"Sir?" asked Serena, somewhat alarmed. "You were staring at me."

"Was I? Forgive me, Miss Norwood."

He hesitated for a moment.

He took a deep breath. It was more than a man could be expected to bring under control. Lord Jack said, in a husky voice, "Yes, I was staring at you, Miss Norwood. It's perfectly true—forgive me. Despite all my assurances, and the very best of intentions, I am quite overcome by your charms. I'm afraid you will also have to forgive me—for this!"

The Rake pulled Serena to him, as he had done with scores of other women, some more experienced, and some more passionate, and some even fairer than she. He covered her lips with his, kissing her deeply, noticing the differences between the desire he felt now and the desire he had felt then, with those others which was only a pale, weak thing, like the moon compared to the sun. It was a mystery how it had arisen, it was a mystery how it taken hold of him, but he recognized something wholly other in the passion that possessed him now. That made Rake Ryland want to possess this girl, and not just now, for an instant, but, to keep her to himself alone. In that new view of her, he was no longer a care-for-nothing rake, but just a man.

Serena, taken by surprise, but not taken without her own warm consent, surrendered at once to his expert touch and let him do as he would, responsive to every move, and every sound, and every tender contact.

No doubt Serena could feel the urgency, the singular intent behind his sudden embrace of her. In a moment, she let fall away all objections to his caress and let her heart lead her on as she began to surrender herself in tender, passionate kisses to this strange, dark gentleman, the notorious rake who, she firmly believed, was soon to become her wedded husband.

Six

The Miss Huntington who re-entered her suite of rooms
in the east wing of Castle Leighton was by no means the
same girl who had left it some hours before. She knew
herself to be a changed woman, but no one in her imme-
diate party but herself was yet aware of this, and she herself sought to conceal it, so moved was she by her
adventure of the afternoon.

Miss Huntington had arrived at the Castle almost at
sunset, with her bonnet askew and her hair disheveled.
Her lovely Pomona-green gown was marred by bramble
scratches, a hem rimmed with dirt, wrinkled, and stained
by grass and mud. Her half-boots were likewise ruined,
not merely scuffed but with the sole separated from the
uppers, filthy beyond repair.

In the commotion that ensued upon her return, no one
noticed the unusual brightness in her eyes, the sighs she
would emit from time to time, nor the dreamy, unfocused
look that was present on her face. Mary White simply
scolded her and took pains to order up bathwater; her aunt
merely scolded her and told her to get dressed at once for
dinner. If a tear fell from her eye from time to time, she
brushed it away with her hand so quickly that her extraordinary inner state passed quite unnoticed: Having been

moved to the very core of her being, Serena was lost in love.

Her aunt saw nothing of it.

"Where have you been, Serena? How could you behave like such a care-for-nothing? I had no idea you thought to go out walking! I had thought you were safe in your chamber, trying on clothes! I have had servants out looking for you for two hours now, with no one able to tell me where you had gone! It's just not done, Serena! What could you have been thinking of?" cried Lady Clayburgh, not waiting for any answers to her questions, rushing her toward Mary's fond ministrations.

"The duke has just come back from a trip to town and is indisposed for the evening, so you shan't be meeting him at all tonight, which I'm sure must be a disappointment to you."

"Oh. Yes, to be sure," replied Serena vaguely, as Mary helped her remove her clothes and enter the hip bath. Serena settled back into the warm waters gratefully, allowing Mary to pour water over her skin, cleansing her, washing all her concerns away. Her skin itself still held such heightened sensation that only the gentlest silken touch was at all bearable; she was filled with such new terror and passion that she thought she might weep for joy.

She sighed again, and let her fingers drift aimlessly in the water.

"Whatever is wrong with you, child?" asked Lady Clayburgh, irritated. "Are you ill?"

"No, Aunt Gillian," replied Serena softly.

"You look as if you are quite in another world. Although the duke will not be present tonight, there will be many of the London ton to dine, of course, as well as many powerful and important local personages. You will be meeting Lord and Lady Mountjoy and their daughter, as well as Lady Shelburne, who is the sole reason that this marriage is being made. You must be prepared to make an excellent impression on her. Child, your mind is clearly otherwhere. Will you attend?"

"Yes, of course, Aunt Gillian. I beg your pardon."

"You must dress to go down to dinner at once. Lady Shelburne will be there, as I said, and you must meet her, and she must give her final approval of you. The Earl and Countess of Mountjoy are close neighbors, whose estate marches with Leighton—their approbation also is vital to you, not in terms of whether or not the marriage will occur, of course, but in terms of your future happiness. You must be accepted within the neighborhood as the first lady of the county. I have never seen you like this before, Serena. Are you quite sure you aren't ill? If so, I have potions you might take. Would you like tea?"

"No, I'm very well, indeed, Aunt Gillian, I do assure you."

"Well, then. Finish your bath quickly. Dress, and do take extra care—you are on exhibit from now on, I'm afraid. Make certain you show me what jewels you're wearing—really, at a place like this, one cannot wear too many jewels. If one wears too few, people tend to think one hasn't many!"

Serena allowed Mary to dress her in all her finery, but it was as if it were all happening at a distance, as if it were all happening in a trance, to someone else. Lady Clayburgh had chosen a jonquil confection made in London at Marbury's. Aunt Gillian had insisted upon traveling straight from Barchester to London, staying three weeks at the Pulteney Hotel in Piccadilly—and at whose expense? Serena had wondered.

Aunt Gillian took her out on the very first day, when

Serena wanted to go to the Tower of London, and to view the Elgin Marbles, and see Big Ben and Westminster Abbey and Parliament and the Egyptian Hall. She wanted to go to Astley's, to Covent Garden, and to the Theatre Royal, but Lady Clayburgh had been adamant—the work of choosing a wardrobe for the young lady soon to become the Duchess of Leighton was serious work. Not until all the styles had been chosen, not until all the cloth had been selected and purchased on Bond Street, not until all her measurements had been taken, and the many dresses that she required were well on their way to being finished, did Lady Clayburgh relent and finally allow her niece to go out and enjoy the other pleasures of London.

The dress she had chosen to wear to be presented tonight to the guests at Leighton was one of the finest in her new, very fashionable wardrobe. Serena had always admired the fashions of London, but had never moved in the finest circles, or even considered so doing. It was simply never a part of her life.

Serena was a country girl, raised in a country way. When she saw herself in the mirror, dressed in the first style of fashion, she almost did not recognize the face that looked back at her, tall and proud, wearing a lovely necklace of pearls with a cross at the center and two matching drop earrings of pearls with diamonds.

There was something else about herself she did not recognize. She put her hand up to the curve in her neck, the curve that her lover had kissed with such extensive ardor, and felt it as if it were new to her. In a way, she had become new to herself. Serena knew that she was never to be the same, ever again.

She had had calf-loves when she was young, of course. Henry Harris used to plague her and play tricks on her from the time that they were seven, and by the time that they were twelve he revealed to her that he had always thought her special. They'd held hands once or twice, and that was that.

When she attended the country balls at Squire Renfrew's, one or two of the older boys would try to steal a kiss from her, and sometimes they'd succeed. It never meant a thing. Her heart had been virgin, completely untouched—that is, until today, until this afternoon.

Now the axis of her whole universe had shifted suddenly. She was aware that the man who had been making love to her was her superior in age and experience, of course, but she thought, or felt rather, that he, too, was involved, and that he too had been surprised by the suddenness of their mutual attraction. She desperately hoped that it was so, that he would not simply toy with her once or twice and cast her off again, returning to his stable of mistresses.

Moved as she was, she also felt tender and vulnerable, wishing she could meet him again at once so he might reassure her of the constancy of his affections. Was it to be so? Could her hopes be realized?

That love could some so suddenly and surely was amazing. That it could happen between her and the man she had pledged to marry, unseen, and untested—that was either good fortune or it was fate.

Whatever it was, the die was cast.

Seven

Turbot and trout, quail and pheasant, beef and lamb and lobster—the dinner was laid out on an enormous table, silver serving plates filled with entrées and their accompanying sauces placed one after another, all the way down the long yards of table. Miss Huntington was sitting in the place of honour, across from Lady Shelburne, who was acting as the hostess tonight.

Lady Shelburne was an imposing figure. She scared Serena to death, and Serena was not a girl normally unsettled. Lady Shelburne had wild grey hair, a sharp, hawklike nose, and penetrating brown eyes that seemed to Serena to be inspecting and assessing her constantly. It made her feel like a creature in a zoo.

Lady Clayburgh seemed well aware of this, for she, seated not too far away, kept staring at Serena as if encouraging her to bring herself forth or to make some witty remark that would amuse Lady Shelburne, but Serena was far too discomfited.

She found that, in the pressure of the moment, all sense had left her brain. She had lost track of her afternoon with the duke, she had forgotten where she came from or even her own name; she could only nod a frozen yes or no when addressed directly. It was all too lowering, and her need to make a good impression on Lady Shelburne, now that she had come to a feeling of attachment for the duke, only made her more helpless and less rational.

Miss Huntington barely breathed all through the many removes of the dinner, and was vastly relieved when at last Lady Shelburne rose to signal that it was time for the ladies to withdraw.

With the ending of the formal dinner and her entrance into the withdrawing room, Miss Huntington thought that her troubles were over, but in fact they had barely begun, for Lady Idelle Mountjoy approached her just as soon as she saw she was alone.

"So, this is to be the new little duchess!" she said in a condescending tone. "Why, I'd wager that this is your very first visit to a ducal seat. Tell me—I am right, am I not? Is it your very first visit?"

Serena reddened, staring at Lady Idelle's sapphire-and-diamond pendant, which, she felt sure, Lady Clayburgh would have told her was unsuitable to be worn by such a young lady.

"It is my first visit, Lady Idelle."

"I wonder that you do not feel completely overwhelmed by it! It must be so difficult for someone who has not been brought up in the first circles to be suddenly thrust among them! Tell me the truth—is this not so? Do you not feel unequal to the task? It would be a vast wonder if you did not! My heart goes out to you, truly it does, for it is quite unfair that such a green girl should be thrust into the middle of the ton, where everyone can be so cutting and so cruel—at least they can to those who are outside their special circle. It is sad, but it is so. I'm sure you'll feel less bereft in time, however. It must be so, for you are to be our new duchess! But pray—don't tell me that you haven't been to a party at a country house before either! Is this your first time for that as well?"

Serena lifted her chin defiantly. "It is, M-miss Mountjoy."

"Oh! Pray, do not call me miss! It is quite incorrect! You must use my title and refer to me as Lady Idelle! All my friends do, and, as we will be neighbours after you marry Alastair, I hope you will as well! It will be such fun having you in the neighbourhood!"

"Will it?" asked Serena suspiciously.

"Yes, of course. It will be so diverting to see how you—manage yourself with all of this. I expect your own household was somewhat—well, rather less grand, am I correct? I am certain that it was—well, it could hardly not be, could it?"

Serena blushed furiously, thinking of her father's small manor house, which would have fit into one section of the servants' wing at Castle Leighton.

"Yes, of course, you must feel so very small and overwhelmed and out of your element. It could hardly be otherwise, Miss Huntington, could it? I wonder that you consented to the match, Miss Huntington. Why did you, if I may be so bold as to inquire?"

The nerve of the girl! thought Serena, suddenly feeling angrier than she could ever recall feeling. *What right has she to say such things to me? This is insupportable!*

"Let me understand you correctly, Lady Idelle," Serena said, disguising her anger as best she could. "You are inquiring as to why I consented to a match with the Duke of Leighton?"

"Yes," she replied, seemingly without a shred of conscience. "I am. It seems such an odd choice."

"Does it? What if I told you I was in love with the duke?"

"Oh! But what a charming thing to say! You have not even seen him, much less met him, to the best of my knowledge, and yet you are ready to swear your eternal loyalty to him! That is very good in you, I'm sure," she said, waving her fan.

Truly, Miss Huntington would rather have boxed her ears, but decided to use wit instead. She began, with dangerous softness, "Well, here is the thing, Lady Idelle. Beyond my deep personal feelings for the duke, I understand that it is quite a pleasant thing to be a duchess. I must confess that rank figured highly in my choice of husband. I am surprised that you yourself would not have wished to rise to such exalted status. Did you not think it would have been pleasant—had he chosen you, instead of me?"

Lady Idelle coloured slightly, which pleased Serena a great deal.

"I-I am sure it would have been a pleasant thing, indeed," agreed Lady Idelle, beginning to see that there was more to Miss Huntington than was at first apparent.

"When I am a duchess," Serena went on, beginning to rise to the occasion, "I will have a great deal of money at my disposal, and, I believe, my tastes and whims will rule the countryside. I will be able to have every dress that I wish, and buy every jewel that I want, and keep every horse that I want, and go where I will when I will."

As Lady Idelle began to look more and more uncomfortable, Serena's imagination became more vivid.

"Castle Leighton will of course become, even more than it is at present, the social center not of just this neighbourhood, but of the entire county." Serena added meaningfully, looking directly into Lady Idelle's eyes, "An invitation to my table and an invitation to my house will be regarded very highly. Those who are for one reason or another not in my good graces will of course remain uninvited. In fact, one's position in the ton could plummet quite suddenly, even quite completely, by losing the good will of the Duchess of Leighton!"

Lady Idelle looked momentarily dumbfounded. Miss Huntington smiled, and her eyes sparkled wickedly.

"I feel sure that you understand perfectly what I mean," purred Miss Huntington. "Do you not?"

"I do understand," gasped Lady Idelle, fully cognizant now of her new position vis-à-vis the duke's intended. "I did not mean to be impertinent, your Gr—I mean, Miss Huntington. I beg you will forgive me if I gave a poor impression. Please, I am so very sorry."

Serena rewarded her new supplicant with a tight, knowing smile, and Lady Idelle, inwardly fuming, left her presence with as much outward calm as she could muster.

The nerve of that woman! thought Serena. *Perhaps I was a bit harsh on her, but it was very necessary to put her in her place! I have never given any one such a setdown, not in my whole life,* she reflected. *I did not realize it could feel so very diverting. Becoming a duchess might not be such an unpleasant thing, after all.*

Eight

Lady Idelle Mountjoy, tall, blonde, and in a very foul temper, repaired to the library to restore her demeanour before the dancing began. It was in this mood, and in this manner, that she came upon Lord Jack Ryland, who was sitting in a burgundy leather chair.

Lord Jack closed his book with a snap. He was attempting to read Herodotus, but with a mind completely invaded by passionate thoughts of the divine Miss Norwood, it was an impossible task. If Miss Norwood did love him, then, he wondered, what was he to do? What if he was falling in love as well?

"Oh, Jack! Hiding from the guests, are we? I thought I had not seen you at dinner," she said. "Alastair is in hiding as well, I think. Runs in the family."

Lord Jack rose at once when Lady Idelle entered, noticing, not without a slight pang of regret, how much her looks were still improving. A beautiful face, with a body completely lacking in heart.

"How are you, Idelle? You are looking very well."

"Am I?" she asked, turning in a small circle to show off her dress and herself "I hope I am, and I thank you for the compliment."

She approached Lord Jack and ran her fingers playfully

across his starched white cravat, complaining, "I am not, however, feeling very well, for I have just spent the last few minutes talking with that scheming little minx Alastair intends to marry. What a shocking girl! Have you met her?"

"I have not yet had the pleasure. I understand she is very handsome, however."

Idelle gave a short laugh.

"Ha! That may be," she snapped, "if one can be satisfied with a thoroughgoing country bumpkin sense of fashion, one which is completely and utterly at odds with the sort of well-bred sophistication to be expected in a duchess!"

Lord Jack poured her a small glass of sherry, which she gratefully accepted.

"Come now, Idelle. I think you are being a little unfair about this girl. Perhaps you are unhappy Alastair did not think of marrying you?"

"Nonsense! What do you take me for?" Lady Idelle said lightly, draining the glass nervously.

"You perhaps don't wish me to answer that, Idelle. I have known you all my life, recall. I know exactly where your values lie, to my own detriment."

Lady Idelle frowned, and gestured toward the sherry. Lord Jack refilled her glass, and Lady Idelle drained it a second time.

She sighed and answered, "Don't tell me you're still flogging that dead horse, Jack. No one in my position would marry a younger son."

"Certainly not," he replied smoothly.

"That's just the way things are. Papa simply did not allow it."

"Yes, my dear. Of course."

"Love had nothing to do with it," she said, planting a light kiss on his cheek and running her hand along his chin. He removed her hand, backed away, and said, "Certainly not. Love has nothing to do with marriage—I understood you very well at the time you refused my offer, and even now I understand your character perfectly. What I do not understand, however, is why Alastair's marriage seems to be causing you so much pain."

Lady Idelle found Lord Jack's seat and occupied it, frowning, saying, "I deny that his marriage in any way affects me. It does not. It could not. It is this chit, this country mouse he has chosen who is—and forgive my frankness—completely unsuitable!"

"Why so?" asked Lord Jack, intrigued.

"She is a callow, self-seeking fool!"

"You are very exercised on this matter, my dear."

"It is scandalous, I tell you! You must talk him out of it, Jack, really you must! Just ten minutes past, this girl revealed to me at length the depth of her mercenary desires. This Miss Huntington spoke to me about what clothes she would have, and jewels, and power, and travel, and luxuries, and how an invitation to her table would be such a compliment."

"All of which is true."

"True it may be, but she was deliberately baiting me. That is the point!"

Lord Jack could not help but smile, adding, "I'm sure that must have been very unpleasant for you."

"It was. I despise this Miss Huntington. I would do anything to prevent her from becoming Alastair's wife. I shall do everything I can to prevent it. I consider it my duty to the neighbourhood."

"Come, come, Idelle. Reconcile yourself to the fact that you have lost Alastair, and that this Miss Huntington, will you or nil you, is going to marry him, and she will have rank and fortune that outdoes yours. I'm sure that is what hurts, and not the girl's behaviour, foolish though it was of her to mention it to you."

"I think she did it on purpose."

Lord Jack smiled again. "Why would she do that?"

"I'm sure I don't know!" said Lady Idelle with a huff. "The horridest thing was her saying she actually loved Alastair! Ha! Loves him! A man she hasn't met! What a fib that was! Nobody loves Alastair. For one thing, he is a complete booby. For another, he is thoroughly self-absorbed. No one could love such a man. Thus, the girl is not merely a vile social climber, but a liar to boot."

"Nonsense, Idelle. It merely shows in her a very nice sense of the duties and responsibilities and privileges of being a duchess. She will have jewels and rank, but she will also profess love for her husband. She'll do very well. Calm down, woman. Have another glass of sherry and sit with me by the fire."

Lady Idelle hiccuped slightly, and remarked, "I am afraid I have already had too much, too quickly. I thank you, dear Jack. You have always been a consolation to me!"

As you have always been a thorn in my heart, my dear, thought Lord Jack, who sat down in his favourite chair and began once again reading about the exploits of the Greeks.

Nine

Miss Huntington was almost weeping when she entered the room, closing the door behind her and leaning against what appeared to be a tall bookcase. She had wandered from place to place, desperately trying to find some refuge from the company, some place where at last she could be alone and try to marshal her feelings. The nerve of that girl! It was only after Lady Idelle left her that Serena found herself shaking with anger, completely discomposed.

That had been the least of her troubles. The next thing she knew, she was being interrogated once again by that harridan Lady Shelburne, who fused intrusiveness and haughty condescension in an unbearable combination. To make matters worse, her own aunt, Lady Clayburgh, seemed utterly unable to assist her, as she was poked and prodded and quizzed and inspected by every old dowager in the drawing room. She had to get away, and so she slipped out through a side door and into a passageway, and then fell into the gentlemen's parlor, where they were all enjoying a brandy and a good laugh at the expense of the Prince of Wales and his mistress. Embarrassed, she slunk away through another side door, only to interrupt the third footman kissing a chambermaid, and retreated

at once through yet another door, until she arrived in this
room, which appeared dark, and relatively safe, and
empty.

It was only when she walked around the end of the
bookcase that she discovered she was not at all alone.

"Oh, my!" she cried, surprised and a little frightened.

The figure turned and rose, saying, "Why, Miss Norwood! This is an awkward place for us to meet, but let
me assure you what a pleasure it is to see you again! I
should have seen you at dinner, but I confess, I could not
bring myself to come down for it. Sometimes I have the
strangest moods that give me a horror of crowds. Odd,
isn't it? Won't you sit down? How came you here?"

Serena gratefully accepted his offer of a chair, but declined his offer of sherry.

"I know just what you mean, sir. I was in the drawing
room, and somehow I had become the focus of all attention, or so it felt, and it seemed that everyone had my
weight and measure and an opinion of me, and of a sudden
I found I could not bear it, and I fled."

"It is good we have so much in common, Miss Norwood. Let me tell you how much I enjoyed our—time
together this afternoon. I hope you will forgive my—how
shall I say? My ardour. It was honestly meant."

"You are so kind, sir. I really had not hoped to find a
man so kind, when I consented to come here. It has meant
so very much to me to come to know you, as a person
rather than merely as a personage."

"I don't quite follow you, I'm afraid."

"As long as we're here, and alone, I have a confession
to make."

Lord Jack rose, went to her, and drew her to him. He
put his finger to her lips and silenced her with a kiss,
adding, "This is no time for confessions, my dear. As long
as we are alone, let us make the best use of our time. You

move me as no woman has ever done, and I do not even know your Christian name. What is it?"

"Serena," she whispered, her knees weak. "You must know I am unused to all this flattery and kindness."

"I have flattered many women in my time, Serena, but what I say to you now is the God's own truth. I am obsessed by you, fully and completely. Every time I see you, I want to touch you. Every time I am apart from you, I want to seek you out and make you mine, for all time, forsaking all others. I know that in my past I have behaved badly. I have been wayward, and reckless, and cold."

"No. Shh," she said.

"You need to know the truth. I believe in honesty above all things between two people, and until I met you, I had all but abandoned hope of finding a woman I could trust, who could place her trust in me. I have behaved very badly toward many, I have broken many hearts, and, worst of all, I have done it on purpose, from feelings of revenge upon your whole sex. It is not a pretty tale, I assure you. One cruel experience was enough to set me against all women and to behave toward them as one cruel, rapacious woman had behaved toward me. It was wrong of me, I know."

He waited for a moment, and she felt tears in her own eyes when she saw those in his.

"Something changed for me today, my dearest, up there on the Norman Tower, and I have been thinking about it all the rest of today. When I tried to steal a kiss from you, it began as just a passing fancy, but I found the more I felt, the more I wished to feel, and that for the first time in my whole existence."

He brought her hand to his lips, kissed it, and said, "I treasure you, my dear."

When she looked at him, she felt that through his deep eyes she saw the depth of his very being. This, she thought, must be what it was like to be falling in love. How lucky that it should be happening so suddenly, and so completely. She felt transfixed.

"I want to make you mine," said he.

"Yes, please," she answered.

He took a deep breath and embraced her fully, just as he had once before—one arm placed carefully at the nape of her neck, the other around her small waist, leaning her back over his arm. He placed his head next to hers and began kissing her softly and gently at the nape of her long neck, the cleft of her chin, on her cheeks, till, finally, his lips met her mouth, which, with a small cry, she opened.

"My God, woman. You make me forget myself," said Lord Jack, pulling away from her with great difficulty. "Lucky is the man who will call you his wife."

"You are so kind and good, Alastair," Serena said shyly, returning his kisses. "I am so fortunate to have found you. I promise, from the bottom of my heart, that I shall love you truly and be a conformable wife to you, your grace."

Suddenly, the tall gentleman's entire demeanour altered. The eyes that had been charming and romantical turned sharp and cold; the mouth that had offered pleasure now transformed itself into a hard line.

He pushed her roughly onto a small sofa near the fireplace, paced briefly, then whirled around, confronting her.

" 'Your grace?' 'Alastair?' What can you mean? How dare you speak to me in that way? Has this all been some kind of joke, some kind of pretence? Were you put up to this by Idelle, by any chance? Or by my brother?"

"Your brother? To whom do you refer?"

"I refer," he said with brutal sarcasm, "To my elder brother, the duke! Alastair Ryland, Sixth Duke of Leighton!"

"Y-you are the duke. You are the man I am to marry!"

"The man you are to marry? Do you take me for an utter fool?"

"No, your grace. I am so sorry. I know the arrangements are not entirely complete. I did not mean to be presumptuous."

"Madam, you seem to be under a misapprehension. I am not the Duke of Leighton. I am Lord Jack Ryland."

Serena's eyes widened.

" 'Rake Ryland'?" she gasped. "That is who you are? Oh, dear. What have I done? Oh, dear. Oh, dear."

"This news does not seem to meet with your approval. Did you have your cap set at my brother's rank and wealth?" he sneered. "I had thought you beyond this, I confess. I have, however, been wrong before about women. It seems that I have been wrong again."

"No, no, you don't understand. When we arrived, I saw you standing on the balcony, and they told me you were he—my aunt did—at least I thought she did. I saw you the first moment I arrived. I thought you were your brother. I assure you, I should never have acted as I did, so freely, in terms of my conduct, had I thought otherwise. I beg you will believe me."

"Oh, I find it easy to believe that any woman would avoid a younger brother. This is not the first time it has happened, believe me. I am just surprised to find your mercenary character revealed. I had thought that you, Miss Norwood, were quite otherwise—the more fool I."

"Miss Norwood? Oh! There is that to explain as well! You see, I am not Miss Norwood! I made that up! I am Miss Huntington. Serena Huntington, of Norwood, Barchester."

"Huntington? Then you are the one—"

"As I said, I am the one who is to marry your brother! Who, as I thought, was you!"

Lord Jack gave her a steely glance, looking at her as if

she were the lowest creature ever made, and saying, "You are a scheming, lying wench, Miss Huntington, if that is your true name. I cannot pretend to understand your little game, madam, but it does not suit you well. You pretended to be a country miss, an innocent, but I see now your slyness and your cunning. I confess, you had me fooled."

"I am innocent, I beg you! I deceived you, thinking you were he!"

"Nonsense. You are a trollop in the disguise of a maiden, no more deserving of my brother's hand in marriage than is Red Nell, whom you resemble not just in colouring, but in quality and in manners. My brother is a fool, and I wish you well of him. I will tell him of your lies, but it may not be enough to dissuade him. I am only grateful that I have discovered your treachery before my own heart became hopelessly entangled in your web of selfish grasping. Yes, it's true, my girl. I'm not the one with the title, and I'm not about to be seducing my brother's bride, if that's the kind of entertainment you had been thinking of. I admit I was captivated by your beauty and was beginning to lose my heart—until my lucky discovery just now that you have none!"

"My lord! I swear, I did not know it was you! You were on the roof, you were pointed out to me—"

"Oh, save your excuses. I'll have none of them. Pray, allow me the intense pleasure of escorting you within, where they will by now be dancing, and where Alastair, your intended, at last will greet his bride-to-be! I will so enjoy presenting you to the real heir to title and fortune, the title and fortune you find so compelling that you have sold your very heart and soul for it, if soul you ever had."

"Oh, Lord Jack, please—"

"Don't turn on the tears for me, my pretty, for it won't work. I now know who you are and what you are, and of what wickedness you are capable. I don't think for a minute that you were lost when you went to the Duck and Crossroads yesterday. I think you are a brazen tart, and I would warn my brother against marrying you, only I can promise you that he cares no more about finding love in marriage than do you!"

"Lord Jack!"

"Shut up, woman, will you?" He turned and looked at her, furiously, and then gave her a last, long, and desperate kiss.

"How dare you?' cried Serena, humiliated.

Lord Jack Ryland shrugged and wiped his lips with his hands, saying, "Why such a show of virtue? Stealing a kiss from a strumpet is hardly a crime."

"Lord Jack, I beg you will listen to me—"

"Leave my presence, woman, do you hear?" he thundered. "Begone, before I strike you!"

Ten

It was all upside down. What had been right and good
and filled with love an hour before was filled with wrong
and hateful misunderstanding. There was not even enough
time for tears, and certainly not time to fully feel the regret
that had taken control of Serena's heart.

It had been a simple enough error, of course, but that
small error was enough to set her universe askew, with
lasting, fearful consequences. She could not believe what
a fool she had been, thinking that somehow this arranged
marriage, arranged by her for mercenary reasons, just as
Lord Jack had accused her, would turn out for the best.

She said she would marry the duke. She had let a man
she believed to be the duke make love to her. She had
fallen in love with the man. The man with whom she had
fallen in love turned out to be another, someone who hated
her for the mercenary contract she had agreed to.

Serena could hardly disagree with his opinion of her.
She was beginning to hate herself as well.

Any thought she might have had of fleeing to her room
was swept from her mind when Lady Clayburgh found
her.

"I've been looking for you this last half hour. Wherever
have you been? The duke was not down to dinner, but he

has ordered that there be dancing, and he expects to meet you, tonight, at once! What is wrong with you? Have you been crying? Why should you cry, girl? You haven't even met him yet!"

Serena flashed her aunt a horrified glance, to which her aunt replied, "Just a jest, my dear. You seem a little agitated this evening."

"Oh, Aunt Gillian, I can't begin to explain what has happened."

"You are correct. You cannot, because there isn't time. Here, let me fix your hair—that's better—and let's just pinch some colour into those cheeks."

"Ouch!"

"Don't be such a goose. There. Come with me at once, for it will be a vastly exciting evening for you. Imagine, meeting for the first time someone who will make you his duchess! Could any occasion be happier?"

Serena shook her head compliantly, feeling like a prisoner being taken away to gaol.

"You look very lovely, Serena, so keep that in mind, and remember to be confident in your demeanour," said her aunt, scrutinizing her gown of silk pistache. It had small silk roses embroidered on the sleeves and on the line of the bodice; there was an overskirt, which at its raised hem was ornamented with a line of matching silk roses and lace, to incomparable effect. "You look every inch a duchess. Take care to behave that way as well—I want to see nothing from you that is impulsive or even ill considered. Remember to be friendly, not too forward, and do curb your tongue. When high rank is yours, you will be allowed some eccentricities, but you are not married yet, young lady. Heed my words, will you?"

"Yes, Aunt Gillian," said Serena, as meek as a lamb.

"Let's be off, then."

Lady Clayburgh led Serena down a long hallway that

connected the old wing with the center of the house. As they approached, Serena could see the flickering light from the sconces and hear the sounds of laughter from the crowd that was gathering in the main hallway.

Serena and her aunt emerged at the top of the grand staircase. Looking down, Serena could see Lady Shelburne waiting at the first-floor landing, staring directly at her. She exchanged a glance with her aunt, allowed a frozen smile to fix itself on her face, and with as much courage and elegance as she could muster, proceeded down the stairs. For a moment, all thoughts of Lord Jack had ceased, for she had been hurled into a performance for the London ton, and, no matter what her own feelings were, this marriage must go through. Her family was depending upon her to make a go of it, and she would not let them down, no matter what kind of fellow this duke turned out to be.

She took the slippery marble stairs very carefully, one step at a time, anxious not to make a fool of herself but finding that especially hard tonight, all too aware that every eye in the house was upon her, weighing her, measuring her, curious to see the duke's choice of his duchess.

A small murmur went around the crowd when they got a good look at her, which made Serena blush. She felt a mixture of admiration and approbation wash over her from the crowd. She glanced again at Lady Clayburgh, who smiled at her more encouragingly, and after only a minute or so, she had managed to make her way down the steps without breaking an ankle.

There was a dark-haired gentleman of about thirty waiting next to Lady Shelburne, someone she had never seen before. He was smiling at her in a stiff, formal way, and she smiled back.

Serena did not give his identity a second thought until the countess waved her fan first in her direction, and then in his, saying to her, "Miss Huntington, may I present to you Alastair, Duke of Leighton."

It took all of her intelligence and all of her training not to drop her jaw like a rock. Her eyes must have widened, and certainly those standing around heard Serena's sharp intake of breath. This set off a rapid round of commentary.

Her breath quite knocked away from her, it was just as if she had suddenly taken a hard fall from a horse. It was uncanny. Like a doll, she dropped a deep curtsy to this utter stranger whom she had agreed to wed. As much as she had liked his brother on first sight, she felt herself unaccountably repelled by the duke, and not merely because he was not the man she had first met. Repelled was too harsh a word, but she certainly disliked him.

What had her foolish, rash nature gotten her into now?

It was like some horrid nightmare. She felt that she might faint, and indeed, the duke, seeing the girl's unsteadiness, held out his hand to her, which she took and clung to for support. She noticed his hand was hot and covered in perspiration, which made her wish she could withdraw hers, but it was too late now. Everything was too late.

She smiled at the duke and allowed him to lead her toward the ballroom, passing through the crowd like a reflection of herself, smiling and nodding as the people parted to let the couple through. Serena could hear one of the old women saying, "The girl was quite overcome with awe at meeting his grace. That was well done of her, was it not?" Another added, "It is a shame about the hair, though. I wonder that his grace would marry into a family that had rusty hair."

She could hear snippets of conversation, barely, as she moved along, something to the effect of "she looks well enough," to "silly way to make a marriage, if you ask me," to "where are the refreshments? I really must find something on which to nibble—why don't they just go in, so we don't have to stand around here all evening?"

Serena tried to turn around and glance at Lady Clayburgh, but her aunt was walking along behind, chatting away happily with Lady Shelburne. They did not seem discomfited at all.

As they entered the grand ballroom, Serena screwed up her courage and turned to take the measure of the man next to her. He was of medium height, a little fleshy around the chin and the abdomen. The duke resembled his brother in general build and in the dark color of his hair and eyes, but resembled him as an inferior plaster copy resembled a marble bust.

Every deficiency she noticed in the duke pointed out the superiority of the brother. She looked around to see if Lord Jack was there, somewhere, but she could not find him. Not that it would make any difference, she said to herself. Everything in her world was just as it was, this man, this duke, she must marry. She had her duty to her family, and meeting that duty was paramount.

They had reached the head of the ballroom. The duke turned to her and led her out onto the floor. His grace turned to signal the orchestra, which began to play a minuet.

Other couples joined them on the floor, joining almost in precise order of social precedence. When the duke and Miss Huntington began to dance, the rest of the company followed.

Serena felt relieved that she could pass some time in this manner, losing herself in dancing, while she tried to unravel her emotions. From time to time she would pass her partner close enough for him to say a few words to her, as he tried, in a vague and uninvolved way, to make himself agreeable.

"Miss Huntington," he began, "I suppose you have had time to admire the architecture of our little castle?"

"I admire it very much, your grace."

One whirl around, a few steps, and they were face-to-face once more.

"Yes, the house spans the generations, for generations of the family have worked their wiles upon it."

"Yes, your grace."

A few more steps, rise on toes, and turn around again to face her partner, the man with whom she was going to spend the rest of her natural days. A long promenade made for a longer monologue.

"There is a Norman section, which you will of course have appreciated, and the Tudor section, a Gothic wing, and finally, the entire restructuring that is being done to it under my aegis. One must, of course, improve the property, for it would be so wrong not to, don't you think?"

"I th—" was all Miss Huntington got out as to what she thought before her noble host was off and running again. Had he not been her near-betrothed, he would have been almost amusing.

"Yes, I thought you would agree that it does take work and, of course, a goodly sum of money to leave a mark upon one's estate."

"Yes, your grace," she said, glancing at him to see if he were paying her the merest bit of attention, but of course he was not. The dance had ended, and the duke was leading her off the floor, still chattering on uninterruptedly.

"Some persons say that due to this mixture of styles, Castle Leighton is a mishmash, but that is poppycock!"

The duke drew her to a pair of large gilded chairs, upholstered in dark blue velvet, which had been set out on a dais at one end of the ballroom, with a small table in between, and a footman standing nearby, ready to offer refreshments. The duke seated Serena, then himself.

A wave of his grace's hand produced wine for himself and ratafia for Miss Huntington, along with a small plate of food, of which Serena partook.

"Generation after generation of Rylands have put their imprimatur on the place, each one according to their propensity and means, and it is our wish that such practice shall continue on down the generations." And here the duke gave her a wily, knowing leer, leaning over to pat her knee. "Those generations being a work in which we expect and look forward to your participation, Miss Huntington."

Miss Huntington was so horrified by this brazen reference that she began to choke on a bit of biscuit.

The duke did not notice. At that moment, he stood up and proposed a toast.

Serena felt the whole company rising around her. There was a certain amount of bustling as servants, who had been warned of a toast but not warned as to when it would occur, made sure that those who wished for wine had been provided with a glass. Serena remained in her seat, feeling very self-conscious but trying to keep a polite smile on her face.

The duke was making a long, flowery, idiotic speech about her, and as he gestured in her direction, she looked up across the ballroom. In a space that occurred around a few couples, she saw first Lady Idelle Mountjoy, staring at her in an unfriendly fashion, without a glass, and next to her, Lord Jack Ryland, looking at her with the same ardour one might feel toward an insect. Serena Huntington wished she were dead.

Her humiliation was not at an end, however.

Suddenly Serena felt her hand being grabbed by a larger, fatter, bejeweled hand—it was raised up, the duke leaned over and kissed it in full view of the company, and then he raised his glass in her honour.

"To my dear Miss Huntington, in hopes that at the end of her stay here at Castle Leighton, she will do me the honour of becoming my wife, and your duchess!"

"To Miss Huntington!" the company replied.

It was beyond mortifying. She wished she could crawl under her golden chair.

She turned to her host and whispered, "Thank you for your good wishes and kind words, sir. Your condescension is very much appreciated."

"Of course, of course, my dear. Would you care to dance again?"

"Oh, perhaps not quite yet. I am a bit fatigued."

"Fatigued? Of course you are. I say, I am often fatigued myself I believe it is a common occurrence."

Serena shot him a look of disbelief, but the duke was quite beyond comprehension. Miss Huntington thought for a moment that in all her life she had never met anyone filled with such empty self-consequence. Of course, this duke was her first duke, she reasoned; it might be simply a matter of the rank itself. Who knew? Who wished to?

I deserve it, Serena thought to herself. *It is just as Lord Jack said. I have done a mercenary thing in undertaking this marriage, and now I shall receive my punishment for it, and my just deserts, by becoming leg-shackled to a clumsy, vacuous, self-important fool.*

Serena, resigned to such inane conversation, replied, "It is a bit fatiguing, being among so many people with whom I am not acquainted."

The duke clapped his jeweled hands, and his footman, who had been leaning against the wall trying to keep himself awake, jumped.

"But my dear, you must meet everybody, everybody! Oh-ho! Speaking of meeting, here's someone else you must meet!"

The Duke of Leighton signaled to a gentleman across

the room. It was Lord Jack! As she recognized his identity, Miss Huntington's discomfiture increased exponentially. Would this evening of humiliation never end?

"This is my brother Jack, Miss Huntington! Lord Jack Ryland, as he is. Rake Ryland, as he is more usually called," he said, leaning in with a wink and having the audacity to pinch her on the cheek, "for he has a wicked way with the ladies."

Lord Jack had the grace to give his brother an evil look at this comment, but he would not meet her eyes as he swept her a quick bow, which she returned with a slight curtsy.

Serena did not know with whom she was more furious—herself, the duke, his wretched younger brother who had virtually seduced her and played with her heart, Lady Idelle for being so miserable to her, or Aunt Gillian for leading her, wide-eyed, into this madness.

Her anger suddenly made her bold, and she said, lightly, tauntingly, "Why, Lord Jack and I have already met! We are old friends—just since yesterday, your grace!"

Lord Jack now favoured Miss Huntington with an evil look, which he transformed into a look of challenge.

"That's true, Alastair! We became the very best of friends, almost upon our first meeting! Why, I think we were taken with each other almost at first sight, as we hear about in legends. We became so very close that if you knew of it, you might become jealous! I would feel privileged to continue our acquaintance, dear brother. So, may I have this dance, Miss—Huntington, I believe it is?"

The duke's voice boomed forth, saying, "Certainly, Jack! You must dance with her! She is a wonderful dancer, our Miss Huntington, but I must ask you this—you must not steal her heart!"

Serena blushed beet red at this, and even Lord Jack looked discomfited.

"I will forgive you for falling in love with her at first sight, and I will forgive you close acquaintance, but I shall not forgive it if you make her fall in love with you, as we know you do with all of the ladies, for dear Miss Huntington is as good as promised to me, Jack, and I shan't allow you to captivate her away from me, do you hear?"

"What hope could I have with Miss Huntington, weighed against you, dear brother? I feel sure she is a sensible girl, not a hot-headed one."

This remark made Serena furious, and she shot Lord Jack a look of real wrath. He gave her a tight, mean smile and took her hand, leading her out onto the floor.

Again, the rest of the company lined up below them. They began to perform the steps Serena knew by heart. She wanted to slap the man, she wanted him to take her in his arms, she wanted to know why he was seeking her out at all, save from mere perversity of mind.

Again, she took up the challenge as they passed shoulder to shoulder, saying pertly, "Thinking so little of my character, Lord Jack, I wonder that you can bear my company for an entire dance."

"Thinking so little of your heart, Miss Huntington, I wonder that you can bear the company of my brother for an entire lifetime. But then, that itself would explain it."

"You wrong me, sir."

"Do I? How is that?"

"You do not know my heart, sir."

"I know that your actions are not guided by your heart, madam. That tells me quite enough."

"You are unkind."

"Do you try to tell me that you are not marrying my brother merely for his rank and his fortune?"

Miss Huntington coloured.

"Y-you do not know the particulars of the case."

"Spare me your 'particulars,' madam. At least you have

the grace to call a spade a spade. if my brother marries himself off to an adventuress, it is hardly any concern of mine."

"You are cruel."

"I think it is you who are cruel, my beauty. It is unfortunate that somehow I have been drawn into this tangled plot, but I will seek to extricate myself and heal my heart."

"This is the most foolish, wretched misunderstanding. I took you for your brother. What else can I say?"

"You can tell me why you lied to me about your name, Miss Huntington. That would be an interesting start. Not that it really matters, the reasons behind your mendacity. I am a little curious, however."

The dance ended, and Miss Huntington and Lord Jack remained together on the dance floor for a moment. Lord Jack was about to bow and leave when Serena whispered to him, "Is there a place nearby where we might be private?"

Lord Jack's eyes glittered dangerously, but he led her to a door at the end of the ballroom. He opened it; they passed through a small parlour into a sitting room lit by a small fire.

"I told you before, I made a simple mistake. I thought you were the duke," said Serena.

"Did you? How convenient."

"I did. It was a simple misunderstanding," she said. "Why can you not believe me?"

"Yes, there is that. However, leaving aside your thinking of me as being my fabulously wealthy, titled brother, and even giving you the benefit of the doubt on that score, you will have difficulty, I think, explaining away the bold-faced lie about your name, and then it will be so very hard to explain away your conduct."

"My conduct?"

"Thinking back on it, you were rather free with your

favours, were you not, Miss Huntington? Freer than would have been expected in a young lady of quality, certainly."

"You are a horrid, desperate man! I tell you I thought you were the man I was to marry!"

"Yes, it is all so complicated, isn't it? A girl who agrees to marry a man, sight unseen. What kind of young lady would ever do that? A girl who conceals her identity. A girl who conceals her identity from the man she mistakenly assumed is her extremely wealthy husband-to-be. What kind of girl would do that? A girl who is free with her favors almost on first meeting? A girl who walks alone to an inn? A girl who walks around unchaperoned? I can tell you, it is all very unusual, do you not agree?"

Lord Jack walked over to the door through which he had entered, and he locked it.

"What are you doing, sir?" said Serena, feeling frightened for the first time.

"Don't play the fool with me, girl. I don't know how you and your aunt managed to worm your way into Lady Shelburne's good graces, for she is usually awake upon every suit. Nevertheless, I will thank you to remove your talons from my poor brother and leave this house at once. You should be hostessing a house in Soho rather than dining at the table of a duke. For shame, madam. Your conduct from the very first has been unsuitable, worse than that of a serving wench. If your conduct on the Norman Tower was not bad enough, look at your conduct this evening. Introduced to society as the intended of the Duke of Leighton, then asking to be private with an unmarried gentleman and willingly to go with him to his rooms. Don't make me laugh, madam. I know what kind of woman you are. I am famous for it."

This time, Serena was not taken by surprise; she wound her hand up and struck Lord Jack full in the face.

"How dare you say such things to me! You! Rake Ryland, as you are called! You must be drunk, for there is no other excuse for you to have spoken to me as you have! I made a simple error, taking you for your brother, and from that, you have the audacity to try to turn it into some kind of evidence that I am a plotter and a schemer after your family's fortune! I wanted to know the character of the duke, as I thought you were, and thought it would be better to learn his character without the usual pretence of courtship and society. When I met you I was vastly relieved, and touched, and I did feel for you just as I said. My words were honest! My actions honest! My feelings for you were true! I never thought that you would be the kind of person who you now are showing yourself to be, bad-tempered, and cruel, and unforgiving."

He grabbed her roughly and pulled her to him.

"And not rich enough for you, isn't that the real truth, wench? That's the kind of person you expected and wished me to be! Beyond that, you're a hoyden."

Lord Jack crushed her to him, kissing her; Serena, quite unable to help herself, kissed him and clung to him, beside herself with tangled emotions—sorrow and joy and fury.

"I wanted you, Serena, as I have wanted none other in my life."

"And I you," Serena whispered. "Believe me, Jack."

Lord Jack pushed her away, saying ruefully, "You wanted me well enough, my girl, until you knew my fortune. There is a rising passion in you, my girl, for I know that feeling well. If you say you're not a harlot, well then, maybe you are and maybe you're not. If you say your feelings for me were deep and true and are deep and true, well, maybe they are. And maybe not. But I'll tell you one thing about yourself—any girl who would marry that fool of a brother of mine, sight unseen, is marrying him for money, say what you will, argue what you will."

He patted her hand, releasing it. He went to the door, unlocked it, turned around, and faced her again.

"That's the kind of girl I'll have none of. No matter how I feel. And that's a promise. I wish you well in your sham marriage—your bed, poor girl, is like to be a cold one, and lonely."

He bowed, exited, and left her alone.

Eleven

Miss Serena Huntington slept all day, not waking up until four o'clock in the afternoon. The luxury of having hot chocolate brought up to her, which yesterday had seemed part of a gay adventure, today was a hollow and meaningless event. It seemed to Serena that the life she had consented to stretched forth in front of her, a grey passageway to be filled with a similar series of meaningless, empty events. Yes, she would choose her clothes for the afternoon, and for the evening. Yes, she would have her hair dressed for the afternoon, and for the evening. Yes, she would choose among suitable jewels; yes, she would dine on the finest of foods; yes, she would mingle with the most exalted company. All of it signified nothing.

What awaited her as Duchess of Leighton would be more of the same, with finer jewels, finer dresses, fine company. A husband who cared no more for her than he cared about a leg of mutton. How could she have been such a fool as to think her mad scheme would turn out otherwise?

Serena rang a bell to have her tray removed, and the maid who came up for the dishes brought a silver salver as well, with a letter on it. She waited for the maid to leave, then broke open the wafer. Her heart began to beat heavily. The letter was from her father.

It read:

"*My dearest Serena,*

You have been gone to London and to Leighton a whole month now, and to me it seems a whole year. The brightness of our household seems to have faded. You know full well, my child, that if I had had any notion of your Aunt Gillian's plan, I would have taken steps to foil it.

Our situation is not as grave as you and Gillian seem to think. My health, although not the best, is steadily improving, I believe, despite the dreadful potions that Dr. Collum tries to give me. James, Frank, Maria and Sybil are all doing very well, and their prospects in the future are not unacceptable to them. I beg you, Serena do not sell yourself into this loveless marriage!

Please return to us, at once. Leighton can easily find another wife to ornament his table; we can never hope to find another Serena to brighten our lives.

> *God bless you,*
> *Father*

Tears welled up in her eyes and fell down her cheeks as fast as she could brush them away. That was all that was needed, she thought. *I am selfish to think of my own happiness when the future of my family, and the health of my father is at stake. They must be my first goal. Thoughts of them will make this castle life supportable.*

Filled with new resolve, Serena went out to face the

day. She would see the duke this afternoon, he would ask
for her hand in marriage, and she would say yes. She
would marry him and belong to him forever.

Twelve

Rake Ryland left Castle Leighton in the late hours of the night, after his quarrel with Serena Huntington, and repaired directly to the Duck and Crossroads Inn, where he finished the night in bitter, drunken revelry. When he awoke, late in the afternoon, his head ached like the very devil and he wished he were anywhere else. Red Nell woke him with a knock at the door; Jack noted that in the light of day, she appeared a worn-out, disheveled creature, lacking in all intelligence and grace. He wondered how he ever could have mistaken Serena for her.

The very thought of Serena Huntington was enough to cause his head to throb with a vengeance.

"Nell!" he cried, trying to drag himself into consciousness. "Stop your knocking. Say what you came for, and then be off with you. Have you something for my head, lass?"

"Fred said I should wake you. He'll have some tonic fer ya, if you have the need," Nell said, scowling at him, angry and hurt that he had forgone his usual attentions last night. "Go down and get it yourself."

Lord Jack poured some water into a ewer and splashed his face with it. Looking in the mirror, he saw that he looked as evil as he felt. *Blast all women, anyhow,* he thought to himself. *I'm off to London.*

He went downstairs and hailed Fred Styles, the inn-keeper, whom Lord Jack had known since he was in leading strings. Fred, a jolly man, slapped him on the back and welcomed him to the day, and, as Red Nell had promised, the innkeeper began to prepare for the Rake a special concoction of gin and juice and bitters.

"There, lad. Drink this down so ye may feel that life is worth living again. It tastes like the very devil, but it makes the morning after revelry near as pleasant as the night before."

"Don't ask me about that, Fred. There's nothing worth living for, my good man."

'That's as may be, Lord Jack. I'm sorry to hear you're not in the best of moods today. I would have thought that young lady who's come to be the duchess might have brought some gaiety to the castle as well. Were you not there last night?"

"Yes, I was there," he said gloomily. "Pray, don't remind me. I should have known better than to accept Alastair's invitation."

"We saw that girl—a fine, red-headed lass—when they stopped off here on the way to the Castle, she and her aunt, as is. Horse threw a shoe, and it had to be mended. Talked some time with one of the lady maids—told us a terrible sad story about the girl's family. You know it, of course."

"Of course I do," replied Lord Jack testily. "Here's for your trouble, and here's for your potion, which tastes like the devil, just as you said, and here's for the room. I'll be off to London."

"Very good, your lordship."

Lord Jack decided to bring the flagon up to the little room upstairs, and encountered Red Nell in the stairway.

"You off for London, Jack? Aren't there more parties out at the Castle that you should be goin' to?"

"I've made my appearance. I can't be bothered with the rest of it."

"Still, she's a pretty thing, ain't she, that girl your brother's picked to marry."

"You've seen her, too?"

"She stopped here for a bit. What a story we heard! So sad. Makes you think, don't it?"

"I know nothing sad about her. Whatever do you mean?"

"Styles told me all of it. He had it from the maid—Mary, her name was. Oh, it was terrible sad, the things that families can do to one of their own blood. Awful."

"Whatever are you going on about, girl?"

"That girl. Her family name is Huntington, I think, and they come from Norwood Manor, Barchester. Her mother married Mr. Huntington against her father's wishes. He'd picked some rich old nobleman for her to marry, but she refused to do it! That was the cause for all the mischief that followed! It was love, you see?"

"Oh, poppycock, Nell."

"No, Jack, it's true—'cause she was already in love with her family's tutor, who was this Mr. Huntington, ya see. His was a good family, but had no money at all to speak of. Her father took it furious bad and cut her off without a shilling! He never spoke to his daughter again! Can ya credit it, Jack?"

"Has all the makings of a penny novel, Nell," said Lord Jack gruffly. "I didn't know you were such a reader. What has this long tale to do with me?"

Red Nell gave him a playful slap, saying, "Attend! It gets even better—I mean, sadder. Girl's aunt made the marriage to the old geezer to please her father while, Catherine, her mother, married the tutor that she loved, Huntington. That marriage was very good and very happy. They had five hopeful children and were expecting a sixth, though Mrs. Huntington did not yet know of it. Then, one day, everything seems fine and dandy, but she and her husband are out riding, when the lady's horse shies and bolts; it ran off at breakneck speed, and her husband rode off after her, trying to help her. The lady's horse came to a ditch, tried to jump it, fell, and the horse fell on top of her. The gentleman's horse did the same."

"How very unfortunate."

"That's what I mean, Jack! Everything's going along swimmingly, and then, with a snap of your fingers, it's gone! All gone! After the accident, poor Mrs. Huntington lived for a full two weeks, in terrible pain, their maid said, and she was right there attending, so as she knows. Her dreadful father, as had cut her off—he never once sent word to her! Can you credit anyone with being so wicked? He'll get his just deserts, and it'll be down in the hot place, that's for sure. Poor Mr. Huntington survived the fall and still lives at Norwood, but as an invalid, dependent on others for his every need and full of guilt and sorrow at his dear wife's death."

"A sad tale, indeed," remarked Lord Jack. "I am very sorry to hear it. I must be off now. I'll see you when I pass by again. Be a good lass."

"You wait, now! I haven't finished."

"Yes, you have, my dear," said Lord Jack, eager to be off. "The girl marries my brother. The end. Finis."

"Yes, she does, but you must understand—it's all about the accident, is how young Miss Huntington comes to marry your brother. Her Aunt Gillian, the one who had been married off to the old nobleman her wicked father'd chosen—the old coot died soon after, the couple childless—well, she felt very badly about the fate of her dear sister. She had tried to give them money when Catherine was still alive, but Huntington would not have it. She tried again after the accident, but Huntington still refused. Lady Clayburgh, as she became, went to visit the family and see what she could do for them, and that's when she found young Serena and thought she might make amends by helping her make a good marriage."

"Oh?" remarked Lord Jack, suddenly interested.

"Now you're gettin' it, Jack! That's why she said she'd marry him out of hand, sight unseen! That's why she'll be a duchess! She done it to save her family," said Red Nell. "I think it's heroic-like. Don't you?"

Lord Jack was taken by surprise. "I hadn't thought of it in that light, Nell."

"Well, you should've. She's a good girl."

"I thought she was marrying for fortune and rank."

"Aye, but she did it for her family—to provide for her poor invalid father, and for her sisters and brothers, for quite a few of them they had. It's a good story, ain't it? Now she'll be in your family, and I thought you should know, if nobody's told you. What you doing now, Jack? You're off to London in an awful hurry."

"I'm off to have a little talk with my brother, Nell. It seems I've been an utter fool, and I mean to change that, if it's not too late."

Thirteen

When would it end? Miss Huntington wondered. When would the gentleman in front of her, down on his knees, finish his interminable monologue of self-praise and self-worth and ask for her hand? She would say yes just to get him to stop boring her to death!

But it was not to be. The duke droned on and on.

"I pray, Miss Huntington, that you will forgive my approaching you directly on this matter of lineal importance, for I am well aware that I should be approaching your excellent father. I understand from Lady Shelburne and Lady Clayburgh, however, that he has been for some time indisposed, and I further understand from these estimable ladies that he is not opposed to this match, which is, of course, really very advantageous to yourself and your family."

Really, it was all Serena could do not to strike him, the obnoxious fop!

"I know that your father's family is an ancient family, though regrettably not a noble one. Your mother's family, the Hardwickes, are extremely respectable, as well as being more directly connected with the nobility. I have heard of your excellent qualities of temperament from your aunt and from Lady Shelburne, and I can stand witness to your beauty and charm. Your gracious manners will certainly suffice for carrying out the many duties that might be incumbent upon you as mistress of this great house."

Would the man never come to the point? It was maddening!

The Duke of Leighton took her hand in his and squeezed it. Miss Huntington's heart sank, only to feel her spirits fall even farther into the abyss when the duke saw fit to bring her hand to his lips and kiss it ardently.

Heaven help me! she thought. *This is indeed my punishment for rashness!*

"I esteem and value your person, your lineage, and your countenance. I wish to make you my wife. Tell me, Serena, can you love me? Will you consent to be my bride and my duchess, cleaving to me forever, in order to continue the Ryland lineage?" said the Duke, still kissing her hand.

Serena withdrew her hand, thinking ruefully how differently she had received the attentions of his brother, sighed once, and stood up.

"Certainly, sir," she said in a businesslike manner. "Now I should like to withdraw to my chamber. I have the headache."

"Oh, no! Not so quickly! You have done me the honour of consenting to be my wife, and you shall not escape me so quickly, not without a kiss to seal the bargain!" the duke cried, grabbing Serena and pulling her to him.

She cringed inwardly, but could hardly resist, she reasoned, allowing him to cover her with wet kisses. After all, she had just consented to marry the man!

The Duke of Leighton was still pawing his fiancée when the door to the parlor slammed open and Lord Jack Ryland entered the room, a scowl on his face.

"Unhand that girl at once, Alastair!"

"Whyever should I, Jack? She's just said she'd marry me. Didn't you, my dear?"

Serena, miserable, nodded.

"I did, indeed, sir."

Rake Ryland laid his beaver and riding crop on a side table, and strode over to where his brother and Miss Huntington were seated. He stood over his brother's kneeling form, dwarfing him.

"I don't care, Alastair. You will simply have to find yourself another duchess. Try Idelle."

He held out his hand to Miss Huntington. She gazed questioningly but gratefully into his eyes, and placed her small hand in his. Lord Jack raised her to stand beside him and placed his arm around her waist.

The duke stumbled up from his knees into a chair, removed a lace handkerchief from his pocket, and began waving it around as he whined, "Idelle? But—all this is settled! I don't wish to go through all this rigmarole *again!*"

"I don't care what you want, I'm afraid, Alastair," Lord Jack said simply. "I found her first, and I shall have her."

He turned Miss Huntington by the waist so that she faced him, smiling, and placed his hand tenderly beneath her chin, raising it toward him, saying, "That is, if you will have me! Will you have me, my dear? Will you forgive my boorish behavior last night, and my unpardonable pride and ill manners? Will you understand that it was only my pain at the prospect of losing you forever that caused me to behave in such an idiotish manner?"

"Don't think of it, Jack."

"I should tell you that I have just now learnt of the circumstances of your family. If I had understood the nature of your difficulties, I should never have said what I said, or done what I did."

"It is nothing."

"Will you consent to be my bride, Serena, the bride of a mere younger son?"

"Forgive me, your grace!" said Serena, warmly, "Oh, yes, Jack, yes, I will! Please!" She threw her arms around Lord Jack, her own beloved Rake Ryland, and he returned her embrace. After a few moments, she turned back to the Duke of Leighton, who was still sitting in a great silk-covered chair, waving around his handkerchief as if to ward off some lurking evil.

Miss Huntington, still standing, took the duke's left-hand fingers in hers, squeezed them, and released them, saying, "I am very sorry, your grace, to cry off so abominably, but I think—we should not suit."

"What? What's this? Stealing my bride, are you?"

"I am," Jack admitted.

"Well," replied the duke, shrugging his shoulders and using his handkerchief now to wave them away, "I suppose that's why we called you Rake Ryland! I feel sure that those days are behind you now."

"Of that there can be no doubt," said Lord Jack, smiling broadly at his dear Serena, and then planting a kiss upon her lips.

"Very well, then, you two, smelling of April and May! Let it be so!" commanded the duke.

In this manner, Miss Serena Huntington, the young lady of quality who came all the way down from Barchester, instead of becoming an unhappy duchess, became instead Lady Jack Ryland, a beloved and happy wife.

Epilogue

As it turned out, Lady Idelle Mountjoy's estimation of the financial worth of a younger son, or at least the financial worth of Lord Jack Ryland, had been grievously underestimated. Not long after the wedding of Miss Huntington and Lord Jack, which took place in a lovely chapel in Barchester so that Mr. Huntington and all Serena's family might attend, it became clear that the Rake was not only awake upon every suit, but that he was also as rich as a nabob.

Lord and Lady Jack Ryland purchased a splendid manor house, Comstock, complete with extensive grounds and park and moved Mr. Huntington and the younger children there to live in comfort, style, and splendor. In due time, their marriage, a happy one indeed, produced several children: young Catharine, Gillian, and John. Serena's brother was able to purchase the commission he desired and to marry the young lady of his choice. There was money for doctors for Mr. Huntington and tutors and drawing masters for Frank, Maria, and Sybil.

Frank eventually went on the Grand Tour of Europe, while Maria and Sybil, following their mother, enjoyed formal presentations at court, complete with lappets, feathers, and hoop dresses. The girls, of course, enjoyed admission to Almack's, and, provided by their stepbrother with a dowry as handsome as they themselves, had no problem attracting suitable *partis*. Maria eventually married a Mr. Edgeworth, who had a great estate in Derbyshire, while Sybil became Lady Spawling.

As to the Duke of Leighton, much to Lady Idelle Mountjoy's misery, after his debacle with Miss Huntington, he pronounced himself uninterested in further attempts at matrimony. He settled his estate formally upon his younger brother, Lord Jack, and his heirs, and thereafter continued his ducal life of uninterrupted self-satisfaction.

Mary White, Lady Clayburgh, and Lady Shelburne mutually agreed that never again would they engage in either making or breaking a love match.

More Zebra Regency Romances

__**A Noble Pursuit** by Sara Blayne   \$4.99US/\$6.50CAN
0-8217-5756-3

__**Crossed Quills** by Carola Dunn   \$4.99US/\$6.50CAN
0-8217-6007-6

__**A Poet's Kiss** by Valerie King   \$4.99US/\$6.50CAN
0-8217-5789-X

__**Exquisite** by Joan Overfield   \$5.99US/\$7.50CAN
0-8217-5894-2

__**The Reluctant Lord** by Teresa Desjardien   \$4.99US/\$6.50CAN
0-8217-5646-X

__**A Dangerous Affair** by Mona Gedney   \$4.50US/\$5.50CAN
0-8217-5294-4

__**Love's Masquerade** by Violet Hamilton   \$4.99US/\$6.50CAN
0-8217-5409-2

__**Rake's Gambit** by Meg-Lynn Roberts   \$4.99US/\$6.50CAN
0-8217-5687-7

__**Cupid's Challenge** by Jeanne Savery   \$4.50US/\$5.50CAN
0-8217-5240-5

__**A Deceptive Bequest** by Olivia Sumner   \$4.50US/\$5.50CAN
0-8217-5380-0

__**A Taste for Love** by Donna Bell   \$4.99US/\$6.50CAN
0-8217-6104-8

Call toll free **1-888-345-BOOK** to order by phone or use this
coupon to order by mail.

Name_____

Address_____

City _____ State _____Zip_____

Please send me the books I have checked above.

I am enclosing   \$_____

Plus postage and handling*   \$_____

Sales tax (in New York and Tennessee only)   \$_____

Total amount enclosed   \$_____

*Add \$2.50 for the first book and \$.50 for each additional book.

Send check or money order (no cash or CODs) to:

Kensington Publishing Corp., 850 Third Avenue, New York, NY 10022

Prices and Numbers subject to change without notice.

All orders subject to availability.

Check out our website at **www.kensingtonbooks.com**